KIDS THESE DAYS

Also by DREW PERRY

This Is Just Exactly Like You

KIDS THESE DAYS

A NOVEL

Drew Perry

ALGONQUIN BOOKS OF CHAPEL HILL 2014

Published by
Algonquin Books of Chapel Hill
Post Office Box 2225
Chapel Hill, North Carolina 27515-2225

a division of
Workman Publishing
225 Varick Street
New York, New York 10014

Printed in the United States of America.
Published simultaneously in Canada by Thomas Allen & Son Limited.
Design by Anne Winslow.

LIBRARY OF CONGRESS CATALOGING-IN-PUBLICATION DATA
Perry, Drew.
Kids These Days : a novel / by Drew Perry.—First Edition.
pages cm
ISBN 978-1-61620-171-5
1. Life change events—Fiction. 2. Fatherhood—Fiction. 3. Parenting—Fiction. 4. Florida—Fiction. 5. Domestic fiction. I. Title.
PS3616.E7929K53 2014
813'.6—dc23 2013024029

10 9 8 7 6 5 4 3 2 1
First Edition

for Tomás

May you turn
stone, my daughter,
into silk. May you make men better
than they are.

—STEPHEN DUNN
from "Waiting with Two Members of a
Motorcycle Gang for My Child to Be Born"

Watch out boy she'll chew you up.

—DARYL HALL/JOHN OATES/SARA ALLEN
from "Maneater"

I'd agreed to it—the baby—because I'd decided that was what was owed. That if your wife, who you loved beyond measure, wanted a child, you were supposed to think it was a fine and perfect plan. While we were trying, Alice was all the time asking me if I was sure. If I was still OK with it. Yes, I told her, yes, which was not quite a lie: I could easily enough see us having a child, or children. I imagined we'd keep them fed and watered, that we'd find ways not to kill them, or ourselves.

And then I lost my job, Alice quit hers, and we moved, cartwheeling and pregnant, five hundred miles south to a vacation condo her family owned to try to paste some shell of a life back together before the kid arrived. Florida. Like something heavy dropped on us from overhead. We'd been there a week, and the two things left I knew were these: One—I couldn't understand what it was you were meant to *do* with a child, past the easy stuff like taking her to ballet practice or Indian Guides or the dermatologist. Two—every morning, a man flew up our beach, same time, same direction, in a homemade motorized parachute.

About the first thing I had no answers, no plans. As for the second, we'd taken to waiting for him each day out on the balcony, mainly because it seemed like we should. That if the universe was going to deliver unto us a flying man, we should pay attention. We'd watch the sky—so much of it, so wide-open—and I'd tell Alice we were stranded, we were lost, we were wayward souls. We're not, she'd say. We're luckier than most. Then the parachutist would appear: The wing a black inflated sail that said POW-MIA on it in tall white capitals, and the guy slung down below, hanging from all these ropes and lines, riding in a kind of grocery cart/dune buggy made of neon green metal tubing. Some days Alice would pull her shirt up over her stomach when he flew by, hold her hands in an open diamond around her just-rounding belly, and say to the baby, "You probably ought to take a look at this." She'd turn like a lighthouse, tracking the parachutist with her body. "Don't forget about this," she'd say. Some days he had a DON'T TREAD ON ME flag strung out behind him. Some days he wore mirrored goggles. Once, a pale blue leather flight suit, zippered neck to toe. See? I kept telling Alice. We were down the rabbit hole. Stop it, she'd say. I don't know why you think that's funny.

■ ■ ■

The condo belonged to Alice's great-aunt Sandy, or had until that spring, when she'd died after a series of strokes. The first ones worried everybody the requisite amount, but they were small, survivable. The last one, though, was catastrophic—a whole-system power surge that left her stone dead on the pink chair that was still right there in the bedroom. Everything of hers was still there, actually, except for the clothes. Those we'd taken to Goodwill. We hadn't figured out what to do with the rest of the stuff yet, and anyway, we needed it: We'd sold most of what we'd ever owned when we moved from Charlotte. We'd winnowed. Downsized. We didn't even have our own forks any more. And we didn't need them. We had Aunt Sandy's.

Alice's sister Carolyn and her family lived half an hour north, up near St. Augustine. They were the ones who'd taken care of Sandy, who'd found her sitting there that morning, but they didn't have any use for the place—they had four girls. Plus they'd just finished building a huge house, five or six bedrooms and as many bathrooms, a pool with a poolhouse. Mid, Carolyn's husband, showed us the blueprints the last time they were up to visit, went on at length about how they were putting in a wine pantry instead of a wine cellar because there were no cellars in Florida. Water table, he'd said, shaking his head like he'd landed on some universal truth. Water table.

The family plan had been to rent the condo out, make a little money off it, but things turned on me at work. I'd been eleven years at the same regional bank, on the mortgage side. We weren't crooked. We were too small to be crooked. But we got pummeled anyway, right along with the rest of the country, and once I'd started on my six months' severance, it felt like nothing fit us quite right any more: Alice was a counselor for the school system, was more and more weary of having to explain to the kids why huffing gutter glue in the bathrooms wouldn't help get them into community college. Two separate mechanics told me my car needed a valve job and a new transmission. We found fire ants in the lawn, carpenter ants in the eaves. When we called Carolyn and Mid, way too soon, to tell them the drugstore test said positive, they asked how we were, and we told them that other than the baby, we were basically waiting for an asteroid. Carolyn said what we really ought to do was just move down, take the condo. Mid offered me a job working for him. We hung up the phone and sat there in the still of the den and stared at each other and thought, well, what the hell? Why not?

Everything happened in a hurry: We put the house on the market, took a bath on it, threw a couple of yard sales, sold my car to the kid who cut our lawn. He had ideas about converting it to run on fry oil and bacon grease. When the school year ended, Alice sent her contract back unsigned, we figured out a way to wildcat along on the insurance for a while, and we took off with whatever we had left that fit in her hatchback. Oceanfront living. The Sunshine State. Done and done.

And that part of it *was* exciting, I had to admit. I'd take a cup of coffee out by the pool, find what shade I could, watch the shrimp boats go back and forth out on the water—when it didn't all feel like some kind of wild accident, it almost felt good, like we'd managed to rig for ourselves a completely new life. Conjured it from dust. When the baby came, all that would evaporate in a hail of mirror-bellied crib toys, but still.

I was convinced it was a girl. Alice was holding steady, said she didn't have a sharp feeling one way or the other.

I hadn't gone to work for Mid yet, hadn't hammered out what to do with my days other than buy limes and check the tide tables. Alice had plenty to do: Take naps for the baby, eat sandwiches for the baby, start thinking about what to do with the baby's room. She'd stand in there and twirl the blinds open and closed, and I'd walk the rest of the condo, staring at the pictures and paintings of birds hung up all over the walls. Sandy had been a birder. We'd found lists of birds in the kitchen drawers. I'd been wondering what you might tell a daughter about birds, once she got old enough to want to know—how they had hollow bones, how some were migratory and others weren't. And I'd been wondering, too, what you might tell a daughter about strokes and seizures, or about bundling securitized loans, or about selling off your whole life and moving to Florida. I guess I'd been wondering what you might tell a daughter about anything at all, how you'd ever learn to stand there and answer all the questions she was bound to have. I was pretty certain the hollow bones thing was right. So I had that. For everything else, I figured what you'd want to do was look up what you could, lie about the rest, and hope she'd never learn to tell the difference. Or at least that she'd forgive you when she did.

■ ■ ■

"We have to bring them *something,*" Alice said. We were riding up A1A, the only real road on the island. She had the shoulder part of the seat belt hooked behind her, convinced that if we rear-ended an ice-cream truck, the baby would be safer without it.

"Like what?"

"Flowers? Or a plant?"

We came up on a guy selling shrimp out of a cooler by the side of the road. The sign hanging off his tent said FRESH, LOCAL. I put the blinker on.

"No," she said. "Please, no."

"Why not?"

"Because we can't show up with something we have to cook. Or peel. Also, you'd eat shrimp you bought from some random stranger?"

"I think that's how it goes every time I eat shrimp."

"Can't we just stop somewhere and get a bottle of wine? And maybe something for me?"

We were due at Mid and Carolyn's for dinner. They'd been over a couple of times—once with the girls to make sure we were moved in OK, and once just the two of them to have a drink on the balcony, but this was our Welcome Home dinner, or Welcome Down, at least. This was also supposed to be when Mid explained to me exactly what it was I'd be doing for him. On the phone, when we'd talked about it, all he'd said was, "Don't worry, Big Walter. You kids just get yourselves here, and we'll work on finding you something." I was supposed to start sometime that week.

Mid owned things. He owned a sea kayak rental place, a locksmith service with a few vans, a sunglasses-and-beach-umbrella shop out by the interstate. He owned Island Pizza. What he did was find some place he liked, but that he thought could do better, and he'd buy in, make suggestions. Then he'd get back out of the way, start taking his cut. He was an almost-silent partner, was how he put it. He was rich. I liked him fine. He'd always treated me well. I don't know if we were friends, but we were buddies. And I had no idea what he had in mind. Maybe I'd drive around and scout out potential investments—lemonade stands and bake sales and hot dog carts. Maybe I'd answer the phones.

I found a grocery store, picked up a couple bottles of white wine and some sparkling water. I grabbed a half-dozen ears of corn because they looked good. "What are you doing with those?" Alice wanted to know when I got back in the car.

"I thought we could have them for lunch tomorrow," I said.

"Lunch?"

"Or dinner."

She shook her head. "I'm not feeling so hot."

She'd been bad the last few weeks, morning sickness in high gear. I felt awful for her, but there hadn't been much I could do other than bring her damp washcloths, try not to make too many sudden moves. "You need me to find you a bathroom?"

"Let's just keep going."

"We don't have to eat the corn," I said.

"Maybe that would be best."

"I'll throw the corn away. Or we can give it to Mid and Carolyn."

"Thanks for inviting us over," she said. "Thanks for moving us down. Thanks for saving our lives. Here is some corn."

"Something like that," I said.

"Drive," she said. "We're late."

We hadn't seen their new house yet, only had half an idea where it was. Alice navigated. I watched us get farther and farther away from anything that looked like somewhere people would live. They were well inland, in a subdivision called Pelican Pines, and they'd warned us—theirs was the only house in there. "Only *finished* house," Mid said. "We got in on the ground floor." We made our turns, drove off the island over a bridge and another bridge and through plenty of nothing, and then there was the development, planted in what seemed like five thousand miles of pine and palm and kudzu. We stopped up front at a guard house with no guards in it, no gate. Just a brick hut with holes where you imagined somebody'd eventually want to hang windows. Alice checked her directions, looked at the hut. "Jesus," she said. "Is this it?"

There was a stone Pelican Pines sign, and a smaller wooden sign that said PRE-SELLING! WHY WAIT? "It looks like it," I said.

White sewer cut-ins and green electrical boxes stuck out of the ground at regular intervals stretching back along a main road, bright new grass growing knee-high in the empty lots. There weren't any houses except for one at the far end of the street, which ran straight in and ended, we could see even from there, in a cul-de-sac. "I guess that's theirs?" she said. It was a brick-and-stone three-story, rambling and enormous, two tiny trees in the gaping front yard.

I said, "I guess."

"It's huge," she said. "And creepy."

"It's OK, isn't it?"

"I don't think I quite believe she did this."

"Maybe Mid knows what he's doing."

"I wouldn't have done this," she said. "I mean, does this seem like her to you? They don't have any neighbors." She kept looking back at the sign, at the rock fence that edged the front of the property. She said, "Would you live here?"

"We don't have this kind of money."

"But would you?"

I said, "It depends."

"On what?"

"On factors," I said, reaching, trying to keep things steady. "Various factors."

"That doesn't mean anything."

"I wasn't ready for the question."

She said, "Do pelicans—do they even have anything to do with pine trees? That's not where pelicans live."

I said, "We should look in the books when we get home."

She piled her hair up on top of her head and rolled her

window down. In profile, she looked like pictures of herself as a little kid—short sharp nose, long eyelashes, not quite smiling, not quite sure of the camera. I reached over and traced the few freckles on her neck. She closed her eyes.

The cicadas had cranked up for the evening. The tree frogs, too. A little breeze blew. It smelled like the water might be about where it was, a few miles behind us. There were turns off the main Pelican Pines road, or places for turns, places where the paving just quit and dumped into sandy gray soil. The area they'd cleared for the subdivision was maybe the size of twenty football fields. After that, there was forest. It was nice, in a devastatingly isolating way. "We can't just sit here," she said.

I said, "We can if you'd like."

"I would like," she said. "But we definitely can't."

I dropped the car back into gear and rolled us into Pelican Pines. By the time we'd made it to the driveway, Mid and Carolyn were already out the door. No sneaking up on them in a place like this. One selling point. But Alice was right: The house did feel odd, standing alone like it was, like a scaled-up dollhouse—the even grass, the flowers blooming pink and yellow, the shutters squared so nicely to the sides of the windows. It was as if they'd helicoptered in a finished house and lawn from somewhere else, somewhere like Missouri. There were concrete statues of pelicans at the bottom of the driveway. We got out of the car and already Carolyn and Alice were hugging, and Mid was shaking my hand, grinning the grin of a tall tan man with a good shave and a good jaw, standing in an immaculate front yard, not wearing any shoes. He had a drink going in a wide tumbler. "Come on ahead," he said. "We'll give you the grand tour."

Alice said, "You guys really are the only ones in here."

"I told you we were," he said.

"I know, but I don't think I totally had it pictured," she said.

"Wait until we tell you the rest," said Carolyn, who was in all green, shirt and skirt, like a bridesmaid.

"What rest?" Alice said.

Carolyn turned to Mid. "You tell them."

I looked around, at the flat land stretching back to the highway, at all the places where houses were supposed to be, and I had it. I knew it. "You bought in," I said.

"One-third," said Mid. "And we got our lot for free."

"He wanted to wait until you saw it to tell you," Carolyn said.

Alice said, "Do you mean—"

"When all this sells," Mid told us, "when they build all this in, we'll be sitting pretty. You're looking at luxury lots here, folks."

"Luxury?" I asked.

"Has something to do with what kind of house you intend to build on it," he said.

"You mean like this kind?" said Alice.

"We know it's big," Carolyn said. "But the architect kept coming back with new ideas, and we just decided, you know, let's go for it."

Alice ran her hands over her dress, a thin-strapped thing with flowers on it I'd never seen before, something she must have bought down here. There was a line of sweat on her lip. She said, "You went for it, alright."

"Well, the girls each get their own room now, and we got the master we wanted—"

"I didn't mean it like that," Alice said. "I'm sorry. That came out all wrong."

"It's alright," said Carolyn. "It looks strange right now. We know that."

"Sure," Mid said. "But wait until we've got a few other houses in here. Wait until it looks like a real street. Picture some kids riding bikes up and down, folks in their lawns in the evenings, out walking their dogs—"

"Are they selling?" I asked him. "The lots?"

"They will be. We had somebody through today to look at 34 for a second time."

"Which one's that?" Alice asked.

"Over there, I think," said Carolyn, pointing at one of the sewer stubs, and everybody turned around.

Alice said, "Is that a good one?"

"They're all good," Mid said. "Every last one of them."

"They look good," I said, trying to imagine a neighborhood where there wasn't any.

Carolyn took a long breath, said, "Why don't I take Leecy and show her the pool? You guys can meet us out back." Leecy was Carolyn's nickname for Alice growing up. I'd never heard Alice use one for Carolyn.

"Great," said Mid. "Will do."

She handed him her glass. "Freshen me up?"

"Absolutely," he said, and I watched them walk away, my wife and her older sister, same tallish height, same red hair, Alice's cut a few inches longer. Same basic build, even, though Alice was a little slighter. Carolyn wasn't heavy—just athletic, like she was maybe ready to do some pole vaulting. It was clear she went to the gym, picked things up. Alice asked her a question, and Carolyn laughed, the sound echoing back to us from the trees. Mid put his hand on my back. "Let's go show you the castle," he said. Carolyn and Alice rounded the corner, and I turned and followed him up the stairs.

Inside, their twin daughters—the middle ones, twelve years old—were practicing what looked like karate in the living room, which was cavernous, astonishing, had cathedral ceilings and an obscene entertainment center taking up the bulk of one long wall. The girls were wearing white robes, white socks. Matching blond ponytails. They hollered out vowel sounds after every move. "Hi," I said. One of them turned and waved, and the other pivoted, shouted, kicked her neatly in the side.

"No fair," the kicked one yelled. I always had trouble telling them apart at first.

"Tae kwon do tests the mind as well as the body," said the kicker. "It tests concentration." The other one lunged at her, tried a roundhouse punch, took down a lamp.

"Jane," Mid said. "Sophie. Could you do that upstairs, please? Or outside?"

"This is our dojo," Sophie said. Or Jane.

"This is not your dojo."

"We have to practice for the meet."

"Outside," Mid said. "Or upstairs. The living room is not the place for—" He turned to me. "Help me out here, Walt."

"Is kicking allowed in tae kwon do?" I asked.

"I guess it is," he said.

"Hello?" said Sophie-Jane. "It's called a snap kick?"

"No snap kicks in the living room," said Mid.

"Dad," she said, complaining.

"Not while company's here. Say hello to Uncle Walter."

They said, "Hello, Uncle Walter," at the same time.

"Just Walter's fine," I said.

Sophie-Jane said, "Can we watch TV, at least?"

"If you do it quietly," he said.

"Can we watch the one in here?" the other one asked.

Mid pulled a glass from the cabinet. "So long as you don't snap-kick it." He gave me a *what-can-you-do?* look, held the glass up. "What's your poison?" he said.

"Whatever you're having is fine."

"Vodka and pineapple. Little soda water on top."

"Perfect," I said, because he could have said almost anything, and it wouldn't have mattered—there was a lot coming in at one time, a lot of family. One quick piece of what was headed our way. The girls sat down next to each other on the sofa. I wondered if Mid and Carolyn had a system for knowing which was which. I'd probably just have one of them dunk her thumb in ink every morning.

"So," Mid said. "What do you think?"

"Of the house?"

"The house, the development, the whole package. This was sort of your gig, right?"

"I did mortgages," I said, though that already felt like some other life, a cartoon badly drawn.

"These'll have mortgages. Come on. Tell me."

Luxury lots. In the jungle. I have some swampland, I was thinking. "We've only been here five minutes," I said. "What I've seen so far looks good."

"It really could be," he said. "It really, really could."

"So long as you don't think you're too far away, I guess."

"From what?"

"From the beach, from civilization, whatever. You know this better than I do."

He broke into a wide grin. "Let me tell you this part, OK? You're gonna love this. Next year, they're building a high school right—" He walked me over to the back door, pointed out a stand of trees that looked exactly like all the other trees. "—over there. Kids'll be able to walk through the woods to get to it. This place is a gold mine, Walter, I'm telling you. They will *walk to school*. It is a sparkling goddamn gold mine."

"Dad," Sophie-Jane called, without looking away from the television.

"We're cursing less in the house," he said. "Had a family meeting, came to an agreement. Now we have a curse jar."

"Sounds great."

"Fucking chaps my ass," he said, too quietly for them to hear. He shook his head, headed back to the kitchen to finish up the drinks. I poured some of our water in a wine glass for Alice, and we went outside. "Check out the pool," he said. He cracked an ice cube in his mouth. "Heated in winter. We special-ordered the tiles around the edge from Italy."

There was a waterfall on one end. The tiles he was pointing out were green glass. What they'd done was build themselves a hotel. "They're terrific," I said.

"I mean, maybe it wasn't exactly worth it, but what ever is?"

Their oldest daughter, Olivia, was sitting off to the side in a low wooden beach chair, reading a magazine. I couldn't remember if she'd turned sixteen yet. She was wearing jeans and a red long-sleeved shirt with what I assumed was a band name on it. The Cattle Prodded. It was way too hot for long sleeves. She had impossibly small earphones in her ears, lipstick on that was something close to brown. She was skinny in a way that made me want to feed her a burger. "Hey, Walter," she said, when we walked past.

"Hey, Olivia," I said.

"It's Delton now."

"What?"

"If he can go by Mid, then I've decided I can go by Delton."

Mid was short for Middleton, their last name. I worked it through. "But wouldn't it have to be 'Dleton'?"

She made a face that looked like it took some effort—bored and interested at the same time. "Yeah, but then nobody would know what was going on, you know?"

"Sure," I said.

"You like it?" Delton asked.

"I do."

She looked at Mid. "He hates it."

"That's his job," I said.

"She's going through a charming phase," said Mid.

"I'm not going through any phase," she said. "This is how I am. This is the picture in its entirety."

"In its what?" he said.

"He'll come around," I told her. "He'll get better."

"You're going to make a great father," Mid said. "Also, you're fired."

"How can you fire me?" I said. "I haven't started."

Right then their three-year-old, Maggie, ran shrieking across the yard—where she'd come from, I had no idea—and jumped into the pool. She was wearing an inflatable purple turtle around her waist. "You two are keeping an eye on her?" Carolyn called. She and Alice were by the driveway, back where it wrapped into a three-car garage.

"Of course," Mid said. Maggie bobbed in the deep end, smacked her hands against the water. Olivia—Delton—rolled her eyes, went back to her magazine. Inside, the twins were probably watching *The Karate Kid* and putting each other in headlocks. I took a long sip of my drink, and then another. Mid held out his glass. "To kids," he said. "This is what you've got to look forward to. You're going to love it."

"I'm fine," I said. "This is fine. Don't worry about me."

"Worry?" he said. "Baby, this right here is as good as it gets, OK? This is the motherfucking dream." He went over to a table and a matching set of chairs, and I joined him, sat in the shadow of his looming brand-new solitary house and just tried to hang on while he cranked himself up talking about the high school, how it was going to be some kind of performing-arts powerhouse, how they were going to build the county's largest auditorium. Delton's phone rang and she answered it, never took her earphones out. Maggie started calling for Mid, begging him to pay attention to something she'd decided was vitally important. "Watch me," she was yelling. "Daddy Daddy Daddy look!"

Delton and the twins were planned, or planned enough. Maggie was an accident. Mid and Carolyn thought they were done, and then they'd had to start all over. I looked at Alice, who was pointing up at something with Carolyn, the roof, maybe, or the chimney nobody'd ever need down here, and I caught myself thinking holy, holy shit, tried to remember one more time what we could possibly think we might be doing.

■ ■ ■

I stood down in the parking garage, waiting for Mid to pick me up. Alice had said she'd watch for our parachutist, and even that signaled a kind of truce—we'd gotten into it the night before on the way back from Mid and Carolyn's about how I'd apparently been distant at dinner.

"Just quiet," I said at breakfast, once we'd resumed combat operations. "I was taking it all in."

"Meaning the kids, right? Meaning Maggie?" Maggie'd stayed up past her bedtime, melted down in a serious performance that left everybody a little bleary.

"Meaning everything," I said. "I get to think about things."

"It was like you were on a whole other planet. Carolyn asked me if you were OK."

"What'd you tell her?"

"I said you were having your thing."

"I wasn't."

"You absolutely were." She took her still-full cereal bowl to the sink, poured it out, and walked off down the hall, or what hall there was. Being at Mid and Carolyn's had made the condo seem tiny, even though it wasn't.

"What's the matter?" I said.

"You could act excited," she said. "That's all. Every now and then, you could act excited."

I said, "I am excited."

"You're terrified. You have been the whole time."

"Why is that bad? Why can't I be both?"

"You know what? You're completely welcome to be both. I would love it if you were both."

I said, "Why are you standing in the hall?"

She went in the bathroom, closed the door. I got up and stood outside it, looking for some kind of traction. "You're having a thing, too, you know," I said. "What was all that about how there's something wrong with their house that way? About how you didn't understand what they were trying to do?"

"That's me being worried about my sister, Walter. It's hardly the same." I heard her turn on the water, turn it back off again. "Shit."

"What?"

"There isn't any toilet paper in here."

I got a roll from the closet, opened the door just wide enough, handed it through. It was what I could offer. "Thank you," she said.

"You're welcome," I told her, and that was most of what we'd said to each other all morning.

Alice and Carolyn were headed to the doctor later on, to Carolyn's ob-gyn up in Jacksonville. Carolyn raved about him. She said he was great, said on top of that, he was put together like a marble statue. I'd offered to go, too, but Alice said there wasn't any need, that she just wanted to meet him, make sure she felt comfortable. If she liked him, we'd go back together for the regular appointment. So I was riding with Mid for the day, my first true day on the job, whatever the job might be. All we'd gotten to at dinner was that he'd pick me up in the morning.

The parking garage was open on the ground level, the walls only about waist high, which gave a pretty good view of the tennis courts. There were two kids out there, college age, hitting it back and forth with an easy, practiced rhythm. The ball had that good sound coming off the racquets. I was trying to remember when I'd last been in the kind of physical shape where playing tennis in the full summer sun would have seemed like a good idea when Mid came around the corner, driving a yellow Camaro that had definitely not been in his driveway the night before. It had to be fifteen years old, early or mid-nineties, but it looked brand new. Like a brand-new banana. He pulled up next to me, the engine rumbling away. He had the windows down. He smiled. Big. "Is this yours?" I said.

"Belongs to a friend of mine. He's letting me test it. Thought maybe I'd get it for Olivia."

I looked down the length of the car. "It's really yellow," I said.

"Yeah, but it's only got 45,000 miles on it. And it's huge. Unless she rolled it, she probably couldn't kill herself." He smiled again. "And it's way too wide to roll."

"What does it get, like eight miles to the gallon?"

"There is that. Get in."

Inside, the car seemed made for some other species: You felt like you were riding right down on the road, the seats were so low, and the windshield was flat enough that we were all but looking out the roof. Mid was clearly enjoying it. I was having a hard time imaging Olivia behind the wheel. "When does she turn sixteen?" I asked him.

"End of the summer. You think she'd like this?"

"Does she like yellow?"

"Who doesn't like yellow? It's a color."

I held my hands out in front of me like I was driving, pushed at the floor with my feet. "Could she reach the pedals?"

"Oh, hell, I don't know. Probably." He gunned us around a golf cart half-hanging out of the bike lane. "We'll just get her in here and see, let her take a look. That's all. I'm only trying it out."

"I didn't mean anything by it," I said.

"You're OK," he said. "No worries."

"I think it could be a great car," I said.

"You do?"

"Sure," I said. "Why not?" The car smelled not exactly new, but like somebody had tried to make it smell new. It had black leather seats. In Florida. I watched Florida go by out the window, tried to keep count of the blue Hurricane Evacuation Route signs. The signs made it seem like evacuating would be more complicated than just driving away from the water, which worried me in a way it was hard to put a solid shape to. I said, "How long's she been going by Delton?"

"That won't last." He pressed the trip meter button on the odometer a couple of times. "Every few weeks it's something new. At the end of the school year she was wearing these knit caps every time she left the house. Ninety degrees outside, and she's walking around like Swiss Chalet Barbie."

"I don't think I remember being sixteen," I said.

"I'm blocking it out, man, everything I can. We keep getting these goddamn boys ringing our doorbell. And that's if we're lucky. Half the time they just sit in the driveway, hit the horn, wait for her to come outside."

"She seems like a good kid, though, right?"

"It could be a hell of a lot worse. She's got a friend who's already been to rehab twice. Pills. Spent last fall living in a halfway house."

"Damn."

"You know what, though? You never know what's coming. And even when you do know, you still don't know." He shifted gears, let that idea sit between us.

The thing about Mid was that he basically meant well. I had him as a pretty good father, a pretty good husband. He probably knew how to listen when he needed to, how to broker peace deals in the house when that was what was required. It felt possible that his politics might not quite match up with mine, or his understanding about how the cosmos spun around, but he'd always seemed like a good guy, somebody who'd happily enough go to his kids' tae kwon do meets, somebody who'd be alright to drive around with in a borrowed Camaro on a given summer morning. Even so, something still wasn't sitting exactly right about the job, and in the wash of another poor effort on my part at being what Alice needed me to be, I figured I ought to check. Be sure. We stopped at a light. Mid drummed his fingers on the wheel. "So I wanted to ask you a question," I said.

"Do it."

"Don't take this the wrong way." Alice and I hadn't fully chased this through—we'd been afraid, I think, to completely sketch it out. "I wanted to make sure you really did need somebody," I said. "Because I could find something to do. It wouldn't have to be much, on account of the condo and everything."

"I need somebody," he said.

"You're sure."

"I am. I cleared it through the boss."

"You are the boss."

"That did simplify things," he said.

"I guess I'm just trying to say—" I shuffled a few possibilities: I could work aisles at the Home Depot, send people to where the hammers hung in their little rows. I could mow lawns. I could work some breakfast buffet place and make sure the bacon never ran low. What I knew: I could not go back to selling loans. That was done and gone forever. I'd spent those last few months at the bank trying hard to believe the bootstraps-austerity-we-shall-overcome singsong that kept floating through my e-mail, but when the Feds finally knocked on our door on a Friday afternoon, I wasn't surprised. Nobody was. We'd been headed that way for the better part of a year.

And they were good at it, the Feds. Efficient as hell. They locked us down, interviewed us one by one, took their notes, took our keys, and then opened us back up Monday morning as a branch of Piedmont National. New signage, new plants, new everything—except for loan brokerage. No new signs on loan brokerage. They shuttered us entirely. I went home, worked my stack of business cards, made my calls. I did what you were supposed to do. Nothing. Turned out, all at once, that nobody was doing much of any of that anymore. They certainly weren't doing more of it. And I was supposed to somehow have a family.

"Listen," Mid said. "I don't want you thinking this is some kind of a charity case. It's easy math, alright? I could use the help, and you're a smart guy. Plus you got a raw deal, if you ask me. You got fucked where it counts. I feel great about this. You don't need to be thanking me."

"OK," I said.

"OK?" he said.

"Yes."

"Glad we got that out of the way."

We passed a place that sold Dutch Barns. We passed a place that sold bicycles. If the earth fell further out from underneath me, I could sell Dutch Barns sized especially for bicycle storage. "But what is it?" I said.

"What is what?"

"What is it you're planning for me to actually—"

"Patience," he said. "That's what we're taking you to see right now." The light turned green, and Mid started back in on Olivia like that was all we'd been talking about, like I wasn't white-knuckling the edges of what I wanted to do when I grew up. He told me about what it was like to ride with a kid who had a learner's permit, how the first time she turned left, she'd just gone ahead and done it without checking, had pulled right through oncoming traffic. He still wasn't sure how they didn't get killed. He told me they were teaching her to parallel park between cereal boxes out on the street in front of the house. I listened and rode, tried to believe. After a few miles he whipped us into a strip center, stopped the car, sat up a little bit, and said, "Well, here we are."

There was a tax service, a church, two empty storefronts, and a vacuum repair place. There were no cars in the parking lot. I couldn't tell what he was wanting me to look at. "What?" I said.

"Right there."

"Where?"

He opened the door, walked over to a white metal building about half the size of a truck trailer sitting in the middle of the parking lot. It was surrounded by red poles sunk into the ground, I assumed to keep people from driving into it. It said TWICE THE ICE! on the front in large red letters. There were two penguins painted on the side, looking pleased with themselves and sitting on a pile of ice. Mid held his hand out at the building. He could have been posing for a photograph.

I put on my sunglasses and got out of the car. I could feel the heat from the asphalt seeping up through my shoes. "What is this?" I said.

"It's a Twice-the-Ice," he said. "I ordered two. They come in this week."

"You ordered two for what?"

"For this. I've already got the locations leased. All we need to do is get the water and electricity run. They come fully ready to go."

I said, "It sells ice?"

"Sixteen pounds in bags, or twenty in bulk. Twice what you get at a gas station. That's the angle. Twice the ice."

I looked at it again. It was a giant white brick with a slightly less giant white brick of an air conditioner on its roof. "I don't get it," I said.

"There's no 'get.' This is as simple as it comes. You drive up, put your money in, and it gives you ice."

There were two stainless steel chutes on the side of the building. Signs over each said BAG and BULK. There was a blue awning over the chutes so you wouldn't have to stand in the sun while you got your ice. "This is what you want me to do for you?" I said.

"Partly," he said.

I walked a full lap around the thing. There were penguins on the other side, too. "How much does one of these cost?" I asked.

"About a hundred."

"Thousand dollars?"

"They pay for themselves in three years, on average."

There wasn't any window in the Twice-the-Ice. No attendant. "It's self-serve," I said.

"The ice never touches human hands."

"Is that good?"

"The website says it is," he said.

"But what would I be doing?"

"What do you mean?"

"The thing makes its own ice, right? What do you need me for?"

"You check on them," he said. "Once or twice a week, you come by, feed two bucks in, make sure it's making ice."

"I check on them. On the Twice-the-Ices."

"Sure."

"Mid," I said. "That's not a job. Or if it is, you don't need me to do it. Pay some college kid to do drive-bys."

"I don't know any college kids," he said. "I know you."

There was no job. The white paint of the Twice-the-Ice was like a flashbulb that wouldn't stop going off. "You don't have anything for me," I said.

"I do," he said. "Relax. This is only one piece. Let me swing you by a couple of other places and show you the whole system. Tell you what I've got put together."

I looked back at Delton's Camaro, chewed over my new career as the security detail for barrier-island ice-vending parking lot trailers. Alice and Carolyn would be headed for Jacksonville by now, for the appointment with the doctor. Other than going back to the condo and dragging one of Aunt Sandy's aluminum folding chairs down to the beach, I literally had nowhere else to be. "Sure," I told Mid. I was riding along. That was what I was doing, what was left I seemed to know how to do. "Let's do it," I said. "Show me the next thing."

■ ■ ■

"Guy won't let me buy in," Mid said, meaning the man behind the bar. "But I love it here anyway." We were at Pomar's, a shrimp-and-beer place he'd been telling me about since before we'd moved. It was squeezed up against the highway—there was the road, a tiny crushed-shell parking lot, and then there was Pomar's. It had big plywood windows open to the air, big fans in the ceiling. You couldn't see the ocean. It wasn't quite hot. It wasn't quite anything else, though.

"You want to run this place?" I said.

"Why not?"

"What do you *not* do?"

"Until those Twice-the-Ices come in and start turning a little cash, not much else." Our shrimp came out: steamed, in a metal bucket, with a second bucket for shells. There was a bowl of lemons on the table. Also a salt shaker, red pepper, a roll of paper towels.

"You're stretched?" I asked.

"The land thing over at the house has us a little thin."

"Then why the ice machines?"

"Those suckers print money," he said. "The guy who owns the one I just showed you? He's got six more down in Daytona. He doesn't have to do anything else."

"So, OK." I was still trying to grasp what was going on. "You can't have in mind paying me any kind of real paycheck just to drive between your two ice huts that aren't even there yet."

"Here's how I see it." He was dressed like a gym teacher—khaki shorts and a polo shirt a half-size too small. He looked a little like an upside-down pear. "You want to work. And I want to work less. I don't have to pay you a ton, because, like you said, you don't have any housing costs. I come out the big winner: I get a guy like you on a steep discount." He squeezed half a lemon over the shrimp bucket, plowed ahead: "All you have to pay for is insurance for the kid, plus three squares a day times however many people are living under your roof. In my case, that's thirty-seven. In yours, it's two, going on two-and-a-half. I don't need you to do much. Hell, *you* don't need you to do much. So what I've been thinking is maybe you can sort of be me a few days a week. Fill in. Go stick your nose in places, make sure everything's working the way it's supposed to. Free me up to do other things."

I said, "Like I'm your second, or something?"

He pointed a shrimp at me. "Perfect," he said. "We'll call it that. I love it."

"Hold on," I said. "How would I even know if—I don't know, if the locksmith thing is going right?"

"Those guys are easy. You stop in, say hello, ask them if they've been opening a lot of doors and windows. See if anybody thinks the van could use a paint job."

"I don't know shit about locksmiths," I said. I knew derivatives. Depreciations. Not this.

"You know as much as I do," he said, "and it doesn't matter. This is a benevolent dictatorship we're running here, you and me. It's their locksmith service. All I need you to do is turn up from time to time and remind people we still exist. Helps them keep a tighter ship."

My beer was warming in its plastic cup. A TV mounted on the wall played a grainy replay of an old college football game. I felt a little desperate, a little hurried. "You don't know me well enough to bring me on like this," I said.

"Come on. I know you fine."

"Carolyn's making you do it. For Alice."

He shook his head. "Not the kind of thing she'd do. I mean, I won't lie—she's pretty jacked about having you guys down here. Talks about you all the time. But I'm happy, too. I've always felt like you and I might get along pretty well if we ever had the chance."

"We do get along."

"That's not what I'm saying. Here. Listen to me." He waved down the guy at the bar, who pulled us two new beers. "This last year or two, I've been looking for somebody to take over the business. I'm wanting to step back. Maybe pick up a hobby. Maybe painting."

"What are you, forty-four?"

"Forty-three," he said. "But I'm tired."

"Painting?"

"Or triathalons. Or Revolutionary War reenactments. Doesn't matter. I'm just ready for something else. I'm ready to sleep a little later. Once Maggie's old enough for kindergarten, Carolyn and I will have more time to spend around the house. Olivia goes to college in two years. This is the old 'I want to spend more time with the kids' thing, except it's not even that."

"I don't think I'm totally following," I said.

"I *do* want to spend more time with the kids. Of course I do. But I'd also like some more time, period. If the Pelican Pines thing works out—shit, if we sell even half those lots, or two-thirds, then I'll be at a place where I can slow down some. Maybe that's not for a year. Maybe the economy shits the bed again. Maybe we gotta grow the city out that way. But it'll happen eventually. And when it does, I'll need somebody looking after things."

"And you want that person to be me."

"I want that person to be somebody good," he said. "Somebody I can trust. You seem like a pretty even guy. You seem like you wouldn't be walking in the front door and yelling at people." He was sweating a little bit. He pulled a paper towel off the roll, wiped his hands, his face, his forehead. "I like you, Walter, goddamnit. Stop fucking around. Take the job."

I thought I had already. "I'm supposed to be your partner?" I asked him.

"My second. I liked the way you said it before."

"And you're wanting to give me a paycheck."

"Well, about that." He went in his pocket, came back out with a slip of paper. "Here," he said.

It was a cashier's check. For thirty thousand dollars. I waited for the circus music. "Mid," I said. "What the fuck?"

"Paying you a salary's just another pain in my ass. Plus, then I have to report you as an employee. This way you're a contract worker. Easier for everybody."

"You really don't have to— "

"Let's call that five or six months," he said. "Or three, if we do well. We can work out the fine print later. This way you can get your feet wet down here, see if all this feels like home. You can see if you can stand working for me. With me. And now you've got money in the bank. Take Alice to dinner, while you still can."

"I can't keep this. It's too much."

He held his hands up. "Don't cash it if you don't want to. Stuff it in some drawer if that makes you feel better. It's already off my books, so it makes no difference to me."

"Mid. Listen. Wait."

He pushed his half-full cup to the center of the table. "Too much talk about money. We've got more stops to make. Time to get a move on." He stood up. I stayed where I was. "You coming?" he said.

"Do you want me to get this?" I said, meaning the bill.

"Walter, don't go all big spender on me now, OK? This was business. Business is on the company." He put twenty-five dollars under the sugar caddy and walked outside, left me at the table. I wasn't certain what to do. I felt sure when I explained it to Alice, I'd get it wrong. Half of it, anyway. Mid fired up the big engine. I added five dollars out of my pocket even though he'd already tipped plenty, chased him out there, climbed in my side, buckled up, and tried very hard to act like I knew what was going on.

■ ■ ■

"Let me see it," Alice said. I handed it to her, and she unfolded it. "Shit," she said.

"I know."

"Shit," she said again. We were sitting down by the dunes, on wooden benches built into the walkway to the beach. The sun was setting. There was a little wind off the water. Alice had a box of crackers and a glossy booklet called *Loving Your Second Trimester.* She said, "What are we going to do?"

"Put it in the bank, I guess. I can't be walking around with it."

"He really didn't say anything else?"

"Just that it was easier this way. Or that it would be."

"I still don't think I understand what he wants you to be doing for him."

"He took me around," I said. "We went by Island Pizza. We went out to the sunglasses shop. We looked at things."

"You looked at things?"

"Pretty much."

"Are you working tomorrow?"

"He said he'd pick me up at ten."

"What are you doing?"

"Looking at more things, I guess."

"Thirty thousand dollars," she said.

"I tried to bring it up a couple more times, but he'd just talk about something else."

"Like what?"

"Like Olivia, the house, the high school. He loves to talk about the high school."

She said, "Carolyn told me they might not build it."

"What? When?"

"Today in the car. She says it's tied up with the school board or the county commission or something. They haven't voted yes yet. She says Mid keeps acting like they have, or like they will, but she thinks there's a chance it won't go through."

"What else does Carolyn say?"

A bunch of people walked by us on their way down to the beach, all of them wearing matching faded jeans and untucked white button-up shirts. Picture time, a couple of sunburned families' worth. "She says there's something not right with him lately. She says there's something going on where he's not the same."

"Not the same how?"

"That's what I asked. She couldn't explain it. Maybe it's the house. I'm not sure." She ate a cracker. "Carolyn said she thought he was under stress. How does he seem to you?"

I said, "He seemed fine. Like himself."

"Except for the part where he gave you an enormous check."

"Except for that."

"But you felt like he was alright?"

"How would I know better than Carolyn?"

"You wouldn't," she said. She was staring up behind me at the building. I turned around. There were towels hanging off the balcony railings, umbrellas in the corners, hurricane shutters down on the units nobody was in. She said, "This is all starting to feel a little bizarre, right?"

"Starting to?" I said.

"Don't do that," she said.

The group down on the beach had lined themselves up, the kids standing behind the adults, who were kneeling. A flash went off a few times. Then they broke formation, went into some deal where everybody held one kid sideways, smiled for the camera again. I said, "Did the doctor say anything about Kitchenette?"

"Or Kitchen," she said, right away. We'd been fooling with pairs of baby names, joking around—Kitchen and Kitchenette, Azalea and Azaleo.

"Or Kitchen," I said.

"I made an appointment for a week from Monday. He said we'll be due for an ultrasound. If the baby's pointed the right way, we might be able to find out the sex. If we want to."

"Do we want to?" I said.

"Do you?"

I couldn't see how knowing would make anything easier or harder. I said, "Could we wait until we get a little closer to it, see how we feel?"

"We're pretty close to it," she said.

"What do you want to do?"

"I still don't know, either." She opened up her booklet, flipped through the pages. “They gave this to me today,” she said. “It says I’m supposed to get all horny during the second trimester. Here: ‘You may find your sex drive increases. Take advantage of this time with your partner.’” She smiled.

I said, “Are you wanting to have sex now?”

“No, you idiot. Not now.”

“I’m just asking. I was making conversation.”

“That isn’t making conversation.”

“You’re still mad,” I said. “From this morning.”

“I’m not. I’m just weird.” She waved the book at me. “This says I’m allowed to get a little weird. It says we’re not supposed to worry.”

“What does Carolyn say?”

“She said she wanted sex all the time.”

“I meant about the worrying.”

“I didn’t ask her. She wanted to know how you were doing today, how you were with everything, and I said fine.”

“But you think I’m not fine.”

More formations down on the beach. More pictures. Most of the kids laughing, one of the little ones in tears. She said, “Walter, half the time you’re fine, like now, and half the time it’s like you’re at the bottom of a well.”

“I’m not at the bottom of a well.”

“Sometimes you are, though,” she said, and wiped her eyes.

I moved over to her bench. “Are you crying?”

“The book says I can cry.” She sniffed. “It says I’ll have mood swings. It says it’s perfectly normal.”

“Then you’re doing it right. You should cry.”

“Don’t tell me what to do.” She got up and put the crackers on the railing. “I’m going up,” she said. “I’m going to go take a shower. Why don't you stay down here a while, and then later you can come up, and we can maybe see what happens."

"What?"

"Maybe the book's right. Maybe I would like to have a little sex."

"Are you kidding?"

"No," she said, laughing now, wiping her face with her sleeve. "Not really."

"That sounds great," I said. "Anything you like."

"Oh, God," she said. "Watch out for the crazy lady. Crazy lady coming through."

"You're not crazy."

"If you think that, you're worse off than I am. Maybe we're both losing it."

"We're not losing it."

"How would you even know?"

"I wouldn't," I told her. "I wouldn't have any idea."

She walked over to me, kissed me on the top of my head. She left her face there in my hair. She said, "We're going to be fine, right?"

"You're the one who's always saying so."

"Are you OK?"

"Hell, I'm rich."

"We're going to be good at it," she said. "I know it."

"Me, too," I said, even though I knew no such thing.

She straightened up, wiped her eyes again. "Come up in a little while, alright? I missed you today. I don't know why, but I did."

"I'm glad," I said.

"You should be." She kissed me again and walked away. She let herself through the gate at the pool and then out again on the other side, over by the stairwell. I watched her go, and then did what she told me to do. I bided my time. I looked back up at the buildings in our complex—four concrete boxes lined up right on the seawall, three of them five stories tall and ours six, the tallest thing on the beach. Everything else north and south was either houses or two-story deals, red and blue 1960s horseshoe condos with orange roofs. This was still Old Florida, Carolyn and Mid liked to say. Undiscovered. That wasn't quite it, though—it was more like people had discovered things down here, but weren't altogether sure what to do with their find. The light came on in our unit. Alice opened the shades at the sliding glass door. It seemed like it couldn't be her up there, though of course it was. Down on the beach, a county sheriff rode past on a four-wheeler, probably looking for kids drinking beer. A string of pelicans flew just along the first set of breakers. Pelican *Palms,* I thought, but not Pelican *Pines.* Alice was right. It started to get dark, and the picture people came back up and rinsed their feet at the spigot by the pool. Once they were gone, I went upstairs, found Alice.

There were bars across all the storm sewer drainpipes in the roadside ditches. Mid said they were there to keep the alligators out. I was telling Alice about the alligators while we rode north toward Jacksonville.

"But why would alligators want to be in storm sewers?" she wanted to know.

"They just do," I said. "They like it in there."

"Why would they like it in there better than where they live?"

"I think it's the same as where they live."

She changed lanes. "I don't understand why you think that makes any sense."

"When Mid was explaining it, it did."

"Well," she said, "there you go."

I had the day off. I'd only asked for the morning, but Mid told me we should hang out in Jacksonville after the appointment, make a day of it. Carolyn gave Alice a list of all the good baby stores. I'd been eight or nine days on the job, and it was as advertised: Mainly what we did was drive out to Island Pizza, make sure they were selling pizzas; ride over to the sunglasses place, see that the sunglasses were lined up and ready to go. The Twice-the-Ices had gotten delayed at the plant in Georgia, weren't due now for another two weeks. But Mid had lined me up something actual for the next couple of days—he wanted me to go out to a fish camp he had a piece of, have a look at some land they were talking about building rental cabins on. I was supposed to report back, tell him what I thought. "We need an outsider's perspective," he said. "You can tell us if it looks like what we already think it looks like." Alice and I hadn't touched the thirty thousand. We were afraid to.

Alice bled a little the Friday before. That was the big news on the homefront. She called the doctor's office and they wanted to know how much, what color. It didn't sound like an emergency, they said. Everything was probably still fine. Some women bleed early in pregnancy. They said we were still early. Alice worried. I worried. She'd been all over the Internet, diagnosed herself with every possible malady, found lists of syndromes with long hyphenated names.

The waiting room at the doctor's office was a kind of cross between an aquarium and an airport. All we needed was some gentle voice over the intercom announcing flights to Frankfurt and Lisbon, and we could have been in any Terminal C anywhere. The flat-panel TVs in each corner were showing something about flowers blooming in the Serengeti. That eventually switched over to lions hunting zebras at a muddy watering hole, which didn't seem right, but there wasn't anybody to talk to about it. There was only an electronic check-in kiosk and a closed frosted glass window on one wall. While Alice beamed us up, I read an entertainment magazine from the year before, read about sitcoms that had already been canceled, movies that had already come and gone. A nurse eventually materialized and called Alice's name. We went into the back.

Height and weight. Blood pressure. Go behind this door, pee in a cup. Then the nurse put us in an examination room: table, stirrups, plastic model of a uterus on a low bookshelf. Everything was fancy and shined up. If there were multiple plastic uterus models available, this was surely the deluxe edition. The gown they had for Alice was a little better made than some of the clothes I had on. There was even a pitcher of ice water and two glasses on a little stand by the door. The glasses had the clinic's logo etched into the side. "You do get your money's worth here," I said.

"It's like a spa," Alice said. "I like it."

Two or three more nurses came in and did two or three more things to Alice before they walked us down the hall to the ultrasound room. The tech in there got her up on the table, rubbed her down with the jelly, held the magic wand up to her belly, and without much warning at all, there it was—the windshield-wipered image up on the screen, black-and-white, grainy, a channel you couldn't quite tune in. Still, it was pretty clear it was a human baby in there, pretty clear, even, which end was head and which was tail. Our child. On the damn television set at North Florida Fertility. That plus the underwater mouth-sound of the heartbeat. Alice reached for my hand. She was crying. I was, too. It wasn't possible not to.

I'd always cried at significant moments, at public ceremonies. I cried when they played the national anthem before graduations and ballgames. I cried when other people got married, even in the movies. I cried at long-distance telephone carrier commercials, back when there were long-distance telephone carriers. And now I was crying because there was another life up there in that picture, and that was more than I could process, more than I figured anybody could process, really, when or if they tried to work it through. And I knew something in me was meant to be rearranging itself, that I should be undergoing some profound reassessment of the way I saw the world—but instead I was off and gone on my own ride, through the tunnel and into the dark. I was thinking about middle-of-the-night feedings, about chicken pox, about boys sitting in the driveway, laying on the horn, waiting for my child to emerge from the house. It was like those first few seconds after a car wreck, right after you first come to, and you're thinking, Wait. We can still undo this. We can figure something out. Alice said, "Isn't it unbelievable?" I was not lying when I said it was.

But I did not suddenly feel like a father. I did not have some vestigial urge to run out and stab a gazelle in the throat and drag it back to our hut for dinner. Instead, I felt what I'd been feeling all along, since we'd started talking about it, started trying: That I was powerfully, deeply alone. That the rest of the world, the world of ultrasound technicians and locksmiths and mortgage bankers still writing mortgages and center fielders holding their babies in their arms during post-game interviews—all those people knew exactly how to do this, did not flinch in the onrushing face of certain peril. They'd simply come wired with something I hadn't. They knew they were supposed to have children, did it without batting an eye. It was what came next. You survived your twenties, you found someone who felt like she could live under the same ceilings you did without needing to kill you, and you had a kid. You had another. Everyone did it. Everyone.

“Would you like to know the sex?” the tech asked. She kept clicking things, measuring lines on the screen.

I looked at Alice. “Sure,” I said. My voice seemed too loud for the room.

“We can—”

“No,” said Alice, interrupting me. “No. We want to be surprised.”

I said, “We do?”

“I like that,” the tech said. “I wanted to be surprised, too, you know? But my husband said it was driving him crazy.”

“It’s driving us crazy,” Alice said. She looked dead ahead at the screen. “We’re just going to try to keep it a secret anyway.”

The tech smiled at us. “Y’all are sweet,” she said.

Another nurse came in to help Alice get cleaned up, and she took us back to the exam room, told Alice she could get dressed. I felt cut open, run over. It seemed like I couldn’t hear so well. Alice asked me questions, and I answered her. Somehow we landed in the doctor’s office. DR. VARDEN, it said on his door, underneath a suite of little multicolored plastic mailbox flags that sent some secret signal to somebody, depending on which one was flipped out. We sat together on a leather sofa. Dr. Varden wasn’t in there.

I don’t know what I’d expected. Maybe I hadn’t thought far enough ahead to remember to expect anything. I kept looking at Alice’s stomach, checking for some kind of change, and then back up at the hundred or so framed snapshots of happy families all over Varden’s walls: Kids and parents skiing, kids and parents on horseback, kids and parents whitewater rafting. We were going to need a better camera. We were going to need to go horseback riding next to whitewater rapids.

Dr. Varden arrived looking healthy, looking fit, wearing scrubs that were somewhere between pink and purple. He had a picture on his desk of his own family—three boys like nesting-doll versions of Varden, and his calendar-pretty wife, all of them standing in a field wearing tan shirts, tan pants. They were the most deeply content scout troop in history. He sat down, beamed, rifled through a folder. "Well," he said, "you two are doing absolutely great. You just really are." His teeth were so white you wanted to tell somebody about it. He pulled a clear ruler from a drawer, measured something on a large printout of one of the ultrasound pictures. He mouthed some numbers to himself. "All clear," he said. "Sound the bell. Everything's just right." He winked at us. On purpose. He held up the ultrasound. "You take a pretty picture," he said.

"Thank you," said Alice.

Varden said, "So let's talk about this bleeding."

Alice said, "Is everything OK?"

"In this?" He put the picture back in the folder, patted the cover. "From what we can see, yes and yes. Mister Computer spit out a nice set of numbers. No real risk factors except for your age. Good heart. Good stomach. Past that we can't tell much else yet, but those look good. Only real marker is the bleeding."

"Marker?" Alice said.

"Warning sign. Little tiny. But still. Just the one day, the bleeding?" He went back through the chart, found his page. "This says Friday?"

"Yes."

"Brown?' he said. "Not red?"

"Yes."

“Brown is good,” Varden said. “To be expected, even. Or maybe not, but not *so* surprising.” He talked and moved like he was sped up, like his clock wound differently than ours did. “If it happens again, or if we see anything bright red, that’ll get our attention, but I certainly don’t think we need to do anything right now.”

“What would we do?” Alice said.

“Rest. Small procedures. But we’re not there, OK?”

“OK.”

“You’re a champ,” he said. “Blood pressure. Heartbeat. I love it. You and the baby both. Just great.” He leaned over the desk to look at her. “You look fantastic, by the way. I’m not just saying that. You really do. For your age—” He held his hands out, a magician’s apology. “And I don’t mean one thing by that. Not one thing. All I’m saying is that a pregnancy in your thirties is different from one in your twenties. That’s all. And you? You look like you’re in your twenties.”

“Thank you.”

“You’re more than welcome. How’s the nausea?”

“Better,” she said. “A little bit.”

“That ought to keep improving, too. I bet it does, but we’ll get somebody to call you next week to check in. How does that sound?”

“It sounds good,” she said.

“And how about Dad? Questions from Dad? We doing OK?”

Dad was just trying to stay upright. “We’re doing OK,” I said.

“The thing here says you’re from Carolina. Anywhere near Myrtle Beach?”

“That’s South Carolina,” I said.

“Right.” He drank out of a glass of ice water using two hands, like it was a sippy cup. He stood up. It was clear the appointment was over. He was a man with things to do next. "Misty will take care of you up front," he said, "unless there's something else you good folks need." He looked at Alice one more time. "You'll be getting big before you know it," he said. "And you'll look great then, too."

"Thank you," she said.

"Mom, Dad, if you think of anything, *anything,* that you want to ask, call the office anytime. We have nurses on the help line twenty-four hours, seven days. Anything you think of, just call." He pulled a desk drawer open, got out a magnet shaped like an egg. "Number's right on there," he said, handing it to Alice. "You two pop that up on your fridge." The phone number ended in B-A-B-Y, spelled out in pink and blue ribbons. Alice put the magnet in her purse. "So," he said, shaking my hand, then Alice's. "We'll see you in a month, OK?"

"A month," she said.

"Wonderful." He walked—almost ran, he was moving so quickly—to the door, showed us into the hall. He waved when we rounded the corner. We waved back. And we must have paid at the desk, must have walked ourselves out into the blazing parking lot, must have found our car—I just don't remember it. I know I got the AC running. I know we watched a very pregnant woman walk up the front steps to the clinic. Alice opened up the little envelope they gave us, shuffled through the ultrasound pictures. There was a CD, too. She said, "So I guess we're having a baby."

I said, "It looks like we are."

The AC wasn't doing much other than pushing out hot air. "That was a lot," she said.

"Dr. Varden?"

"He wasn't like that last time. He wasn't as— He just wasn't quite like that." There was a drainage ditch off to the side of the parking lot. I checked for alligators. The blacktop shimmered in the heat. Alice said, "Are you alright?"

I said, "Are you?"

She put the photos back in their sleeve. She said, "It all just seems impossible. It's like I can't entirely believe it."

"Right," I said. "It is like that."

"Did you see the way he drank the water?"

"With both hands?"

"I've never seen an adult do that," she said.

"I don't think I have, either."

Alice said she was hungry, so we got out Carolyn's directions, figured out where the mall was from where we were. I found the interstate. Alice held the pictures in her lap, looked out the window, didn't say much. I did not ask her what she was thinking. Back in the office, Varden was probably doing push-ups in between patients. Jumping Jacks. Flossing. Traffic on the highway was slow, but moving. I still couldn't get used to how flat the land was everywhere you looked.

One of the things she'd told me was that it wasn't just that she wanted a baby, but that she wanted a *family*—she wanted me, specifically, to be a father, as much as she wanted to be a mother. She wanted *us* to have a child. I'd tried talking to friends about this back home, coded conversations out by the grill, tired parents who repeated the party line: It was hard as hell, but it was the best thing that had ever happened to them. They all said that, like they'd gone to some day camp to learn the right words: *The best thing that ever happened to us*. It was hard, though, to know if any of that was true, or if, instead, once you had somebody living full-time in the guest room, everything else was scoured so clean you couldn't remember what your life had been before.

■ ■ ■

"Salad Tong?" Alice said. "No way. That's not even in the game." When we played the game, it seemed like a game, and I liked that—it felt less like we were headed for a screaming infant in our laps, and more like this was all some puzzle in an in-flight magazine.

"Salad Tong," I said. "Salad Tong and Salad Shooter." We were sitting in the food court, looking out on a long riverwalk, finishing our lunch. There was a guy outside doing airbrushed portraits on T-shirts. Inside, there were carts where you could buy perfumes, wigs, hats with the logo of your choice stitched in while you waited. The mall went on forever, like a mall of a mall. I had a vague sense of being frightened by it. I had a definite sense of being frightened by everything else.

"But which one would be the boy?" she said.

"Salad Shooter, of course," I said.

"Why of course?"

"You can't call a girl Shooter."

"Don't be a jackass," she said. "Go get us smoothies, OK? Bring me a strawberry."

I stood in line at New World Smoothie. All the flavors were named for explorers—the Ponce de Lemon, the Vasco de Gamagranate. They didn't have plain strawberry. They didn't have plain anything. I ordered Melon Magellan for myself, got an Eric the Red for Alice. EXCITING BERRY BLEND, it said on the menu board. She was on the phone when I got back to the table. I tried to explain about the flavors, but she waved me off. "Carolyn," she said. "Slow down."

I could hear Carolyn on the other end, but couldn't make out what she was saying. A group of kids came through wearing those shoes with wheels. One of them hit a chair a couple of tables over, went down. It looked like he was thinking about crying, but he held it together, got himself up, rubbed his knee, rolled back over to his friends. Alice said, "How is he in jail?"

I snapped right back in. "Who?" I said. "Mid?"

She put a finger in her other ear. "Is he alright?"

"What's going on?" I whispered.

"Did he know?" she said. While Carolyn answered, Alice took a sip of her smoothie, winced. "What is this?" she asked me.

"It's an Eric the Red. What the hell's happening right now?"

"Carolyn, hold on a second." She covered the phone. "Mid's in jail," she said. "The police raided Island Pizza this morning, and somebody was selling pot out of the kitchen. I think. Or out of the stockroom. Carolyn's freaking, so it's a little hard to understand."

"Who was selling the pot?"

"I've been on the phone three minutes."

"Was he there? Why is he in jail?"

She said, "What is it you think I'm doing right now?" She took her hand back off the mouthpiece. "What?" she said. "He's right here. I just told him. Is that OK?" She tried her smoothie again. "Of course we can come. We'll leave right now." Carolyn said something on her end. "That's crazy talk," Alice told her. "It's got to be a mistake. We'll meet you there. We'll be right there. Just tell me how to find it." She made a gesture for a pen.

I didn't have one. She looked around, then went to a counter-height table in the center of the food court where there were customer comment cards and ballpoint pens on chains. She wrote a few things down, hung up, came back to the table. "Let's go," she said.

"What happened?"

"She's half-hysterical, and she probably should be. We're supposed to meet her at the—" She looked down at her comment card. "The St. John's County Jail." She looked at me. "The *jail.* How could he be in jail?"

"Was he selling?" I asked. "Was Mid the one selling it?"

"All I could get out of her is that he was there, for some reason, when the police got there."

"But do they arrest you for just standing around?"

"How would I know? I don't know anything about this kind of thing. Where did we park?"

"Blue level," I said.

"I thought it was green."

"Level G," I said. "But it was blue."

We found our way out of the mall. Everything felt heavy and bent. On the drive back south, Alice kept talking about how she knew something was wrong, how she could just tell.

"But he doesn't seem the type for jail," I said.

"What is the type?"

"Fiercer?" I said.

She chewed on her lip. "Walter," she said, twisting in her seat. "The check. Do you think they can trace the check?"

"Do I think they can what?"

"The police. The check. Do you think we're in this?"

"OK," I said. "Wait. We don't even know if there's a 'this' to be in. And, yeah, they can trace the check. We deposited it. It's ours. But we haven't done anything. If somebody needs the check back, we'll give it back. That's all."

"Are you sure?"

"I'm sure."

"When you were with him," she said. "When you were with him, did you see anything like this?"

"Are you asking me if I've been dealing marijuana for a week without telling you?"

"I'm asking you if there's anything you know about. Anything you haven't told me."

"No," I said. "Jesus Christ. I mean, I can't figure out exactly how all his money works, but we haven't been in any gunfights in the town square, if that's what you're asking."

"That's not what I'm asking."

"What are you asking?"

"I'm not. I'm not asking anything."

I changed lanes, passed two trucks carrying culverts, worked a little bit on the math of what might be happening to me, to us, to Mid. Whatever it was, it was not good. Only motivational speakers and singers were better off for having gone to jail. For your average pizza house owner, jail time was probably not R&D.

"How could he do this to her?" she said.

"We don't know if he did."

"He did something." She put the ultrasound pictures in the glove compartment. "Also, what was going on with the smoothies?"

"They were named after explorers. They were all combo deals."

"Why?"

"I didn't ask."

She said, "Don't ever get arrested, OK? Don't ever make anybody come to jail to get you. This is awful."

"I'll try."

"I'm not kidding around. You don't get to go to jail. Neither of us does."

"I bet he didn't choose this," I said. "I bet this isn't what he had in mind for today."

"I still want us to make a rule."

"OK," I said. "It's a rule."

"Thank you," she said, and right then it occurred to me that if I'd been riding with him that morning, chances seemed better than average that whatever it was that had happened to him at Island Pizza would have happened to me, too.

■ ■ ■

The jail was a low cinderblock building set into scrub, with grassy areas cleared out all around. It was also the sheriff's office, the DMV, the courthouse, the tax and tag, and city hall. It took us four tries to find the right door.

The inside was nowhere near as nice as the waiting room at Varden's office, but it was the same basic idea: chairs and a window with somebody official behind it. You gave your name, you sat down, you held tight. Carolyn was already signed in on the register. We assumed she was in the back, wherever that was, with Mid. We were the only ones in the room. "I hate it here," Alice said.

I said, "I think you're supposed to." The woman behind the glass looked up at us and frowned. There was a Coke machine off in the corner, unplugged, its door half-open. There wasn't anything in it except a few cans of Tab. I asked Alice if she wanted one.

"They won't be cold," she said.

"Still," I said. "They're right there."

"You can't just take one," she said. "You can't steal from a jail."

I went back up to the desk. "Do you have a water fountain?" I asked.

The woman said, "We do not."

"What about the soda?"

"That machine is out of order."

I said, "Would you mind if we—"

She said, "Sir, please sit down. Someone will be with you in a moment."

I walked the edges of the room. Alice sat by the window, staring out into the parking lot. There was a clock, childhood-era industrial, the kind that plugged into the wall and ran its second hand around. Carolyn finally appeared out of a door in the side of the room that said UNAUTHORIZED ENTRY PROHIBITED, and when she saw Alice, she went straight to her, put her face in her shoulder. I couldn't tell whether to watch or look away. I heard her say, "Goddamnit, Leecy, I didn't sign up for this." I looked away.

Alice took her outside to get her calmed down. I sat inside with the Tab. By the time they came back in, I had a plan going where I would just grab one, start drinking, see what happened. The machine bothered me, standing open like that. Alice and Carolyn sat down, and Alice said, "He asked to see you when you got here."

I said, "Me?"

"He asked specifically," Carolyn said. Her face was puffed up.

"What do I do?"

"They call you," said Carolyn. "I asked them to give us a few minutes first."

"I just go back there?"

"They come and get you," she said.

I wasn't thinking right. "Are they not letting him go?" I asked, and Carolyn started crying again.

"They're keeping him overnight," Alice said, almost whispering. "They can't find a judge who can see him before tomorrow."

I said, "A judge?"

Alice mouthed *not right now,* rubbed her hand across Carolyn's back.

The door opened again, the UNAUTHORIZED ENTRY door. A policeman dressed in brown and green said, "Walter Ingram?" I raised my hand. "Come with me," he said. Carolyn pushed her hair out of her eyes, then leaned back into Alice again. The officer let me through the door. "Empty your pockets for me, sir," he said, and I put my keys and my wallet on a beige table in the middle of a beige room. Change and receipts. Little bits of sand. There was a camera up in the corner by the ceiling. The officer said, "Please hold your arms out from your sides." I held my arms up and he passed a small black wand over my body. It beeped at my belt buckle. He made me take that off. Once we were beepless, he let me through another door and into another tan room, and there was Mid, in a pair of jeans and a Hawaiian shirt and sock feet. He was not in handcuffs. He was sitting at a table with a paper cup of water in front of him. The table was too small for him, or the chair, or both. He said, "Did you bring me a beer?"

“They took everything I had back there.” I turned my pockets inside out.

Mid said, “They took my shoes and shoelaces. Apparently I’m not supposed to hang myself.”

“Are you wanting to hang yourself?”

“Not yet.”

“Good,” I said. “Right? That’s a positive.”

“One way to look at it.” He picked up his water, set it down again without drinking. “Thanks for coming.”

“Anytime.” I sat down across from him.

“This isn’t me,” he said. “I wanted to make sure to tell you that to your face. This isn’t me.”

“OK,” I said.

“But I can’t really talk about it. The lawyer’s telling me not to discuss it until we get to court.”

“It’s good you have a lawyer,” I said.

“He’s a tax attorney, but he said he’ll have somebody by tomorrow. Somebody who does criminal.”

“Criminal,” I said.

“It’s just a precaution.”

“Alice says you might be in overnight?”

“We have to set bail. Then I’ll be out again.”

“What is this?” I said. “Are you alright? Are we— ”

“I’m fine,” he said. “We’re fine. Everybody’s fine. This is a setback. I’ll be out tomorrow.” He sounded tired. I felt bad for him, but I also wanted to ask him how he’d managed to achieve this.

“Is there anybody I should call?” I said.

“Just go over to the fish camp tomorrow like we planned. Go on with your day like it was any other day.”

"Any other day I'd be riding with you." It was a stupid thing to say, a kid thing, but I couldn't help it.

"You'll be fine. Go get a lay of the land. I'll be out by the afternoon, and we'll be back to normal."

"That's all?"

"I just wanted to tell you this wasn't me. And I'll tell you the whole thing, too," he said, waving a hand at the ceiling. "But, you know, anything you say, and all that."

"It can't be that bad if they're letting you talk to me."

"That's what I thought. But I still get to spend the night for free." I could hear the lights humming. He said, "Carolyn's OK?"

"She's with Alice. She seems alright."

"You're lying."

"A little. But she is with Alice."

"It's good you guys are here," he said. "I'm glad you're down here."

"Alice is good in a crisis," I said.

"Well, we found ourselves one of those."

The door opened. The policeman put his head through. "Time, gentlemen," he said, and shut the door again.

"They only give us five minutes," Mid told me.

"You're OK," I said. "You're sure?"

He looked down at the table. "It could be worse. The guard back there told me they go out for barbecue for dinner, so that's what they're bringing me tonight." The cop knocked on the door again, but didn't come in.

I said, "Maybe if you just apologize, this'll all clear up."

"I tried that. No dice."

I looked behind him, at another door. "How is it back there?"

"I'm the only one here," he said. "So far, anyway. So I haven't had to make a shiv out of my toothbrush."

"Funny," I said.

"I'm here all night. Tip your bailiffs."

"Mid, what *happened*?"

"I'll tell you tomorrow," he said. "When it's all over. I will."

The cop came in, and there was a moment where I felt like I might be supposed to hug Mid, to pull him close and say something that would get him through the night, but by the time I got any of that worked out, the cop had turned him around, walked him through the door in the back of the room, and he was gone. A minute or two later the cop came back for me, took me out the way I'd come, gave me my change and belt back. He locked the door behind me. Carolyn and Alice were in the same place I'd left them.

"They're bringing him barbecue," I said.

"He likes barbecue," Carolyn said. She blinked, squeezed her eyes shut. "This is so wrong," she said. She stood up. "I need some air."

Alice asked me to finish up whatever needed finishing. I told her I would. I held the door for them, let them out into the afternoon. I went to the desk to ask the woman if we needed to sign back out, anything like that, but she wasn't there. It was silent in the room. No radio, no TV, nothing through the walls. I turned around, and Carolyn and Alice had gone past where I could see them, and for a moment I had this unshakeable feeling that I might be the only person left on the planet. Like Mid and Carolyn and Alice and the woman behind the counter and the baby and Varden and all of them had winked out of existence, and I was who was left. Me. I would survive on Tab and sheer force of will. I would leave messages for future civilizations. I would paint elk on the walls of the jail. Then the woman reappeared behind her desk, stared at me, said nothing. I said nothing. She slid her glass closed, and I went outside.

In the parking lot, Carolyn was sitting in the open side door of their SUV. The clouds were banking up out west like we'd see a thunderstorm later on. This was what happened most afternoons—three thousand degrees, then an afternoon storm, then three thousand degrees again. Carolyn said, "I don't know what I'm supposed to tell the kids."

"Would you like us to come over?" Alice asked.

"Maybe. But I need to tell them first." She seemed far away. You couldn't blame her. "I have to tell them first," she said again.

"We can call you," said Alice. "We can bring you dinner."

Carolyn thumbed her car keys around the ring. "That sounds fine," she said. "Let me get home, and I'll call you."

"Or we call you," Alice said. "Either way."

Carolyn pushed a button on the truck key, and the horn honked once. She pushed it again. Same thing. "Leecy?" she said. She was crying again.

"Yeah."

"What the hell?"

Alice sat down with her. "He'll be home tomorrow."

"What if he isn't?"

"He said he will be."

"But you know, this morning, he didn't mention any of this might happen."

"He probably didn't know," I said, trying to help.

Carolyn looked up. "He better goddamn not have."

"Let us cook you dinner," Alice said. "Get home and get settled in and call us, OK?"

"Settled in?" she said.

"You know what I mean."

Carolyn sat still a long time. "Thank you," she said, finally.

Alice said, "You don't have to thank me. This is what happens."

Carolyn said, "This is definitely, definitely not what happens."

"Go home," said Alice. "Go home, and then call us."

"I guess I'll do that," she said, and she got up, got herself in behind the wheel, hugged Alice through the open window, and then drove away, left us standing in the parking lot. We walked over to the car. I let Alice in on her side and she sat down, left the door open. I did the same on my side.

"Jesus," she said, leaning her head back against the rest. "Is it me, or are we at the jail?"

"I don't think it's you," I said.

She took the keys from me, put them up on the dash. Then she ran one hand down her side. "The Bundle of Joy does not care for this," she said. "The BOJ does not care for this at all."

■ ■ ■

By seven o'clock, we still hadn't heard from Carolyn. Alice wanted to go over there. I managed to get her to agree to at least wait until eight before we called to see what was going on. My position was: Give her some privacy. Alice's position was: Shut up. I'd left her sitting in the condo, at the glass-topped table, holding the phone in one hand, and picking at a shell-shaped pink vinyl placemat with the other. I was out on the balcony overlooking the parking garage. It'd been a tense afternoon. We'd fought about which balcony was the front or the back, whether the ocean side was the front or not. Once we'd worn that out, we moved on to whether there was any food in the house, whether the blinds on the beachside sliding glass doors were rusting, what kind of problem it would be if they were. I guess we felt like we couldn't go at each other over Mid. I kept making the wrong moves, choosing the wrong sides—and through it all, I couldn't stop thinking about the ultrasound room, how dark it had been in there, how bright the picture of the baby on the screen looked. I was certain Alice was working on that, too. She had to be.

I was running the scores and highlights in my head, watching the sun try to go down, wondering if Mid had any kind of view from his room, his cell, whatever it was, when the Camaro showed up, parked itself lopsidedly across a couple of spaces. The driver's-side door jawed open. At first there was nobody, and I had the crazy idea the car had driven itself over, some yellow reinvention of a dead TV show—but then there was Delton, standing on our parking deck. I opened the front door. I said, "You're probably going to want to come out here."

"I'm busy," Alice said.

"Has Carolyn called?"

"No."

"Well, if she calls, tell her Delton's here, OK?"

"Who?"

"Olivia. Delton. She's here."

Alice stood at the other end of the hall. "You want me to tell her what?"

"Downstairs," I said. "On the parking deck. Come see."

"How did she get here?"

"You'll like that, too."

"There's not some chance you're enjoying this, right?"

"Just come see," I said.

Outside, she kept a little space between us, leaned on the metal railing. Delton looked up and saw us, but did not wave. "Oh, hell," Alice said, pushing the heel of her hand into her forehead. "Oh, no."

"Right?"

"I'm going down there," she said.

"Give her a minute," I said.

"Whose car is that?"

"It might be hers. I'm not sure."

"She's fifteen years old. It can't be hers."

"Mid's been driving it. He said he was thinking about getting it for her."

"That? For a child?"

"It's got low miles."

"My God," she said. "He belongs in jail." She walked away, disappeared into the stairwell at the end of the building. When she came out again down on the roof of the parking deck it was like a magic trick, the slap of her shoes coming back up at me as she moved toward Delton, who was sitting now on the hood of the car. They talked, but I couldn't hear anything. At one point Alice held her hand out, and Delton gave her the keys. I wouldn't have thought of that. There was some school counseling for you. Every now and then one of them would look up at me, so I went inside, switched balconies. They didn't need me watching. Alice had it under control.

The beach was mainly emptied out except for a red pickup driving our direction, stopping every few hundred yards for a minute or two, then starting again. There was an orange light going on the roof. I found Sandy's binoculars, fooled with the focus until I was dialed in enough to see that it was a woman driving the truck, that when she stopped, she was getting a rake out of the back and smoothing a path from where the beach was flat back up to these cordoned-off areas in the dunes, places where stakes had been driven into the sand and pink tape strung between them, maybe three or four feet on a side. She got back in, drove a little, stopped and raked in another landing strip. There was a taped-off spot just past our buildings. I hadn't noticed it before. A sign was stapled to the stakes, but even with the binoculars I couldn't read it.

Alice and Delton came in behind me. I heard Alice tell her where the towels were, heard the bathroom door open and close. I still had the binoculars up to my face when Alice came out. "She's taking a shower," she said. "We thought that might make her feel better."

"Is she OK?"

"Well, her dad's in jail."

"Besides that, I meant."

She sat down, let out a long breath. "I don't know that there is much besides that, really."

"Did you call Carolyn?"

"She asked me not to. She said she wanted to do it herself."

"Are you sure we shouldn't—"

"Please don't ask me that," she said. "She asked me to wait, and I decided the ten minutes it'd take her to shower wouldn't make a whole lot of difference. God, I want a glass of wine."

"You could have a half," I said. "Want me to open a bottle?"

"I think I'll just shut my head in the sliding glass door a few times instead."

"It'll work out," I said.

"Empty promise," she said. "You don't know that."

The phone rang, and we looked at each other. It was loud. It rang again. "We have to get that," I said.

"I know," she said, but neither of us moved. The answering machine picked up. *This is Sandy Wilkes,* Aunt Sandy's voice said. We hadn't changed the message. It felt weird to keep it, weirder still to erase it. We'd been meaning to get a new phone and save that one on a shelf in the closet. *If I'm not here,* her voice said, *I must be out. Please leave your name and number, and I'll get back with you as soon as I can.* I was holding her binoculars. We were sitting in her chairs. Delton was getting ready to use her monogrammed purple towels. The machine beeped, and then there was Carolyn's voice filling the condo, saying, "Leecy? Are you there? Jesus Christ, is Olivia with you? She left a note. Pick up. Goddamnit, I need you to—"

Alice was already at the phone, telling her yes, Olivia was here. "She's fine," she said. "She's in the shower. She wanted to call you when—"

Delton opened the bathroom door, stuck her head out. She said, "Is that my mom?" Then she saw me. "Oh," she said, and shut the door.

"Sorry," I said.

Alice slid a stool away from the little pass-through bar to the kitchen, looped the phone cord around her wrist, accidentally pulled the phone off the counter. "Shit," she said, trying to pick everything back up. "Are you still there? Hello?" She pressed the button a few times. Other than the shower running, it was dead quiet in the condo.

"She's gone?" I said.

"She'll call back," she said, and the phone rang again.

"I'm going back outside." I motioned at the bathroom door. "Give her some space."

She nodded, answered the phone. "Hey," she said. "No. I dropped it. How are the twins?"

The pickup was past us, headed farther down the beach. Up north, some kids were setting off Roman candles. Somebody had a grill going on the strip of grass between the condos and the dunes. There was that mineral smell of charcoal in the air.

Alice had come to Florida when Delton was born, and when the twins were. She came for Maggie, too. When she got back that time, the Maggie time, all she could talk about was what a good father Mid was, how involved he was, how many diapers he changed. We'd stopped at some chain restaurant on the way back from the airport. There were hockey sticks on the wall. She said, "But here I am treating him like he's some wonder of the world because he's wanting to be a parent. To his own child." Then she said, "You know Ed came to see them and didn't even pick her up?"

Ed was Mid's brother. "Is he supposed to?" I said.

She looked at me. "What do you mean?"

"Why is it a big deal that he didn't pick her up?"

"She's his *niece*," she said. It was clear exactly what kind of deal it was.

"I get it," I told her. "I'm sorry."

She went back to her cheese fries, got quiet, and I ordered another beer. That was basically how it went for the few years we talked about having a kid, talked about trying: I'd make some error, and things would be sharp between us for a couple of days. What I'd feel afterwards was mainly guilty, and stupid—like I was a failure one more time and one more way, like here was the most primal thing in the world, and yet again I could not figure out how to do it. Or why. Everybody was scared. I knew that. You were an idiot if you weren't scared. But my thing broke along another fault line: I simply didn't *want* to do it, didn't want to think about it. In a bizarre way, Alice being pregnant, finally, was better. The abject dread of getting ready to have an actual kid was better than the shapeless place I'd been before.

I looked in through the glass doors at Alice. She had one foot curled up underneath her on the stool, was dressed in thin sweatpants and a T-shirt with holes worn through the back. The light in there made her look like she was in a store window. She laughed at something Carolyn said, a small laugh. She put one hand on her collarbone. She was beautiful. If we'd had a kid three years ago, like she wanted, we'd already have three years past us.

Delton came out through the other set of sliding doors, the ones off the master, and sat down next to me. She had on a pair of Alice's shorts, one of my shirts. "Hey," she said.

"Hey," I said back. Play it cool, I decided. Play it straight. Just talk to her.

"Thanks for the clothes."

"Anytime," I said.

She said, "They're still on the phone."

"Yeah."

"My mom's going to be pretty pissed."

"Maybe Alice can smooth things out," I said.

"No. This is bad. I'll be grounded." She put one foot up on the railing, started picking at her nail polish. "What's with the binoculars?" she said.

"I was watching that pickup. The woman driving it keeps getting out and raking the sand."

She said, "That's for the turtles."

"The turtles?"

"You've seen the nests, right? They're marked with like string or something?"

"The pink ribbon?"

"Right," she said. "That."

"Why does she have to rake the sand?"

Delton pulled her knees up to her chest, rested her chin between them. "It's so if they hatch, the babies can make it to the water. She's raking out the tire tracks."

"Really?"

"We went on a field trip about it. They can't get over the tire tracks by themselves. They need it flat. It's kind of cool. The turtle people are super serious about the whole thing, though. If you mess with the nests, you go to jail or something." She blinked a few times and turned away. "Fuck," she said, her voice catching. "Sorry."

I didn't know what to do, whether I should touch her on the shoulder, anything like that. "It's OK," I said.

"It's just, this'll be really great at school next year, you know?"

"It'll be over tomorrow," I said. "Maybe nobody will find out."

She wiped her mouth on her sleeve. My sleeve. "You don't get it," she said. "I mean, you wouldn't know. I have friends who buy from there. From Island. It's pretty famous."

I said, "Are you saying you *knew*?"

"Everybody knows. I just didn't know *he* knew. This is so fucking weird."

"Wait," I said. "Wait, OK?"

"What's the matter?"

I thought, How long do you have? Instead, I said, "Maybe he didn't know."

"Maybe."

"Do you think he did?"

"No. I don't know. Listen, you can't tell her this, OK?"

"Who?"

"Aunt Alice. Don't tell her. She'll tell my mom."

"How am I going to—"

"Oh, God, I know, you're married, you're best friends, you tell each other everything. Whatever. Could you just not tell her this one thing?"

"Do you buy?" I asked her, because now I was the cops.

"Sometimes I smoke with my friends. But I don't actually buy it."

"That's good," I said. "Safer, anyway."

"Yeah."

"Does everybody smoke?" I said.

"Not everybody. But a lot of people. So you won't tell her?"

The wind picked up. More fireworks down on the sand. Delton knew about Island Pizza. Mid was in prison and Alice was on the phone. I was who was left to be in charge. I said, "What if we just try to make it through tomorrow, and then see what happens?"

"Can you at least not tell her tonight?"

"OK," I said. "I won't tell her tonight."

"Cool." She relaxed a little, pushed her hair off her face. "I ran over a sign, by the way. But I got out and checked. You can't see anything."

"What kind of sign?"

"Something in the middle of the road, up on the grass. I'm not sure."

"Are you alright?"

"It was just a sign. I kind of lost it and drove over the curb. I'm fine."

She looked out at the water. The shrimp boats were lit up red and white. I wanted a beer. Or a joint, even. Instead, I sat with her, studied her, waited for her to tell me something else I did not know.

▪ ▪ ▪

Alice and Carolyn decided Delton staying with us was easier than somebody driving her back home, so we set her up on the sleeper in the living room. We left her watching a comic explaining the difference between going to bed with white girls and going to bed with black girls. "Are you allowed to watch this stuff?" I said.

"I've seen it already," she said. "It's on all the time. I like him. He's funny." She turned around. "Not this part so much, but other parts."

The comic said, "Now white girls will go like *this*."

I said, "Can we get you anything? Water? Another blanket?"

"I'm good," she said. "You guys are cool. It's cool here. I'm all set." Alice rubbed Delton's hair. I waved. We went to bed.

Through the wall, I could hear the rise and fall of laughter on the TV, and I could hear when it changed over to commercial, but I couldn't make out individual words. I said, "Do you think she's having sex?"

Alice said, "That's what you're worried about right now?"

"No," I said. "But do you?"

"You were, right?"

"She seems young."

"No, she doesn't. She seems fifteen."

"That's young," I said.

"I'd have her on the pill. I'll tell you that."

"Oh, God," I said.

"What?"

"Fifteen years feels like a lot of years from now. That's all."

"Don't freak out about that. Freak out about other things."

"Don't worry," I said. "What did Carolyn say?"

Alice moved her pillows around. "She said the twins handled it OK. She didn't tell Maggie. I think she thinks he did something. But I don't know."

"Does she know what the charge is yet?"

"Intent to distribute," she said. "Whatever that means."

"Holy shit."

"Well, you don't go to jail for a parking ticket, right?"

"Yeah, but—" My head felt a little loose from my body. "We might be fucked."

"I thought you said we were fine."

"We are. In one way, we are. But still."

"Still what?"

"We'll need that money," I said. "That money or other money." I reached underneath the sheet, rested my hand next to her hip. "It's just—you know we can't really move back, right?"

She said, "I don't want to move back."

"But we're here for this," I said.

"We're here. It doesn't have to be *for* anything."

There was a crack running from the window to the corner of the ceiling. It looked years old. "Do you think he did it?" I said.

"Carolyn's pretty pissed off. And sad. She doesn't sound right."

"I don't blame her," I said.

"Yeah, but it's different. She sounds different."

"I just can't see him as the local whatever," I said. "Dealer." Delton clicked off the TV in the other room. The light, too, I saw under the door. "We should probably be quiet," I said.

"She can't hear us."

"Carolyn was fine with her staying the night?"

"She was not. But Olivia wanted to stay, and neither of us could think of anything better. What'd you two talk about out there, anyway?"

"School," I said, the lie coming easily. "Turtles. She didn't really want to talk. I think she more wanted somebody to sit with her."

The AC kicked on, hummed and pushed at us. Every noise, every creak and pop, was still so new. Just don't tell her tonight, she'd said. So fine. I hadn't. I felt like an asshole, and at the same time like I'd done the right thing, or something like it. "I do kind of love that she stole the car," I said, trying to pull us in some other direction.

"You don't want her having sex, but she can be a car thief?"

"Thief's kind of a strong word."

"You think it's cute," she said.

"I think it's harmless."

"Do you think she's done? You think her driving herself over here is all there's going to be?"

"I hadn't thought about it like that."

She turned off the light and held to her side. The room was dark but for the moon shining through the glass doors. We slept that way, though the next morning I couldn't remember falling asleep. All I could remember was a dream of Mid, working a drive-through window, handing out bags of newly hatched sea turtles to car after car after car.

■ ■ ■

The plan was this: Alice would take Delton back home, take care of the kids while Carolyn went to court. I'd go out to the fish camp. Devil's Backbone. When I called to make sure somebody would be there, the guy on the other end of the phone picked up and just said, "Backbone." We agreed on ten o'clock. Alice and I fed Delton a bowl of Mini-Wheats, a glass of orange juice. She sat on the sofa bed watching one of the morning shows. We watched her like she was some kind of exhibit. Eventually, Alice drove her back to the castle in the hatchback, which left me piloting the Camaro. I felt like a child behind the wheel of that thing. I could see how it'd be no great challenge to takc out a sign.

Devil's Backbone was on the Intracoastal side, a sand and oystershell drive running back to two trailers welded longways at the seam. Out where they had the docks, which were a good deal more serious and permanent-looking than the building itself, somebody was keeping an iguana in a homemade cage. There were no boats in the water, no cars in the parking lot. It was hot and bright. It was always hot and bright. The place was a fever dream. I half-wished I had somebody with me—the twins, maybe. Having a couple of people nearby who knew martial arts might not hurt.

Inside, it was refrigerator-cold. The biggest through-wall air conditioner I'd ever seen was roaring away behind the counter, and there were low ice-cream-shop coolers full of bait along the walls: Styrofoam containers of worms, shrimp, fish. Live bait, too, in tanks. No bell on the door, no bell on the counter, no way to alert anybody you were there. Faded pictures of fishing triumphs stapled up everywhere. Hats and T-shirts and beer cozies with DEVIL'S BACKBONE printed on them. And the requisite fishing supplies, line and three thousand different shapes and sizes of lead weights, sorted into tins and trays. A sign up by the counter advertised boat rates. FULL DAY 225. HALF DAY 185. 90/HR. The rest of the board was empty, filthy. I stood in the middle of the floor and waited.

A man came out from a back room, tall, heavy, nodded at me, said, "Be with you in a minute." He took a tray of fishing weights outside. I could hear him walking along the dock. He came back in carrying a big plastic cooler, set it by the bait tanks, stood up straight, wiped his hands on his jeans, and said, "Charter?"

I said, "What?"

"My charter. You it?"

"No," I said. "Sorry. I'm—"

"So you gotta be Mid's guy. Pleasure. You want to see the cottages."

"Walter," I said.

"Hurley," he said. "Nice car."

"It's borrowed."

"Never seen one yellow like that before."

"I think somebody had it done," I said.

"I guess we can hope for that." He picked at something behind his left ear. "We'll walk the site, and I can show you the drawings we got made. That seem like the way things ought to go?"

I had no idea how things ought to go, and it didn't matter, because Hurley didn't wait for an answer. I followed him back out into the hot, and he walked us down a fresh-cut path into the weeds, around toward the water. I tried not to think too hard about snakes. Or about whether Hurley might be carrying some kind of weapon. It wasn't that difficult to imagine him turning on me with a machete. We stopped after a couple hundred yards. "So these are the cottages right here," he said, but there was nothing—no sites, no other paths. Just weeds leading down to a thin beach that was as much mud as sand. "And over there's gonna be the pool," he said.

From where we stood you could see the bridges coming over from the mainland, a newer concrete drawbridge built almost on top of an older wooden one. The center of it was knifed open for a long white yacht. The middle of the wooden bridge had been cut away. Across the waterway there were mansions on stilts edging out of the forest. Over here, in the flat, there was nothing. "How big are they going to be?" I said.

"Two bedroom. Kitchen, living room, laundry. And front porches. We're having front porches."

"How many?"

"Two waterfront," he said. "And then four more back poolside. We'll probably break ground in a couple weeks."

"I thought Mid said you guys were still kicking this around."

"Y'all do get a vote, I guess," said Hurley. "How's he doing, anyway? I heard he got a little busy."

"He's fine," I said, on instinct.

Hurley said, "I guess I don't have to tell you, but we don't need a lot of trouble out here, you know?"

"Sure," I said.

"But tell him I feel his pain."

"I will."

"I'd have sent flowers if I could have."

"Flowers?"

"He'll pull through. He always does." The yacht had made it through, and the bridge was sliding back into place behind it. Again I felt lost. Again I felt like there was some book I should have read beforehand. He said, "Ask me about the numbers out here. Ask me about rental prices."

"What'll you rent them for?" I said.

"Guess."

"I have no idea."

"Thirteen hundred a week," he said, rising up on the balls of his feet. "Two-fifty a night. In season, anyway."

"Are you serious? Here?"

He pulled a cigarette out of his pack. "No offense taken," he said.

"I didn't mean that," I said.

"You're from where? Kansas?"

"North Carolina," I said.

"Not the beach."

"No."

He got lit up, took a long pull. The smoke against the salt mud smelled acrid and wrong. He said, "Look. Our whole thing is we get folks down here thinking they want to spend a week fishing, OK? They've got some dream all worked out about how it would go. What they really want to do is fish for one day and spend the rest of the week sitting on their fat asses on the beach watching the little ladies go by, but they don't know that." He squinted into the sun. "Everywhere else down here is houses and condos.

Any town but this one is high schoolers making twelve bucks an hour plus tips to set your umbrella in the sand for you. We call these fishing cottages, though, and who we'll get is dudes with big dreams, dudes who've seen what they think they want on some YouTube video. Drop a pool in the ground for the wife and kids, take these boys out and get 'em sunburned and drunk, and at least for that first day everybody has the time of their lives. After that I don't know. Maybe we'll load up one of the boats and take everybody around front to the real beach, if that's what they want. Run us a water taxi every couple hours or something. I've been wanting to do this for years."

"Why didn't you?" I said.

"Needed you," he said. "You and the jailbird."

"Why not a bank?"

"Can't be dealing with suits all day. I like to keep it local." He flicked the ash off his cigarette. "Mid's good people," he said. "He'll make his money. You tell him we're ready. Tell him if we open up next season, he'll make his cash."

He took me back up to the building to show me the drawings. The cottages looked fine there on the rolls of paper—shake siding, tin roofs. They looked like they'd be perfect almost anywhere. Just not here. I did not say so. I nodded and listened and did my job. Maybe it looked different to somebody who wasn't me. Maybe it'd look right once the cottages were actually standing. But what it seemed like on paper was that somebody was trying to play house at a gas station.

His charter turned up, two guys wearing golf shirts tucked into their pants. They looked pink and hungover. I took my chance to go, headed for the door while Hurley asked them whether they had any gear, whether they might like to rent some truly top-of-the-line stuff. He was precisely the picture of himself they wanted him to be. It was nearly noon. Hurley broke away from them right as I was getting into the car, told them to hang on just a second, gentlemen, leaned through my window, and said again to tell Mid this was a sure thing. "Also tell him I said get well soon," he said, and shook my hand. I got back out on the highway. My head was crammed full and buzzing. Hurley knew things I didn't, but that didn't make him particularly special. It only added him to the list.

■ ■ ■

I found a place for lunch that looked safe, predictable, had a top deck where you could see the ocean. I ordered a Coke and a fish sandwich. The place was open to the air on the beach side, pretty full, and it was not difficult to see who was local and who was not. I sat there trying to figure out if Hurley had meant me, if I was the sort of person who might be his perfect mark—the kind of guy who might, on the strength of a glossy brochure, rent a half-sized cottage on the wrong side of the island. Alice called. "Where are you?" she said.

"I'm eating lunch," I said. "North a little ways." I checked the menu. "The Oasis."

"Mid's out on bond. And they dropped some of the charges. It's down to just possession, and the lawyer says they'll either make some kind of deal or get it dropped completely."

"Possession."

"The lawyer says they had to charge him with something."

"Does anybody know what happened?"

"Mid says the police came through and arrested everybody in sight. Apparently he doesn't know anything about it, but they took him in since he's the owner, or part-owner, or whatever."

"That doesn't sound exactly right."

"That's what Carolyn says, too."

"How is she?"

"They went somewhere to talk. I think she's pretty blown away."

"But he's out?"

"He is."

"That's good," I said.

"I guess so." She didn't sound sure. All around me people started getting up from their tables, walking to the edge of the deck, looking south. I looked that way, too. "Are you still there?" she said.

"Yeah," I said. "Hold on a second." It was the parachutist. Or a parachutist. But there couldn't be two. "I think this is our guy," I told her. "Up here. I think it's him."

"What guy?"

"The vet. The flyer. I think he's up here."

"How far away are you?"

"Doesn't matter. It's him." At first he was just a black kite against the sky, but he kept coming, and there it all was again: the DON'T TREAD ON ME flag hooked back up to the rig, plus two rainbow-striped windsocks hanging from the undercarriage. He had on a full Indian headdress. It looked like his beard might be in a braid. People cheered as he got nearer. He saluted, and people cheered louder. He flew a big loop out over the water and came back around.

"How does he look?" Alice asked.

"He looks—he looks good. He's got more stuff." And then he pointed at me. I said, "I think he's pointing at me."

"Why would he be doing that?"

"Maybe he recognizes me."

"From the balcony?"

"How would I know?" He was turned in his seat, grinning. He was wearing the goggles.

"Do you think he could know you were you?"

"No," I said. "But maybe." If he did, he had to wonder where Alice was, why she wasn't there to show the BOJ the fabulous flying man once more. He quit pointing, flew on up the beach. It was over, just like that. Everybody sat back down.

Alice said, "Hello?"

"Yes," I said. "Sorry."

"I lost you for a minute."

"I just—" He'd spooked me, is what it was. A winged messenger, come for me. "Never mind. It doesn't matter."

"When are you coming home?"

"Now, I guess. When I finish eating." How could he have known? I kept seeing him bank and find me. I picked up the table topper, read down the specials. Clam strips. Cornbread. I felt very far away.

"Walter?" Alice said.

"Yeah."

"Did you hear me? I said I'd see you at home."

"Home," I said.

"Are you alright?" she said.

I gave her the only answer I could.

Saturdays were changeover days. The weekly renters packed up in the mornings, and their replacements arrived in the afternoons. The ones leaving: bleary from all their good fortune, determined now to make good time on the ride back into their daily lives. Arrivals: in a hurry, full of brand-new bodyboards and unrusted chairs and bags of groceries, sugared cereals and hot dog buns and beer. The little kids shrieked. The big kids preened. The adults loaded luggage onto hotel carts, wheeled their way into the elevators, found their spots on the upper floors. Maybe someone was towing a couple of jet skis. Maybe somebody'd brought a college-themed tent big enough for the whole family. They'd get settled in, unpacked, and then they were down on the beach or into the pool, parents trailing the kids, trying to make sure they put on sunscreen, floaties. The refrain of the arriving parents: Wait. Wait. Ronnie, just a goddamned minute. Kayla, come back here right now.

What they did: Sit on the beach, read, make sure the kids didn't drown in the surf. Sit by the pool, drink, adjudicate Marco Polo disputes. Sometimes, on a Wednesday, the beach would go quiet, empty itself out, all the renting families off to St. Augustine for a carriage tour or down to Marineland to watch the dolphins jump through hoops. The cars came back with dolphin-shaped bumper stickers: I'VE BEEN TO MARINELAND.

Fourth of July: Big fireworks in St. Augustine, bigger ones down south toward Daytona, the sky lit up on both edges. On our beach, people shot off squealers, screamers, six-by-six cubes with names like Smiling Dragon and Happy Family. Dads and kids hunched into the wind trying to light matches, ten tries for every one they got lit. Then the scatter and scramble for safe distance, the thing going off too soon, the laughing, the apologies, the promises not to do it again. Then they'd do it again.

Alice and I sat on the balcony, celebrated our independence. Alice was showing more, a quarter-moon there at her waistline, said she was sure she felt the BOJ kicking. I couldn't feel it. "Hold still, hold still," she said. "That right there? You don't feel that?" I told her I wanted to. "You will," she told me. "Don't worry. Soon."

I spent half a week moving the bird paintings around the condo, but the walls were a different color behind the frames, so I moved them all back.

▪ ▪ ▪

Two Tuesday nights after he got arrested, Mid rang our doorbell. It was the first time anybody'd rung the doorbell since we'd been there. It played the national anthem. I opened the door. Mid had a pink duffel bag with plastic glittery handles. "It's Olivia's," he said, holding the bag forward a little. "I couldn't find the suitcases. Mind if I come in? I think I need to sit down."

Alice met us in the hall. "What is this?"

Mid said, "She kicked me out."

"Please say that's not true," Alice said.

"Don't worry. I'm not staying."

"You have a bag," she said.

He looked down at it like he'd already forgotten he had it with him. "I don't know why I brought this up."

"What happened?" I asked him. "What's going on?"

"The guy who runs morning prep at Island? Stevie? He called and asked to store some stuff at our place. In our attic. Carolyn picked up while he was talking. I didn't even get the chance to tell him no."

Alice said, "Stuff?"

"Grow lights," Mid said. "Stuff."

"Carolyn's right?" she said. "You knew?"

"Alice," I said.

"Did you?" she said, ignoring me.

"I had an idea," he said.

"This can't be happening," she said. "This is insane."

"Let him talk," I said, mainly because nobody'd talked about it yet. Mid wasn't talking to Carolyn, Alice reported, and he sure wasn't talking to me. I wasn't asking him, for one thing. I'd been afraid to. We'd been riding stop to stop like nothing happened.

"Did you know?" Alice said. "Will you just please say?"

"I tried not to know," he said. "I knew in the way you can know without knowing."

She said, "Is that what the lawyer's telling you to say?"

"I only ever played with the front of the house. Whatever went on in the back, I tried to just let that go, ignore it."

"That sounds like bullshit," she said. "No offense. Also, I don't think you being here is such a good idea." She turned around, walked away. "I have to call Carolyn," she said.

"I'm not staying," Mid said again.

"You can if you need to," I told him.

"No, he can't," Alice said, from the kitchen.

We heard her pick up the phone. He said, "This is just for a few days. Until she cools off some."

"Sure," I said.

"I spent a couple nights out after Maggie was born, when she was about a year old. This'll solve itself."

"Sure," I said again. Alice was talking to Carolyn now, saying something about getting to the bottom of things. Or hitting bottom. I couldn't tell.

"The county commission met this afternoon," Mid said, looking at the floor. "On the school."

"And?"

"They voted to delay construction indefinitely. No funding. Cutbacks and all that. I guess they're going to try some kind of bond issue in the next election, see if that'll fly."

"That sounds bad," I said.

"Very."

"You OK?"

He switched his duffel from hand to hand. "You know, it's kind of hard to say."

I said, "Grow lights?"

"He was wanting me to hang onto them for a week or two."

"You would have told him no," I said, checking.

"Yeah," he said. "That's what I would have told him."

"What made him think he could ask you that?"

"That's exactly what I was trying to tell Carolyn. This doesn't have anything to do with me."

I said, "It has something to do with you, though, right?"

"I should have told you," he said. "I should have told Carolyn. I never should have let it get this far."

"You knew," I said.

"I thought they had it under control. The place makes a ton of money. Made. I just felt like the less anybody knew about it, me included, the better. I felt like it wasn't my business."

I said, "Even though it was your actual business? That was your plan?"

"I think it was," he said.

"Jesus, Mid."

Alice came down the hall, purse in her hand. "I'm going over to see her," she said. "Mid, it's not that I don't— Anyway, you just can't stay here. I'm sorry. It's Carolyn—"

"I get it," he said. "I'm staying with a guy down the beach a little. I'll be fine. This will all be fine."

"Fine," Alice said.

"Yeah."

"She did ask how you were."

He looked awful, I thought. Cratered. "Tell her I'm making it," he said. "Tell her I'm holding up."

"When will you be back?" I asked her.

"Later. Don't wait up." She kissed me, and then said, "Please be good."

"What?"

"Be good," she said again. She was wanting a joke, but it didn't work—she ended up meaning it. "When I come back, I don't want anything to have happened to you."

"How could anything happen to me?"

"How would I know?" she said, half under her breath, and then she left. We could hear her walking toward the elevators. Mid sat down, leaned against the front door, and thumped his head on it a couple of times. A hollow, metal sound came back.

I said, "Can I get you something? A drink?"

He hit the door again. "That'd be about right," he said. "But I might want some ice cream first."

"Some what?"

"Ice cream. I'd like some ice cream. Doesn't it seem like that would help?"

We didn't have any. Alice had run through it a couple of nights ago, and I hadn't been back to the store. "We can go get some," I said.

"Do you mind?"

"Let me get the keys." I left him there in the hallway, went to get my things. I stood in the back bedroom and looked at myself in the mirror. Ice cream. I didn't quite know him well enough to understand if he was coming unraveled or not. All I knew was that he was in my hallway, holding a sparkly pink duffel bag and banging his head against the door. Nothing in Sandy's bird books for that, probably. I found my wallet, found my shoes, and only then remembered that I didn't own my own car anymore, and that Alice had taken the one we had. "Mid," I said.

"Yeah."

"You drove here?"

"In the banana."

"You buy that thing yet?"

"Still test-driving it."

"You're going to have to test-drive us to the store."

"Right. That'll be fine."

I walked out there. "Can I ask you something?" I said.

"Go ahead."

"What's in the bag?"

He looked up at me. I don't know what I thought he was about to show me. Stacks of twenties. Silver-plated pistols. Pure uncut Venezuelan hash. He unzipped the bag. Clothes. T-shirts and socks. I felt relieved, but also a little disappointed, which was how I knew Mid might not be the only one tuned in to the wrong station. Be good, I could hear Alice saying. Be good, be good.

"You ready?" Mid said, standing up, and off we went.

■ ■ ■

Delton was in the parking lot at the grocery. We passed her coming in. "Jesus Christ in a rayon tracksuit," Mid said. "Another country heard from." He cut a long loop around a row of parked cars, brought the Camaro back to where she was standing with a few other kids, all of them smoking cigarettes. She'd seen us the first time by. There wasn't any mistaking that car. When she flicked her cigarette away, it was more show than any attempt to cover up what she'd been doing. Mid shut the headlights off so we wouldn't blind them. The kids stared at us. They were bored. Not caught. Not afraid. Just bored.

"See?" Mid said. "This is what I'm talking about. She doesn't give a shit about anything."

"Sure she does."

"She doesn't give a shit about me. We've asked her not to smoke."

"Kids smoke," I said. "At least she's not driving."

"We asked her not to smoke until she was eighteen. That's the kind of fuckwad compromise you end up making."

"The other night, Alice said she'd have her on the pill." It was out of my mouth before I even tried to think it through.

"She is on the pill."

"She is?"

"Sure, man. You think we're idiots?"

He left the motor running, got out of the car, and walked over to Delton. He didn't yell. He put his hands in his pockets, stood there and fathered. He'd gone to jail. He'd been kicked out of his own house. He was in search of ice cream. He asked her a couple of questions, and she shook her head no to each one. She had a new haircut, one side longer than the other. She had on that same long-sleeved band T-shirt again, only this time with a pink ballet skirt. She was cute—not Homecoming Queen cute, but you could tell she wasn't going for that. Mainly what she looked like was a kid playing dress-up, trying to play at being grown up. And who could blame her? That was give or take what any of us were doing. Mid asked another question, and she nodded yes this time, leaned into the car they were standing around, came out with her purse. They walked back toward me and Mid opened the driver's-side door, folded the seat forward. She got in. She reeked of smoke. "Walter," she said, in a fake deep voice. "How goes?"

"Delton. It goes."

"Father has suggested I tag along with you two for a while, instead of hanging out with my miscreant friends."

"Fabulous," I said.

"Isn't it?"

Mid drove us over a few rows, found a space by the door. He parked and we sat there, the grocery glowing out into the lot. I hadn't seen Delton since she spent the night in the condo. From the back seat, I heard the scrape and flash of a lighter. "Come on, Liv," Mid said. "At least don't smoke in the goddamn car."

Delton took a long drag, then knocked on the glass with one knuckle. "These windows back here don't open or something," she said.

Mid reached his hand back. She gave him the cigarette like it was a wad of gum. He rolled his window down, dropped it out, and almost immediately a pickup flashing green lights pulled up behind us, blocked us in. Security. Mid looked in the rearview. "Give me a fucking break," he said. Delton giggled. I wondered if maybe she'd been smoking more than cigarettes. A kid got out of the pickup, walked to Mid's window. He said, "Excuse me, sir?"

Mid said, "Yes?"

"I was just wanting to ask if this was your cigarette."

Mid leaned out the window and looked at the ground. "It is not," he said.

"I believe I just saw you drop it out of your window."

"Yes," Mid said, and that seemed to confuse things. The kid stood. We sat. It was a standoff. Then he noticed Delton.

"Olivia?" he said.

"Hi, Ellis."

He looked back at Mid and me, frowning. "Is everything alright?"

"This is my dad," she said. "And my Uncle Walter."

"Oh," he said, clearly relaxing. We weren't homicidal kidnappers. Probably. He reached his hand in. "I'm Ellis," he said. "Olivia and I had PreCal together last spring." Mid shook his hand.

"Mrs. Newell," Delton said.

"Remember how she wore that same sweater every day for two weeks?" Ellis said.

"Yes," said Delton, but not really to him. It was pretty clear what the score was: Delton was several rungs up the social ladder from Ellis. They were math class friends. Associates. Out of math class—at the grocery store, say, with her jailbird dad—she wanted less to do with him.

Ellis said, "You know what? How about I just pick this up this one time, and we go on about our business?" He was magnanimous. Dauntless. He already had the cigarette in his hand.

"Great," Delton said.

"Thank you," said Mid.

"We're supposed to enforce the regulations," the kid said, by way of apology. "You know, rule of law, that kind of thing. Society on the brink of collapse."

"Wow," Mid said.

"It's serious business," he said.

Mid said, "It won't happen again."

"Olivia," Ellis said. "Maybe I can text you."

"Maybe," she said.

"Awesome," he said. He was wearing a white short-sleeve polo. He had acne. He had a blue baseball cap with the logo of the security company on it—a lock and a dog. Finally he gave us what was probably supposed to be a wave, walked over to a trash can by the building, dropped the cigarette in, got back in his truck, and left.

Mid tilted the rearview so he could see Delton. "He seemed nice," he said.

"Dad."

"He's got a job. Tucks his shirt in. Talks like a senator."

"Dad. Seriously."

We went inside the grocery. It was catastrophically well lit. The store was running some kind of promotion having to do with a new deli counter, which looked exactly like any other deli counter I'd ever seen, but they were excited about it, had arches of red and orange balloons up everywhere in all the bright light, stations where free deli samples could be had. It seemed late at night to be having a deli party. Delton broke away, started making the circuit of samples. I hung back with Mid. We watched her eat sliced turkey, sliced ham. "What'd you say to her back there?" I asked him. "In the parking lot?"

"I told her we were getting ice cream."

"She knows about you and Carolyn?"

"Everybody was right there when she went apeshit."

"But why'd she want to come with us?"

"I told her we were going to a party at my buddy's place on the beach. I said she could come."

"We're going to a party?"

"It's one of the kids at Me Kayak, Sea Kayak. It's his parents' place. They're in Europe for the summer. That's where I'm staying. Only he's having a thing tonight, a few people, low-key."

"You're taking her to a house party on the beach."

"We are. I wasn't sure what else to do."

"How about let her smoke in the parking lot with her friends?"

"You know," he said, "that didn't really cross my mind."

We went to look for ice cream. Mid chose chocolate. I got a thing of rum raisin. When we got back to the deli, there was a pirate, in full garb, doing a magic trick for Delton. He was floating a small table a couple feet in the air, lighting a candle on it, saying something into a headset about a lovely dinner for two. "Now I'm going to turn this over to you," he was saying to Delton. "You're going to fly the table, little miss." The tablecloth had some kind of wire rigged into it so that he could do what he was doing, which was to hang onto the corners magic-carpet-style and act like he was the only thing keeping all of it from zipping over to frozen foods. The table danced in the air. It was a medium-good trick, a step or two up from what you could get at a toy store in the mall. Delton was shaking her head, was saying she didn't want to fly the table.

"No, thank you," she said.

"Come on, baby," the pirate said into the microphone.

"I don't think I love the tone of his voice," Mid said.

"Let's everybody gather round and watch the pretty girl do some magic, all courtesy of SliceRite Premium Select meats and cheeses," said the pirate. "Watch the little lady amaze us." The pirate had a peg leg, obviously fake, obviously plastic. I had no idea what a pirate might have to do with meat and cheese. Or magic tricks. Then the pirate was somehow touching Delton on her right hip, right about where her T-shirt didn't quite meet her skirt, and she shoved him, hard, back through a prize wheel that was set up behind him, orange and black and red pie wedges of various discounts and two-for-one offers from the deli. The pirate went down, and the prize wheel and the magic table and a stand speaker hooked up to the microphone went down with him. It made a hell of a noise. He was back up in a hurry, one bare leg sticking out from his costume. "Fuck you, you little bitch," he said into the mike, and that went out over the speakers. He took a step in Delton's direction. Mid started toward both of them at a jog—we'd both just been standing there—but Delton was fine on her own. She stepped crisply to the side and pushed a wire rack of bread at the pirate, baguettes and ciabattas, and he slipped and went down again, this time cracking his head pretty hard on the floor. He stayed down.

Delton turned, saw Mid coming for her. She looked like she might take him out, too. That or start crying. But she didn't do either. She stood still. The pirate groaned. There were store people moving our way, deli employees, and customers standing around like they'd witnessed a crime, which maybe they had. Mid got Delton by the arm, walked her back past me, said, "We don't need to hang around for this." We took our ice cream through one of those do-it-yourself checkouts, and Mid gave the woman supervising the computers ten dollars, made some kind of gesture that I took to mean we weren't waiting for change. The pirate said *cunt* into the microphone. People stared. Mid jogged Delton into the parking lot. He already had the car started by the time I got in. Ellis pulled up to the front of the store in his security pickup, green lights flashing.

"Go," Delton said. "Please go."

Mid clipped a cart on his way out of the lot. He said, "That'll leave a mark."

"You'd be surprised," Delton said from the back seat, not in a faked voice, but not in her real voice, either. She sounded about how you'd sound if the deli pirate had just tried to feel you up. I hurt for her. I didn't know how or whether to say so.

Mid turned right, out from under a NO TURN ON RED sign, aimed us back toward the beach. He drove the speed limit, kept trying to check on Delton in the rearview without her catching him. None of us talked. The car rumbled below us. The radio played. We listened to the DJ tell us what had just been on, what was coming up next.

■ ■ ■

"We don't have any way to eat this," I said. Mid had parked us at a public access for the beach. The gate was closed and padlocked. All we could see was dune grass. No ocean.

"Here," Delton said. She unbent two spoons she was wearing as bracelets, handed them up.

"Are these clean?" Mid asked.

"They're spoons," she said. She pulled a third one off her wrist, wiped it on her shirt. "Pass me some," she said. I gave her my carton. We ate like that a while, sharing the ice cream around. Moths the size of wrens crashed into each other in the lights hanging off the corners of the picnic shelter. A couple came out of the dunes, climbed the gate, giggling. "Great," Delton said. "Young love." They got into a car and drove away.

Mid turned around in his seat. He tried to start talking a couple of times before he finally got going. He said, "Sweetie—"

Delton said, "Here we go."

"What?"

"No speeches, OK? That guy was a creeper. That's all. I shouldn't have walked up to him in the first place. I knew it. I just felt bad for him, and then he was doing the thing with the table, and then, I don't know, it was too late."

"You didn't do anything wrong."

"He probably has a concussion."

"If he does, he deserves it."

"I guess," she said.

Mid chewed his lip. "I'm really sorry," he said.

"For what?"

"For that guy. For the kid from your class in the parking lot. For what's going on with your mom and me."

"Would you guys like me to get out a minute?" I said. "I could go for a walk."

"Can I have the chocolate?" she said. It was like I wasn't there. "Dad. Seriously. I'm all set. You're the one in the shitstorm."

"I think you owe the twins a dollar," he said.

"They're not here, right? I can say what I want. Fucking prudes."

"They're twelve."

"They're the fucking Gestapo."

"Olivia."

"Sorry."

"Your mom and I will be fine," he told her. "Once she forgives me."

She took a bite of ice cream. "Except she doesn't seem all that into doing that."

"What makes you say that?"

She smiled at him. It wasn't a mean smile, but it wasn't kind, either. "You saw her."

"That's how she gets. She's just mad."

"Wait until she finds out you took me to a party."

"How will she find out?"

"She finds everything out. That's how she is."

"Where are you supposed to be right now, anyway?"

"Out."

"Home by eleven?"

"Home by eleven."

I tried to imagine what might be running through Delton's head right then—what might have made her want to be in the car with us instead of out on the beach with some boy, or in a parking lot with her friends. "So, Dad," Delton said. "Are we going to this thing, or what?"

Mid cranked the car, turned us around, put us back out on the road. I started counting Hurricane Evacuation signs again.

After a couple of miles, Delton said, "Will there be any pirates there?"

"God," Mid said. "There damn well better not be."

■ ■ ■

Even though I didn't want any part of being fifteen again, I envied her all the same. Something about that age—young enough to still be a kid, and know it; old enough to feel pretty certain that your problems weren't really kid problems anymore, but to find ways to enjoy wallowing in the pain of that, too. Your dad deals pot out of the back of his restaurant. Your mom kicks him out. Your phone lights and jumps five or six times on the way to a party with your dad and your drifter uncle, the screen filling with the Morse code of everyone you know, and when it goes off yet again, you hunch down farther into the back seat of a monstrous car that could soon be yours, try to make yourself still more hidden. The things she probably typed back: *U will not blv this. LOL. SOS.* Or just as likely, somehow: *I remain, as always, yr hmbl svt.*

She was two months away from sixteen—two months from

the open road and the endless dream of a better tomorrow, her few belongings tied into a bandanna and slung over her shoulder, Huck Finn driving a yellow muscle car, smoking a pack of Winstons, wearing a tutu. And as for me? I was twenty-some weeks away from my daughter's arrival on the planet. I could feel the pressing weight of how little time that was. What I wanted to do was hand a spiral notebook and a pencil into the back seat and ask Delton to jot down, longhand, everything she knew: Should we make the BOJ take piano lessons? Gymnastics? When does a kid go to sleepover camp for the first time? When was the first time you remember being actually happy to play by yourself in your room? Or in the yard? If we had one kid, did we have to have two? Was that some kind of rule? Just write it all down, please, I wanted to tell her. All of it. Write down everything I'm going to need to know.

■ ■ ■

Mid turned at a driveway, pulled up to a little gray clapboard house. It was tiny, fifty or sixty years old. The houses on either side were not—they were behemoths, the products of bulldozings of places like the gray house. The house on the left had its own pool, covered in a clear geodesic dome. The one on the right had marble railings on the upstairs balconies. The gray house had rusting gutters, a cracked storm door. It gave the impression it was leaning. There was an inflatable kiddie pool in the lawn. "Damn," Delton said, once we were out of the car.

For the first time, I saw her fingernails were painted lime green. "Nice fingernails," I said.

She looked down at her hands. She had rings on both thumbs. "It's supposed to be how far you'll go," she said.

"How far?" I said.

"Yeah. All the girls do it. Like, stuff you'll do. Sex stuff."

"Really?" I said.

"I mean, some girls do that, I guess. Or I heard they do at other schools. We don't."

"What's green mean?" I said, pretty sure I didn't want the answer.

"Green means green," she said. "Green means that's what I had."

"Good," I said.

Mid rang the front bell. Nobody answered. We could hear people out back, though, and that's where we found the party, or what was left of it: Kids not vastly older than Delton sprawled over lawn chairs, dining room chairs, stuffed armchairs that looked reclaimed from the side of the road. Almost everyone was up on a wooden deck that hung off the back of the house. There was music going. A few guys had a TV set up on a card table. They were playing a video game. Hockey. "I don't know about this," Mid said.

We hadn't brought anything except for the ice cream that was melting in the car. I was about to ask Mid how we might go about getting a beer, maybe a soda for Delton, when a huge brown dog barreled out the open kitchen door. The dog was a hundred pounds, easy. It was a small bear. A skinny kid wearing shorts and no shirt came running after it, yelling "Roscoe! Roscoe!" The dog never slowed down. It ran across the deck, down the steps, and out onto the beach. "Roscoe!" the kid yelled. "Goddamnit, dude, come back!"

Delton already had her shoes off. "Hey," she said. "Do you need help?"

The kid turned around. "Come on!" he shouted, and took off again. Delton handed Mid her shoes, hesitated for maybe a beat or two, and then she was down the stairs and gone, too, hollering out *Roscoe!* on her way over the dunes.

Mid stared into the space where she'd been. He sat down on the stairs, fit Delton's flip-flops together front to back. He said, "Holy hell."

"Should we go after them?" I said.

"They're gone."

"We could catch up."

He shook his head. "We couldn't. That's the thing."

I said, "You don't think—"

He'd let his chin fall down to his chest. "It's a beach. It only has two directions. She'll be alright."

"Are you sure?"

"No," he said. "But what's the alternative?"

Panic, I thought. Choppers with searchlights. I sat down next to him. We were the oldest people there by fifteen years, maybe twenty. One of the hockey gamers scored and celebrated. Inside the house, it sounded like somebody fell down. There was a lot of laughing.

Mid said, "I've got to be honest with you—I'm not really sure I know what to do right here."

"About Delton?"

"About too much of anything, if you want to get right down to it."

I wanted Alice. She was better at these kinds of moments than I was. I said, "How do you mean?" because I at least knew I was supposed to ask.

"Carolyn keeps telling me I'm crazy," he said. "I think she means it."

Music. Cars out on A1A. Sound of the waves just down the steps. I said, "And?"

"And what?"

I figured, go ahead and find out. "And are you?" I said.

"Let's call her," he said. "You can ask."

"You don't seem crazy," I said.

"Have you seen our house? It turns out I built our house at the Alligator Farm."

"At the what?"

"It's a place up in St. Augustine. Like a zoo. Or a theme park. They have alligators."

"You guys are near that?"

"No, but Carolyn's just waiting to find one in our pool. That's the first thing she does in the morning—make coffee, check out the window to see if we've got gators in the shallow end. That's all she wants. To have an alligator come out of the woods, take a swim. Then she'd have it on me airtight."

I said, "I thought she liked it out there. The house and everything."

"That was back when we thought we'd get the school built. When we thought somebody might actually build out there with us."

"No takers?"

"We live in a demonstration home."

"Somebody'll buy out there, right?"

It was like I hadn't even asked the question. "Hurley went ahead and broke ground at Devil's Backbone," he said. "And you saw those things. That place is a train wreck." He picked at a nailhead pushing up out of the deck. "You know why he really wants to do it? The vacation thing is bullshit. He needs to wash money off from this black-market saffron thing he's got going. He grows fucking crocus in a greenhouse on some island out in the river. Crocus. He's got like three or four migrants who spend all day long dusting those fuckers with Q-tips. It's some special variety, not approved for import, and he sells it to a guy he's got in Vegas who turns it around and sells to private restaurants. He's making a fortune."

"What's your part in it?"

"I'm hooked into him from a while back. He cleaned something up for me."

"What does that mean?"

"It's nothing dangerous. Just some paperwork."

"If he's trying to hide money, what does he need yours for?"

"You don't want to know."

"Maybe I do," I said.

He ignored that, too. "The Twice-the-Ices come in this week," he said. "Maybe tomorrow. I don't know, Walter. I'm not really sure how I'm supposed to pay for all this."

"You don't have the cash?"

"I need to move some things around."

I said, "I can give you that check back if you need it."

"The thirty thousand? Shit. I owe a hundred alone on the Pelican land in September. Plus sixty-five for the Twice-the-Ices, plus monthlies thereafter. And Hurley thinks he wants a deep-water dock once he gets the first run of cabins in. It is possible, my friend, that I may be relatively screwed." He looked up at the sky. "And here's something for you to chew over later with your little family. This is the pièce de résistance. The nom de plume. The guy who called tonight? Steve? The grow lights?"

It was too fast, all of it. Black-market spices. Whatever the hell else he was telling me. I wanted to stop him right there, walk away, never know anything more. I could pack Alice and the BOJ and all the canned food thirty thousand would buy onto a sailboat and just hope for breeze, hope for the best. Instead, I said, “Yeah?”

“Last Friday? When I went to Daytona?”

“Right.”

“It was to have lunch with these agents. I didn’t tell you. It wouldn’t have helped anything to tell you.”

I said, “Agents?”

“It was the whole package—two dudes in a Crown Vic, gray suits, sunglasses, all of it. They kept calling me sir. It was wild. Anyway, they were wanting to know if I could maybe get a little more involved over at Island. If I could perhaps provide them with some useful information, was how they put it.”

“What are you talking about? Who were they?”

“Some kind of revenue task force. Special Agents Johnson and Smith. I said they had to be kidding me. They said they in fact did not.”

“I’m not following,” I said.

“They seem to have me on tax evasion,” he said.

“What kind?”

“The evasive kind. The real kind. Only it’s not so much evasion, I keep telling them, as a sort of unfortunate series of mistakes.”

“The same guys who arrested you want you to become some kind of informant.”

“No. The county arrested us. The regular police. These guys are different. They’re trying to cash in after the fact. My name popped up on their screen, or on a new screen, and now they want to lean on me, and here we are.”

It wasn’t real. It couldn’t be. I said, “Does Carolyn know?”

"She does not."

"So the thing with the phone call—"

"I'm supposed to say yes, let Steve move his stuff in, give these gentlemen a call at their special number. I lied to you and Alice back there. I'm sorry. I just couldn't have her, you know, going over to Carolyn—"

"She knows nothing?"

He said, "The whole thing's batshit, OK? Completely. I'm not surprised she thinks I'm losing it. But it's not just me. It's not just the cops. It's bigger than that. It's the house, the girls, all of it." He lay down on his back, his hands over his face. "We don't talk so much anymore, Carolyn and me. And you know why?" He looked at me through his fingers. "There's no time, is why. Because eventually it's just all carpools and science fair and tae kwon do. Somebody always needs a new pair of shorts in a specific color. And now, with Olivia, it's her goddamn phone beeping and ringing off the hook, without end."

"Mid—"

"She's got college tours in the fall. Somehow she wants to look at Georgetown. She has a Hoyas sweatshirt she got from some boy, wears that thing around the house." He was getting louder. "Georgetown! And then you go to the grocery store, where all you want is a fucking pint of ice cream, because your fucking wife has asked you to step away from the operation for a few days, and what you get is a community theater pirate trying to cup your daughter's ass in the meat department. I mean, what are you gonna do?"

"I don't know," I said, which was the truth.

"You're goddamned right you don't know. Nobody ever knows. And all these people who think they're special, who think they've got it cracked? Fuck them all the way to Sunday." He popped his knuckles. "You should have seen these guys. The agents. Badges. Everything. They wanted to know if I would wear a wire."

"A wire," I said.

"Like in the movies," he said. "Like in the shitty movies with the guy trying to make things right."

I lay down, too, not even trying to take it all in anymore. "You have to tell her," I said. "Carolyn."

"I know that," he said. "You don't have to tell me that."

Something was blinking up above us in all the stars. A satellite, maybe, watching us—two old guys at a party we had no business being at, Delton a half-mile away chasing a shirtless boy and a dog named Roscoe, Mid confessing the whole wrecked catalog of his life to me. I felt dizzy. I said, "I thought you said it was the dream."

"What's that?"

"Kids," I said. "The dream. That's what you said the other night."

"It is," he said. "But sometimes it's everything else, too."

"I thought you had it all neat and organized," I said. "You and Carolyn."

"Surprise," he said.

"I can't get my head around it. The kid."

"Don't tell Alice that," he said.

"Too late."

"Then you're fucked," he said. "Join the crowd."

"Great."

"Just be happy you're not me."

I said, "Are you going to jail? Is that what this is?"

"I'm trying to work on that," he said. "*That's* what this is."

Delton came back up the steps before I had a chance to ask him anything else, to find out if I'd still have a job in the morning, or in a week. To ask him all over again if he was crazy, and mean it this time. Delton was out of breath. She leaned over, hands on her knees. When she came up for air, she said, "You guys have to come right now. The turtles. You have to come see the turtles."

Mid said, "Are they hatching?"

"Come on," she said. "Hurry. It's amazing."

■ ■ ■

What I was thinking as we trailed Delton down the beach: Even if he does go to jail, somebody still has to run the pizza shop. Somebody still has to sell sunglasses, rent kayaks. Also, I was trying to do long division in my head, simple messes like 42 into 613, remainders and carry the one—because seeing those numbers lining themselves up gave me some little corner of order, let me feel like I was back at the desk, with my own pencils, my own paper, my own phone lighting up and being for me. There'd be some deal we were putting together, the numbers run, the facts and figures, the due diligence. A word like *client*. Like *account*. Thirty-year fixed. Five-year balloon. Home in the car through traffic I knew to a house I owned, the familiar rhythms of weeks unfolding one after another—

Delton stopped, looked around. "I thought it was right here," she said. "But that lady's gone."

Mid said, "What lady?"

"The turtle lady. Walter knows."

"The pickup?" I said.

"Right. And there were all these people. She kept making them turn their flashlights off. She said the babies get confused and think the light is the moon."

Mid said, "Are you sure it was here?"

"I think so." She walked up to the dunes, up to one of the taped-off nests. "Yeah," she said. "This was definitely it. I guess they're gone." She came back toward us. The moon was up over the water, about three-quarters full. Everything was lit up white. "OK, look." She pointed at the sand. "You can see the tracks. Oh, man, you guys should have seen it. It was unbelievable." She started telling us about how small they were, about how they crawled up out of the nest and aimed themselves toward the water. And if you stood right, you could see the tracks in the sand, like she said—like someone had dragged a bunch of thin reeds from the dunes down to the ocean. "There were people picking them up," she was saying. "If they started crawling the wrong way, you were allowed to pick them up and turn them around. I didn't do it, but people were doing it. There must have been a hundred of them. They were tiny. It was incredible." Her phone rang. She answered it. "Hey, Mom," she said, and walked away from us. "No. I'm with Dad."

"My daughter, international woman of intrigue," said Mid. "Savior of the animal kingdom."

"On the beach," she said into the phone. "Looking for turtles." She paused. "Like sea turtles. One of the nests hatched." Another pause. "At the grocery." She gave Mid a shrug. "Having ice cream. We ran into each other. I just felt like it."

"Close enough," Mid said.

"Yeah, he's here, too," she said, and then handed me the phone. "Aunt Alice wants to talk to you."

I said, "Me?"

"I'm pretty sure," said Delton.

"Hello?" I said.

"What are you doing?" Alice asked.

"Delton found some turtles hatching, and now I guess we're looking for them."

"I called your cell," she said.

I checked my pocket. "I must have left it at home. Sorry."

"I'm bleeding again. I called the hotline thing, and they want us to come in tomorrow."

"Are you alright?"

"It's more than before. But the nurse said we didn't need to go to the hospital."

"What color is it?" I said.

"Redder than last time."

"How red?"

"Not that red."

"What else did they say?"

"They said it could be fine, or that it could be not fine. They don't know. All they really said was that we could wait until tomorrow."

"That's got to be good, right?"

"I'm trying not to look things up. The nurse said not to. She said doing that was a bad idea. She said I was supposed to try to relax."

"Do you need me to come over there?" I said.

"No," she said. "I'm OK. We're OK."

"What time is it?"

"Almost ten. I'll come home in an hour or so."

"I'm sorry," I said.

"It's not your fault." She sounded worried, but calm. She did not sound like she was bleeding.

"How's everything else?" I said.

"You mean like Carolyn?"

"Yeah."

"Is he right there?"

"Yes," I said.

"Not so good," she said. "It's pretty much a mess. How's he?"

"Same," I said, trying not to look at him. "The same."

"Will you talk to me a minute?" she said. "Can you? Are you busy?"

"I'm not busy," I said. "I'm good."

She said, "I think I'm getting afraid."

"About the baby?"

"About everything. There was a news report about earthquakes. Now I'm afraid of earthquakes."

"I don't think Florida has earthquakes."

"The news seemed to know a lot about them," she said. "We're all going to die, I think."

"We're not all going to die."

"The news says we are."

"The news always says that."

"The news also says crime is up."

I said, "I have to say that actually seems right."

"Is ten-thirty OK for the doctor tomorrow? That's the earliest they had."

"Any time is fine," I said.

"Do you need to check with Mid?"

"I'm sure it's fine," I said. "Ten-thirty. We're good."

"I should go," she said. "Maggie's still not asleep. Carolyn said she's been awful all week. I think we've read her a thousand books. I'll bring you the one about the horse and the seahorse."

"Sounds riveting," I said.

"They learn to share. Tell me not to worry."

"Don't worry."

"I'm worried," she said.

"I know. Me, too."

"What if something's really wrong?" she said.

I looked south, back down toward where our complex was. I was pretty sure I could actually see it from there, the outline of the buildings sticking up above everything else. I had ten different answers for her. I chose the easiest. The one I was least sure of. "Then we'll try again," I said.

"Do you promise?"

"I promise," I said. I felt like if I didn't dig my feet in just right, I might float up off the beach, fly away.

She said, "You three are eating ice cream?"

"More or less," I said.

"That sounds nice."

"It is, sort of."

"I just really wanted to talk to you," she said.

"I'm right here," I said. "It's good you called."

"I love you," she said.

I said, "I love you, too."

She botched the hanging up on her end, so the line stayed open another minute or so. I could hear Mid's house in the background, Alice and Carolyn talking, Maggie doing something that wasn't quite screaming. Then we'll try again, I heard myself saying. It was problem enough to be pregnant. That was plenty. But to have something go haywire—I stood there with the phone up against my ear, the beach running all the way to Miami in front of me, and then the skinny kid walked out of the dark with Roscoe. He had the dog leashed with an extension cord. "Hey," he said to Delton. "Thanks for your help."

"I know," she said. "I'm sorry I lost you."

"No, I really mean it. That was cool of you to even try."

"Nice leash," Mid said.

"Some dude down the beach caught him. Roscoe ran straight up to him. He gave me the cord right out of his place."

"Oh, yeah?"

"Yeah, man," the kid said. "You know what I like? How some people will just help your shit out when you need it."

Mid said, "I like that, too."

Delton never had a chance: Skinny kid, muscles, beach dog, extension-cord leash. It wouldn't have been too hard for me to be in love with him. The kid stuck his hand out, the wrong hand, the one he wasn't holding Roscoe with. He said, "I'm Nic. It's short for Nicodemus." Delton giggled and told him her name was Olivia. Mid took a couple of steps back, looked up at the sky. It was time for me to go home. I asked him if what looked like our place was in fact our place. He said it was. It was maybe a mile away. I told him I'd just walk it, and I told him about Alice, about the bleeding, asked if it would be a problem for me to take the morning. Of course not, he said. He said he'd call to find out how it went. Delton was down on one knee, patting the dog around the neck. The kid was asking her if she surfed. "You're alright here?" I asked Mid.

"Don't worry about me," he said. "For now, you is who we worry about, OK? You and Alice."

"She's fine," I said. "She's got to be."

"Good luck," he said. "You won't need it, but tell her we're thinking of you guys."

"I will," I said, and I left him there with the dog, the kid, Delton, the party.

■ ■ ■

I watched Aunt Sandy's TV, all the higher channels fuzzy for a reason I couldn't figure out. It got worse the further up you went. I could see them trying to sell onyx necklaces well enough, but I couldn't find the ball in the Marlins game. I tried to watch a movie I was pretty sure was about cowboys. I couldn't follow what was happening, though, couldn't tell who to root for, so I gave up, turned the TV off, sat in the dark. I kept thinking of Alice, just Alice, no Florida, no kid, no nothing—just Alice on one of those blank blue screens they did the TV weather against. And I didn't mean to, but I fell asleep.

I woke up on the sofa, not sure where I was, morning light bombing in through the sliding glass doors, the sound of something being torn in another room. I wandered down the hall, the cool of the tile on my feet something I still wasn't used to. That and the pervasive smell of Aunt Sandy in the rooms, the drawers, the closets. Powder. She was haunting us via powder. I found Alice in the front bedroom, and found the sound: She was tearing long sheets of aluminum foil off the roll and thumbtacking them to the window frames. She was running masking tape along the seams. "I tried not to wake you," she said.

"I'm sorry I fell asleep," I said. "I tried to wait."

"Don't you want to ask me what I'm doing? Don't you want to tease me?"

"Yes," I said. "No."

"Carolyn told me they did this for Maggie, to make it completely dark so she'd sleep. Last night she said they were thinking about putting it back up in her room. Here," she said, and held out the box of foil. "Hold this."

I said, "But why are you doing it now?"

"I'm getting a head start. I'm practicing. It's good to be ready."

"This ready?"

"Just let me do it," she said.

"The bleeding," I said. "Are you still—"

"Not this morning. A little more last night."

"Aren't you supposed to be getting rest? Or sitting down?"

"They didn't mention that on the hotline."

"I thought Maggie had some kind of nightlight," I said, watching her tape edges. "I thought she didn't like it dark."

"She hates her nightlight now. She hates everything except books. And chicken nuggets shaped like dinosaurs. Have you seen those?"

"Why didn't you wake me up when you got home?" I said.

"You looked so peaceful, I just left you. I thought if you woke up, you'd come to bed, and if not, you were fine where you were." She took the foil back. "How was your night?"

I rubbed my face, trying to sift out what was dream and what was not, trying to account for what to tell her. I decided to go with everything all at once. "Mid might be going undercover," I said. "And also broke. Delton beat up a pirate at the grocery store. A kid in her class tried to arrest us in the parking lot."

Alice stopped herself mid-motion. She did not turn around. Then she started again, pulled a new sheet off the roll. She put a couple of thumbtacks in her mouth. "Start over," she said, quietly.

"I kind of can't."

"Why not?"

"It's hard," I said. "That's why. It's a lot."

"OK," she said. "Let's go slowly. Undercover how?"

"There are these cops," I said. "I guess they want him to wear a wire. At Island. You can't tell Carolyn."

"I think," she said around the thumbtacks, "that I can tell Carolyn anything I like."

"He's going to tell her."

"What cops?" she said.

"I don't know."

"How could you not know?"

"He wasn't making a ton of sense," I said. "It was hard to keep up."

She said, "Carolyn wants you to spy on him for her. That's what she told me last night."

"Spy on him how?"

"I don't think she meant it like that. Or not exactly. It's just, she doesn't quite know what to believe from him right now, and she doesn't think he's telling her anything, which it turns out he's not, and you're around him all the time— Anyway, I told her yes."

I said, "You told her what?"

"What I didn't tell her was that I'm starting to think you should stay the hell away from him."

"How am I supposed to spy on him and stay away from him at the same time?"

She put a thumbtack in the wall. "She's my sister," she said. "This is all so fucked up." She turned around. "Should I be scared right now? Is that where we are?"

I said, "I think we're still OK."

"But what if there's more? What if he gets you into something? Or us into something?"

I said, "That's not what's going on."

She said, "Who goes undercover? What is this?"

"Maybe it'll all work itself out."

"And that's the kind of thing Carolyn says he's spouting off all the time." She retaped a corner where the foil was pulling away. "I don't want to have to be scared," she said. "OK? It's already hard enough."

"But you want me to watch him. You want me to report back. Like I'm some babysitter."

"Will you just explain everything, please? Will you start at the beginning?"

I said, "I need some coffee."

She pulled another sheet of foil. "Come back when you're ready," she said.

"You're not bleeding," I said, checking again. "You're sure?"

"Not right now."

I wanted—badly, even—to touch her, to reach out for her, but I couldn't make myself walk across the room. I didn't know what I'd say when I got there. Instead I headed for the kitchen, for safety, for juice and coffee, and then for the balcony, to try to find five empty minutes. I needed to get my head clear. There was a fat paperback on the glass-topped table outside—*Your Baby's First Year.* Alice must have brought it home from Carolyn's. I thumbed through it. After every chapter it listed all the new ways your baby could concuss itself or suffocate, all the warning signs that meant your baby had feline leukemia or diptheria or lazy eye. Inside, I could hear Alice foiling the windows five months too soon. I worked back through the pieces of what Mid had told me, tried to see how that all strung together. I didn't want to spy on him. I didn't want any part of anything like that. I put the book back down on the table just as the parachutist came into view. I called for Alice. She came out and stood behind me, hands on my shoulders, and we watched him fly past, no flags, no windsocks, no banners, no extra anything. Just the green cage and the black sail. He did not wave or point. He never even looked over. Probably it was early for him, too.

■ ■ ■

The kiosk, the glass, the polished wood, the technicians, the blood-pressure check, a scan for the heartbeat—still going—and then back into smiling Dr. Varden's office. His teeth were whiter than before, his happy family in the picture on his desk happier than before. It was getting to where I could not fully understand where I might find the borders or boundaries of our life. Dr. Varden sat at his desk and beamed across at us. He said, "Well, Mom, we're completely fine, OK? Let's just let that right out of the gate. This is just baby checking in to be sure everybody's paying attention. Nothing more. No big deal."

Alice said, "But what's happening?"

He held his hands up, palms at us. "You know, we don't know. Could be a hematoma. Could be there was a twin way, way back at the beginning, and the body's flushing itself. Could be some kind of small abrasion in there. Could be lots of things. But since all your numbers look like you've got a little president of the United States cooking away in there, I think it's probably best not to do anything too invasive. Best just to let things move along on their own."

"A twin?" said Alice.

"Not in the way you're thinking," he said. "It's utterly, perfectly normal. You'll get a second fertilization that doesn't take, a clump of cells that hangs out in there until the body says, 'Whoa, what's this?' and then sends it along. But it's probably not even that. It's probably some small scrape that'll take care of itself."

Alice blinked. I thought, Cessna *and* Cessno.

"What we could do," he said, "to ease the mind a bit, is to set you up with a fetal Doppler."

"A what?" I asked.

"You've seen it. It's what we use to quick-check the heartbeat. Some mothers—some *parents*—just want one at home for peace of mind. Might be good in a situation like yours, give you some rest if the bleeding starts again. Though we'd still want you to call in, of course." He went rummaging through a stand-up file cabinet behind him. "Here's the information. You folks can look it over and decide. If you want one, you don't even have to come back in. You can order it through the desk, or off the website." He gave us a brochure that had pictures of Dopplers. They looked like calculators with wands attached to them, salt-shaker-sized microphones with no holes.

"Is it expensive?" Alice said.

"It can be if you buy it. But we've got a rental program. Maybe thirty bucks a month, if I'm remembering right."

Alice said, "And we'd be using it—"

"To check for heartbeat. That's right."

"So if I had some spotting again—"

"Then you could listen out for your little one, make sure everything's humming along, not too fast, not too slow. Then, when all's well," he said, smiling harder than ever, "we've saved you a trip all the way up here. It's mainly, like I was saying, for peace of mind. We don't want Mom under stress. Or Dad."

"OK," Alice said. "We'll talk about it."

"Outstanding," Dr. Varden said. "And remember: Anything at all, you call us, day or night." He stood up, opened the door for us, shook Alice's hand with both his hands. "Anything else?" he asked us.

"Am I still OK to exercise?" she asked.

"If you could do it before, you can do it now. But maybe let's not add in anything new. Maybe no rock climbing, alright?"

"Right," Alice said.

"And Dad?" he said. "Are we OK? Are we still on board with all of this?"

He'd startled me. I'd forgotten I was part of the conversation. I was thinking about heartbeats. About twins. I didn't know what to say right away, and they could both tell. Finally, I said, "Sure I am."

His smile came down a few watts. Alice took a half-step into the hall. Varden said, "Good, good, super," but it was a different show now. I'd made him unhappy, and Dr. Varden was never unhappy. I could see him telling the story later that night around the dinner table, explaining to his happy kids and his happy wife about how he'd had one today, had somebody who didn't know how blessed he was—they'd all shake their heads, smug in their enormous disappointment in me, and then go back to passing heaping bowls of food back and forth, chatting about extracurriculars and volunteering. Varden touched Alice on the shoulder, a funereal gesture. He sent us on our way. We paid. We walked back through the atrium. We sat in the car. Alice handed me the brochure, and I read the names of the makes and models. SweetBeats. Peaceful Beginnings. One of the photos had nearly naked Mom and Dad in bed, soft-focus and resplendent in their joy, Dad holding the Doppler wand like some kind of sex toy over Mom's lower belly.

Alice said, "What was that back there?"

"I'm on board," I said. "Dad's on board."

"Except you're not."

"Do you want one of these?" I said, refolding the brochure. "We can get one if you want."

"That's not what I'm talking about," she said.

"I get a little freaked out sometimes," I said. "I'm on board. I just can't quite fake not being freaked out."

"I'm not asking you to fake it. I'm asking you to get better at all this."

I pushed the door lock up and down. "How am I supposed to do that?" I said, thinking, for some reason, that it was possible she might actually tell me.

"I don't know," she said. "But we're having this baby unless I manage to bleed it away, so figure it out. At least figure some of it out. I'm tired of doing this by myself."

"You're not doing it by yourself. I'm right here, remember?"

"You're not. You're out on the goddamn balcony, or you're off somewhere with Mid. And I don't want that. That can't be us. I don't want us to be Carolyn and Mid."

"I don't want that, either."

"What *do* you want?"

I wanted to go back to how it had been before she wanted a kid. I wanted to go back to having a job I half understood. I wanted my own car. "I want to be with you," I said. "I want whatever it takes to be with you."

"You sound so resigned to it. Like you're settling."

"That's not how I mean to sound at all."

"It's how you sound."

"I do get to feel like this," I said. "I get to carry this flag. I'm sorry. I'm just not ready. That's it."

She reached in behind her sunglasses, rubbed one eye. "I'm not ready, either," she said. "That's not what I'm asking you for."

"I know."

"But do you?"

I did not. I had no idea what she was asking me for. Or: I knew I had such little chance of giving her, right there in the car, whatever it might be she wanted or needed, that I was willing just to let it go.

"Walter," she said.

"Yes."

I think she'd said my name just to see how it felt. The muffler sounded like it was trying to achieve a rattle. I was a miserable prom date, a disaster on all fronts. I wanted to fade away and disappear. A nurse came out the front door, looked at us a while, then went back in. After that, I drove us home.

■ ■ ■

At the condo, Alice said she wanted a nap, went into the bedroom, shut the door. I stood in the hallway thinking of all the easy things I could say to make her feel better. At least to make her feel like I was somehow with her. Through the door, I said, "I love you."

She said, "I know that."

I felt like an asshole.

The phone rang. I picked up in the kitchen. Mid said, "Twice-the-Ice, my man, Twice-the-Ice."

"What?"

"They are here. They have arrived. I am watching one getting ready to come off the truck as we speak. You need to come see this shit. There's a crane. How's Alice?"

"She's good. She's fine." She came around the corner, made a face at me, a question. I mouthed *Mid* at her, and she frowned.

"You all are all clear?"

"It looks like it," I said.

"I told you, didn't I? Great news. Great. So come out here and watch them do this with me. Then we can get some shrimp at Pomar's. We'll celebrate." I wanted to ask him how he'd come up with the money to get them delivered. I wanted to ask how it had gone sleeping at the beach house, what he'd done about getting Delton home. I rearranged some fruit in a bowl on the counter. He said, "You still there, buddy?"

"Right here," I said.

"You coming, or what?"

"I have to see if Alice needs the car," I said.

She shook her head, whispered, "Go."

Mid said, "What we need to get you is your own transportation. Maybe the company can find something for you."

"You sound better," I said. "I mean, today. You sound OK."

"Moved a few things around. Flowed up the cash flow, if you know what I mean."

I said, "Where are you? Which one?"

"Anastasia Station," he said. North, up past the grocery.

I checked the clock on the stove. "I can be there in fifteen minutes," I said.

"You want me to get them to wait?"

"Sure," I said.

"OK. Let me go slow them down," he said, and we hung up.

Alice said, “Off to work?”

“His Twice-the-Ices came in.”

“Will you be back for dinner?”

“I think so.”

“Call me if you’re going to be later than that.”

“I will,” I said.

“Twice-the-Ice,” she said. “It doesn’t sound like any way to get rich to me.”

“I didn’t think so, either.”

She said, “Do you think he knows what he’s doing?”

“I think he thinks those things are little college funds.”

“What do you think?”

“I think they’re trailers that sell ice,” I said. “But I’m just the yes man.”

She looked at me. “You are, aren’t you?”

“For now, anyway.”

“And then what?”

One I knew the answer to, finally. “And then I have no idea.”

“And then you go undercover.”

“Something like that.”

“Whatever that even means.”

“He’ll get it worked out,” I said.

“Sure he will. We all will.” She put her hair on top of her head, straightened a painting of a pelican that hung over the toaster, and went back in the bedroom without saying anything else. I don’t know why I did it, but after she closed the door, I reached out and nudged the painting crooked again. Then I took the keys and left.

The first Twice-the-Ice worked like a dream. You shoved in your seven quarters, chose between the buttons that said BAG and BULK, and you either caught your bag or shoved your cooler under, depending. Sixteen pounds of glistening, frozen-solid ice, delivered instantly while you stood there in the sanctified glow of the very future itself. Mid and I each bought probably twenty dollars of ice the first day we had the thing up and running. We gave bags away for free to anybody who came up to see what was going on. Public relations, Mid said. Marketing. Grand Opening. We gave bag after bag to people who weren't prepared to take them, who put them sweating and melting into their trunks, down onto their floorboards. Mid said the thing about it being twice the ice was that even if they lived a long way away, they still had an even chance of there being a regular amount of ice left by the time they made it home. People seemed to appreciate that line of reasoning. Mid handed out business cards with the two locations of the Twice-the-Ices listed. "Twice the Twice-the-Ice," the cards said.

The second Twice-the-Ice made only very cold water, which

was a problem. You put your quarters in, and the building gave off a groan like it was trying to work, like it wanted to, but then out of the bulk chute came a pretty steady stream of water, and out of the bag chute came an empty bag. Mid fed five rounds of quarters in and got the same thing each time—empty bag, water on the ground—and then he was on the phone to the home office, and they were telling him they'd have somebody out by the end of the week, Monday at the latest.

We went by a few days later on our way out to see Hurley and the cabins at Devil's Backbone, and Mid had gotten a banner made that said COMING SOON. It was hanging across the front of the trailer.

"Twice as soon," I said.

"No," he said.

"No what?"

"Just no."

Mid was still sleeping at the beach house, but he and Carolyn and the kids had started eating dinner again as a family. Carolyn's idea, he said, which he was taking as a good sign. He was thinking he'd be back home in a couple of days. Alice was telling me, over our own quiet dinners, that she thought it'd be a little longer than that. Still, he seemed better, seemed pasted back together reasonably well. This was perhaps Mid not on the very edge of the precipice, or of prison. This was Mid with half his Twice-the-Ices up and running. We rode down A1A, him telling me what they'd done the night before, how he'd dragged the kettle grill into the yard and done a whole turkey, how the twins had ended up fighting over the wishbone. "They fight about everything lately," he said. "They fight about fighting."

We passed a stuccoed church that had a yellow fire engine parked out on the lawn, lights turning, teenagers all over it holding posterboards that said PRAY N' WASH. "That seems unlikely," Mid said.

"What was that?"

"If we're supposed to believe the signs," he said, turning around in a gas station, "it's a Pray N' Wash."

"I don't think I get it."

"I feel like it's self-explanatory," he said. He pulled us into the turning lane, set the blinker.

"What are you doing?"

"Seeing if it's self-explanatory."

"Mid. Come on."

He said, "What's the worst that can happen?"

"We get raptured?"

"I think that happens differently." He eased us through an opening in the traffic. "But I'd have to look it up." The kids on the fire engine waved us in. "This thing could use a wax and polish, anyway," he said.

"The sign didn't say wax and polish," I said.

He said, "Maybe we'll get lucky." We got in line behind a red minivan. A boy, maybe sixteen or seventeen, had his forehead pressed against the van door, and he had his hand in through the open window. He was praying with whoever was driving. The windows were tinted, so beyond a postcard-sized movie that was playing on a drop-down screen in the back seat, we couldn't see much. The movie had geese in it, flying by in Vs. On the ground, there were people watching the geese. There was a girl. All this was taking place somewhere very green. The kid finished his prayer and sent the van over to a Quonset hut that looked like it was probably the meetinghouse for the youth group. Several kids in ponchos and modest-length shorts were soaping and rinsing down cars. The prayer kid signaled us forward, and Mid rolled down his window.

"Hey!" the kid said. He had a plain kind of good looks, like somebody in an orange juice commercial. "Are you guys feeling full of the spirit today?"

"We are," said Mid. I said nothing.

"That's terrific," the kid said. "I'm Jason."

"Mid," Mid said. Then he took my hand. "This is Walter."

"Peace, Walter," Jason said. I nodded. Mid did not let go of my hand. Jason said, "What would you guys like to ask God's guidance in today?"

"We could use some technical assistance," Mid said. "For one thing, I've got an ice machine that won't make any ice."

"OK," said Jason.

"Walter got the water hookups in just fine, so that can't be it. We're thinking it's something internal. Gears and wires, you know? It's a bitch. And so long as we're being honest, I've got a little thing going with law enforcement that could use some oversight. Plus a domestic situation."

"Wow," Jason said.

"But more importantly, Walter's wife is pregnant." Mid held my hand tighter, held our two hands up in the air. "Things have been difficult," he said.

"Wait," Jason said, squinting in at us. "I think I know this one. What we could do is just ask for God's love to be brought more completely into your lives. How would that be?"

"We were hoping you could do something about making it a boy," Mid said. "I think if he's got to have it, then he really wants a boy."

"Mid," I said.

"Walter," he said, "everything is going to be just fine." He turned back to Jason. "Right?"

"Right," Jason told him.

There were several things I could have done. I could have told Jason that there wasn't any point in praying for a boy, and that it didn't make any difference either way, regardless. I could have told Mid to stop fucking with the poor kid, to get us out of line and on with our afternoon.

"Can he be tall?" I said. "And left-handed?"

I'd never seen Mid so pleased. "Yes," he said. "Left-handed is going to be key, Jason. It'll be a hell of a lot easier for him to break into the majors. He can be a pitcher. Middle-inning relief. He'll make us all rich. We won't need any ice machines. If you can make him a left-handed reliever with a good breaking ball and a handlebar mustache, we can see what we can do about cutting you in on the deal."

Jason said, "I'm not sure it would be right to ask for something like that." He said, "God has a plan for each of us."

"I guess that could be true," Mid said. He sounded like he might actually be considering the possibility.

"It *is* true," Jason said, warming up to what he knew. "He has a plan for each of us. Each of us is special in His eyes."

"I have to say I sometimes don't feel all that special," Mid told him.

"But you are," Jason said. "Each of us is so unique. That's what we all have in common."

"Are you sure?"

"Pastor David says that each of us carries a toolbox of gifts."

"A what?"

"A toolbox," Jason said. "Each and every one of us possesses—"

Mid said, "Jason, Walt and I need to go speak with a gentleman about some rental villas he's building in a tidal swamp, so maybe we should just get this taken care of. What do you say?"

It was clear Jason wanted to push ahead with the toolbox, but he also had a kind of customer-is-always-right thing going on, and the latter won the day. He took Mid's other hand—Mid was still holding mine—and without much more warning he started praying for us, an overarching request for grace and mercy and something about opening a door, behind which there would be a light showing us the true and gentle nature of God's eternal might and glory. I had in mind a bare bulb hanging from a closet ceiling. Jason could have been praying for anybody. He did not mention giving my daughter a quick move to first, a workable knuckle-curve. He moved along into some boilerplate about how abidingly good God was, about how He was so good, and ridiculous as it was there at the Pray N' Wash, with Mid holding my hand and Jesus Christ's very own personal Tropicana spokesboy raining down favor upon us, there was an idea I felt come over me, a vague communion, a feeling that if something like the rapture or perhaps minor coastal flooding were to arrive right then, that we'd still be alright, at least in the short term. I was suddenly sure that we'd hash something out, Jason and Mid and me. We would triumph against long odds. Then the kid finished praying, and that passed, and I dropped back to my baseline reading, a kind of gentle, hazy panic. Though there was comfort in that, too—in drifting back to what I knew. Mid let go of my hand. Jason pulled his arm out of the Camaro, told us to shine, and sent us on to get hosed down.

"That was nice," Mid said, while the rest of the youth group washed the car. "Probably I don't need that every day, but I'll take it."

Comfort in panic: I'd felt it all along, since I'd stood in the kitchen flipping French toast while Alice went in the bathroom to pee into one of our juice glasses, afraid she wouldn't be able to go long enough to hold the stick in the stream right. She'd determined that dunking would be the superior method. And it was—it worked—I had the second sides browning when she made a little noise, a sound like she'd shut her finger in something not all that heavy, and I knew well before she came around the corner that the stick would have its two pink lines. Are you happy, she wanted to know. Sure I was. Sure and sure. I flipped the toast. We ate breakfast and I got pretty convinced there was a hum in the room, that the house had developed some new vibraphonic frequency, that in time the harmonics would find their way to the exact right pitch and point to shake us all to dust. I made more French toast. Alice sat at the table, pregnant. The hum set in.

What surprised me was that I'd come, in a way, to like the hum—or at least to recognize it, to reach for it first thing in the morning. Our daughter, Hall-of-Fame relief pitcher Rollie Fingers, was out there, waiting, getting ready in the bullpen. I knew what that was. I had an idea. The books told us how to measure: The fetus was the size of a paper clip, then a Damson plum. I did not know what a Damson plum was, but I could guess. That was not the problem. It was the *after* that was the problem, that seemed so unimaginable. No amount of praying and washing could get you ready.

The youth-groupers soaped us, rinsed us, buffed us dry with a Superman towel. Mid thanked them and passed ten bucks through the window. The kids told us to be careful as we entered the mission field, and Mid told them we'd do what we could. We pulled back out around the circle drive, waited at the road. The sun shone down clean and bright. The hood gleamed. Mid flipped the visor down on his side. A light blue scooter went by in front of us, hugged up against the curb, close enough that we could have nosed out and knocked it over. It was the boy from the other night, from the beach, Nicodemus, and there was Delton, riding behind, wearing no helmet, arms wrapped around him, hands on his chest, hair blowing in the wind. "Well, hell on a cracker," Mid said.

"On a scooter," I said. They disappeared around a curve. I said, "That's that kid."

"Yeah."

"How old is he?"

Mid said, "He's nineteen."

"Nineteen?"

"Believe me," he said. "I know."

"Is that even legal?"

"Doesn't seem to matter so much," he said.

"Doesn't matter how?"

"He calls. He comes by. And that was her on the back of that thing, right?"

I said, "It was."

"That's how."

"Is he a nice kid, at least?" I said.

"He seems like it, I guess. She's seen him every day since that party. He's supposed to come by for dinner one of these nights, show us what a fine upstanding young man he is. She wants us to get to know him."

"Nineteen," I said.

"He's probably getting ready to enter her mission field."

"Don't even—"

"Or maybe not. I can't really tell. When we ask her how it's going, she says they're friends." He leaned back against the headrest. "I've been meaning to have a talk with her," he said. "You know, another talk. We've had *the* talk with her. There's one you can look forward to."

"Sometimes, when mommies and daddies love each other very much," I said.

"It's just lately I've been thinking another talk might be good. I could say something about making sure the kid's literate, that he's kind. That sort of thing."

"That sounds—"

"But I'm trying to decide: So I go on and do that, buy her a frozen yogurt and sit her down, will she then determine that I'm some kind of world-class jackass and end up on the back of a forty-five-year-old pedophile's Harley, instead of on a mainly harmless college kid's Vespa?"

"It's hard to say," I said.

"Kid can't be all bad if he drives a powder-blue Vespa, right?"

"Probably not."

"So maybe this is one of those times where you cut your losses, is what I've been thinking."

"I don't really know anything about this," I said, thinking no advice was better than bad.

He said, "It is a cosmic fucking secret, is what it is."

The way she'd been hanging onto him didn't look at all like the way you'd hang onto a friend, but I did not say so. The hum picked up, got a little louder. A good part of me wanted to get back in line, wait for Jason, pray for those same things all over again, except harder. But somebody else who'd been prayed and washed drove up behind us, hit the horn, and that was it—Mid snapped to, pulled us out onto the road, drove us away in the opposite direction from where Nic and Delton had been headed.

■ ■ ■

The problem was with the foundations. There were four of them—two right down on the water, and two closer to a big pit that was supposed to end up being the pool. It had about a foot of black water in it. Hurley kept trying to say things were mainly fine. Mid broke a piece of concrete off with his hand, held the chunk out in front of him. "When'd you pour them?" he asked.

"They still need to cure up," Hurley said.

"Right, but when?"

Hurley looked off across the Intracoastal. "Last week," he said. "It rained the second day."

"We'll have to tear them out," Mid said, but gently, almost.

"I know that."

"How much are you in right now?"

"Forty-five hundred."

"That's it?"

"I worked a deal with my cousin."

Mid knocked off another section of what might have been living room. "I think your deal is maybe not such a deal."

"Shit," Hurley said. "Don't show it to me, for fuck's sake." He left us there at the water, walked back up to the main building.

"Is he alright?" I asked Mid.

"He comes and goes." He kicked at the back wall. I expected the whole thing to come down, but it held. He said, "Progress-wise, I guess we'd have to call this a little bit of a setback."

I said, "I still don't see what your stake is. If all he's trying to do is cover up his—"

"Don't talk about that out here," Mid said. "Not a great idea."

"Fine," I said, "but—"

"I'll map it out for you later on," he said, tossing his piece of concrete in the water.

"I'd like that."

"Wouldn't we all."

A car came up the drive, that crunching sound of shell and sand, stopped on the rise, sat there idling. A silver Crown Vic. Blue lights in the grill flicked on, flicked back off again. Mid said, "I imagine that's for me." I didn't know whether to wish it was or wasn't. "Hang on a second?" he said.

"No problem," I said.

He climbed up there. Somebody on the passenger side rolled the window down. I think I'd been trying to hope he'd made up the part about the agents, or at least stretched it into a bigger, badder story—but now there they were, in plain sight, and I got a fairly clear vision of all this unspooling itself badly, of Mid, Inc., going under, of Mid himself doing actual jail time in actual jail. And if that happened, if Alice was right and all this went to shit, what then? What if there was nothing left to caretake? Maybe I could find a local and beg my way into a drive-through teller spot. I'd break my suits and ties back out, cling like a goddamn child to the very final shred of what I knew. Roll nickels. Run the vacuum tubes back and forth full of deposit slips and driver's licences. Lollipops for the kids, biscuits for the dogs. Is there anything else I can do for you today, ma'am? Sir? Thank you for banking at Coastal Coin & Trust.

Mid was nodding his head a lot. It looked cool inside the cruiser, and suddenly I wanted to be in there instead of out in the heat, wanted a badge in my pocket and the safety and security of a grateful citizenry to serve and protect. That would be one way to chalk through the days. I pressed a finger against my sunburned arm, watched the skin go white, then fade back pink. A cattle egret—I'd been studying Aunt Sandy's books—landed right down at the water, walked back and forth. Across the waterway a couple guys were trailering a flat-bottomed boat down to the edge of the sand. I spied. I waited. Mid finished what business he had up on the hill—sales figures, ages of consent—smacked his open palm twice on the hood, and the cops backed up, drove away. Once they were out of sight, he looked back at me like he was only just remembering I was still there. "So," he said. "Let's you and me go talk Hurley into getting these things built right."

I said, "You're not going to tell me what the hell that was?"

"More of the same. Nothing new. Well, sort of. Now they want to bug the store."

"They what?"

"I told them I was no longer truly in a place where I could be telling anybody what they could or could not store in my home. Said if they wired me up, all they'd hear was Carolyn telling me how it was. So they said, OK, Plan B."

I said, "If you bug the store, won't everybody quit when they find out you're secretly taping them?"

"Fuck, man, won't I have to fire everybody anyway once they're all arrested?"

"I guess that makes sense," I said.

"It sucks," he said, "but it does make sense."

I said, "I think I need to know how bad this is."

"The cabins?"

"All of it." I'd tried to go small, figure out one thing at a time, and that wasn't working. "I don't really understand anything out here," I said.

"Welcome to Florida," he said. He pulled on his shirt collar. "Alright. These foundations aren't as bad as you think. Even if we have to get somebody to haul all this off and start completely over, it only puts us under a week or two. And it probably doesn't make much difference. He can't open until next season as it is."

"But what about the rest?" I said.

"Hard to say. Looks like all they want is to set up their little cloak-and-dagger gig, sit in some van all day long wearing headphones, maybe find the guy who sells to the guy who sells to the kids. They want to make the papers, run for office."

"That's what they want," I said. "To set up a cop show at the pizza shop."

"That's what they said, anyway."

"With your help."

"With our permission, more like."

"Ours?"

"Mine."

"Are you in it?"

"I'm attached to it, let's say. It belongs to me. It's happening on my watch."

"I can't be involved in this," I said. "Whatever this is, it can't be me."

"Don't worry," he said. "Let's get you involved in these cabins right here. That's it. This can be your thing."

"Except you said these were crooked."

"I said they were complicated. Whatever he does with his money is his thing, on his books. We're investment partners, free and clear. These are rental cabins. We'll build them and rent them to real people who'll love them. They'll come back year after year. Come on—this is right in your wheelhouse. It's got your name all over it."

"I'd have to see the books," I said.

"I love it. You're doing it already. Let's go in there and have you lay some financial mumbo-jumbo on him, maybe frighten him a little bit."

"He doesn't seem like the type to get frightened," I said.

"Just jerk a chain in his ass. A knot in his chain. Whatever."

"You want me to scare the black-market guy."

"Don't piss him all the way off," Mid said. "Just make it a little less likely he'll hire cousin Jimmy to pour the foundations."

"I'll try," I said.

"Great. Then this can be your baby."

I said, "I've already got a baby."

"This can be your other baby."

I looked around, made measure again of how close we were to the water. "All I know is I'd never build down here like this," I said.

"Perfect," he said, smiling down at me like I was the son he never had. "You'll figure it out as you go. You'll improvise. The foundations can't be any worse than they already are. The stakes are very low. You'll be great."

■ ■ ■

Alice had a baby monitor set up when I got home. She was sitting in the den looking at it, a black-and-white picture of the front bedroom on the little screen. You could see the foiled-over windows, the crib in the corner, some bags of clothes Carolyn had brought by—the smallest jeans in the world, tiny sun hats. It looked like Alice had set the camera up on the floor, which did strange things to the perspective. There was a low static hiss. I said, "How was your day?"

"No bleeding," she said. "No nausea. All clear. How was yours?"

"Fine," I said. I was working out how to tell her: Mid is operating according to some other set of rules, ones we don't know anything about. "I think the cabins might be mine now."

"How are they yours?"

"He wants me to be the project manager. I'm supposed to get them built."

She turned around. "What do you know about building cabins?"

"These ones seem like they need new foundations."

"That doesn't seem like enough to really go on," Alice said.

"I'm mainly supposed to threaten this other guy to make sure he builds them right." Our voices echoed back at us on the monitor. "Where'd you get this thing, anyway?"

"I ordered it in the mail." She spun some dials, and the picture got clearer, then fuzzier. "So that's what you do now? Threaten people?"

"I'm more like the bouncer. I'm the heavy."

"You're not big enough to be a bouncer."

"I'm not big enough to be anything."

"Well, this makes plenty of sense." She flicked another switch, and the picture zoomed in. We were right up against the crib. "Carolyn called. She wants us to go to that pancake supper later on."

"I don't know what that is."

"Mid didn't mention it?"

"I think he was too busy running the world."

"I said we'd go."

"What we?"

"Mid and Carolyn, the girls, you and me. All of us. She thought it'd be fun. It's a fundraiser or something for the volunteer firefighters."

"We don't have a regular fire department?"

"We do. This one's for wildfires, I think. Off the island. Over by them."

I checked the monitor again. The crib looked like it was glowing. "How does it see in there without the lights on?" I said.

"I just turned it on, and it worked."

"Is this what we're going to use?"

"I don't know," she said. "Why?"

"Will we have to be watching it all the time?"

"No," she said. "Of course not."

"I didn't mean—"

She clicked it off. "I told Carolyn we'd be there by six. I'm going to take a shower."

It was five-thirty. I said, "We're going to be late."

"Then I'll hurry," she said, and got up, left the room, and shut the bathroom door—hard.

It was Mid. It was the cops on the hill, and it was what was true and what was not true, and all the space in between. It was the fucking crib, my own childhood crib, which my parents had FedExed us right after the move. It came in a huge crib-sized box. I'd cut the hell out of my hand putting it back together. I sat on the sofa and looked at the blank screen of the monitor. When I heard the water come on, I chased her in there, sat on the toilet, watched the steam collect on the mirror. "I'm sorry," I said.

"It's a monitor," she said. "That's all it is. It's a video game."

"I know."

"I don't know why you can't stand there and watch the thing and at least pretend like you're interested."

"I didn't know we were getting a video monitor," I said.

"You didn't know we were getting any monitor."

"You didn't say anything about it," I said.

"Would you have cared? At all?"

I opened the sink cabinet, looked in at Aunt Sandy's cleaning supplies all lined up. "Here's what I don't get," I said.

"What?"

"If she wants to have dinner all the time, why won't she let him come back home?"

"You're changing the subject?"

"I'm asking you a question."

"And you're taking his side."

"No side," I said. "I just want to know."

She was quiet a minute. Then she said, "Because he hasn't asked. She was the one who said they should have dinner as a family, and now she's ready for him to have an idea."

"He has ideas," I said.

"He has schemes. And she doesn't think she should be the one to have to fix everything every time."

I picked up a bottle of grout cleaner. "Do you think they'll be OK?" I asked.

"I don't think she'd divorce him until Maggie was older, if that's what you're asking."

"That is definitely not what I was asking."

"Oh."

"I don't think Mid has any clue at all that that's an option."

She wiped a circle clear on the glass door, looked out at me. "I don't really think he's got much of a clue about a lot of things."

"He's trying."

"Oh, bullshit, he's trying. He's taking his fifteen-year-old daughter to parties."

"One party," I said.

"Plus he's letting her date that boy."

"You know about that?"

"Carolyn told me. He told you?"

"We saw them today, riding around. But come on—that can't be by himself. Carolyn's letting her date him, too."

"I have no idea what Carolyn's doing or not doing."

"Sure you do."

"All I know is, our fifteen-year-old doesn't need to be dating any thirty-year-olds."

"Nineteen."

She said, "You cannot be for this. You don't *get* to be for this."

"I'm not," I said. "But weren't you the one who was so ready to have her on the pill?"

"That was so she could have safe, clumsy sex with awkward boys her own age. I don't know why she doesn't have anything better to do."

"Like what? SAT prep? Volunteering at soup kitchens?"

"Either of those would be fine."

"I don't know what we're arguing about," I said.

"I know you don't," she said, her voice thin.

I said, "What's the matter?"

"What's your real problem, anyway? Is it that you feel like you *can't* raise a child, or do you just not *want* to?"

I listened to the water hit the tile, run down the drain. "Sometimes it's both," I said. "I don't want it to be, but it is."

She pressed her belly against the shower glass. "You do see this thing, right?"

"I do."

"You don't, apparently, because this is the same conversation we always have. Why can't you just surprise me once? Would that be so hard?"

"I'm trying," I said, though I wasn't sure if I actually was.

"I'm ready. I'm ready to be a little fucking surprised." She was crying. "You're a bastard sometimes," she said. "This was supposed to be the fun part."

All I knew was that I needed to be doing something, anything other than what I was doing, which was sitting on my ass. I stood up. I took my clothes off. I got in there with her. I stood behind her, close. She had the water too hot. I squeezed some shampoo from the bottle, started washing her hair.

"I already did my hair," she said.

I said, "I'm doing it again."

She leaned back into me. "How does this make anything any better?"

"It doesn't."

"You're the only husband I have," she said. "We should get to be a team."

"We are a team."

"You don't ever want to talk about it. You don't ever want

to *do* anything about it. All you do is ride to the doctor and not talk to me, and ride back home and not talk to me. It's not fair."

I rinsed the shampoo down her neck and back. I could taste it in the water coming up off her skin. "There's nowhere here to build a swingset," I said.

"What?"

"I was thinking the other day—there's a pool, and the beach, but there's no yard. We don't have a yard. There's nowhere to put a swingset."

"You were thinking about that?"

It was clear she didn't believe me. "I was," I said.

"Mid and Carolyn have a swingset," she said. "We can use theirs."

"A kid's supposed to have a swingset," I said.

Alice said, "A kid's supposed to have a lot of things."

She had red hair right then, our two-year-old child. Luzianne. Spartica. She was sliding down the slide in her red hair and her red dress in Mid's clear-cut backyard, and Alice was standing at the bottom, arms out, waiting for her. Carolyn was filming the whole thing on an old sixteen-millimeter camera, all chrome and black plastic. The twins flipped a jump rope, chanted out rhymes about Delton and Nic, sitting in a tree. Maggie sat in the grass watching the rope spin. And me? I was in the pool, up on Mid's shoulders—we were wanting to play the game where one team tries to topple the other, push the top man into the water, but there was no one else in the pool. No other teams, no other takers.

I picked up the bar of soap, started in on Alice's shoulders, her arms, the backs of her legs. All that familiar ground. I didn't tell her about Mid, or about Hurley, or about the agents. I couldn't. We stayed in the shower until the hot ran out, until the water ran so cold we couldn't take it anymore, and we had to shut it off.

■ ■ ■

The volunteer fire department was a glorified metal garage, the parking lot full of pickups and SUVs and motorcycles. The air smelled like shrimp. Alice and I hadn't talked much on the way over, but a thin truce had settled down between us, and I was grateful. Every now and then I'd reach over, put a hand on her leg, and she'd let me keep it there until I had to shift gears. I was counting that as a positive.

We were late, but Mid wasn't there yet, and neither was Delton. Alice went inside, leaving me to wait with Sophie and Jane. Feral cats lived in the scrub off to the side of the building, and the twins wanted to stay outside to watch them slink in and out of the open, pick at bowls of food the firemen left out for them. They got bored, though, and started in kicking sand at each other until finally Sophie pissed Jane off enough for her to kick back so hard her flip-flop came off, landed in a grimy puddle. "You're a total a-hole, Sophie," she said, which was how I knew she was Jane. She pointed at the puddle. "Get my shoe."

"You're the one who kicked it off."

"You're the one who made me."

"You're the one who can't take a joke."

"You're the one who's acting like a giant B."

They both looked at me, checking for a judge's opinion. I felt like using the first letters of disallowed words might not be an entirely fair way around the curse jar, but I let that lie. I didn't want to get involved. I got the flip-flop out of the puddle, wiped it on my shorts, handed it back to Jane. “Here you go,” I said, holding it out. “Good as new.”

“Make her give it back to me.”

“I don’t think she wants to.”

“You’re on her side.”

“I’m not on anybody’s side,” I said.

Jane took her shoe. “You are,” she said. “Everybody is.” She sounded so sure that I almost believed her, and I was wondering how I might even the score when Mid pulled into the lot, saving me from having to wade any further in. They both ran to hug him, made an older couple driving a Cadillac stand on the brakes to keep from knocking them down. It wasn’t close, but it launched Mid into some prepared remarks on looking both ways.

“We know,” they said.

“I know we know,” he said. “But we didn’t do it.”

“We will,” they said.

“What should I tell them, Walter? That safety is a virtue? That it’s the better part of valor?”

“Dad,” one of them said. Or both. Here was Mid in all his paternal splendor, smoothing over the fight, a hand on each girl’s shoulder now, steering them safely through another afternoon. The storm blew itself out just like that.

“Everybody’s inside?” Mid asked me.

“Delton’s not here yet,” I said.

“She called. She and Captain America are running late. She said we should start without them.”

“The kid’s coming, too?”

"Should be a show," he said. "Fun for all ages." He looked at me. "You seem off."

"Alice and I were into it some." I held the door for Sophie and Jane. "But we're good."

"You need some fire department pancakes, is what you need," he said.

I said, "I need something," and followed him into the cool of the room.

There were long tables running the length of the space, red and green tablecloths alternating down the rows. Alice and Carolyn had staked out some space along the far wall. There were snowmen and reindeer and Santas posed in various scenes at each table, cotton balls spilled around them to look like snow. A banner hanging on the far wall said XMAS IN J.U.L.Y. There was no immediate explanation for what J.U.L.Y. might stand for. Mid tried to pay at the door—there was a huge jar with about five hundred dollars in ones and fives—but the woman sitting there said, "They already paid." She thrust an arm out at Alice and Carolyn. Then she sucked on a massive asthma inhaler she had strung around her neck on a pink cord. The twins stared. I couldn't blame them. The woman's mouth was huge, like a puppet's mouth. It took up half her face. She pointed at two fat rolls of tickets on the table in front of her. "The pink ones are for the kids. Yellow for the adults. Everybody get one, now. We're running a raffle every ten minutes." She pulled hard on the inhaler again. "Keep good track," she told Sophie and Jane. "We've got coloring books."

"We're too old for that," Jane said.

The lady appraised them. "You may be right," she said.

"Well, we've got certificates to the go-carts, too. Do you like the go-carts?"

"We've never been," Sophie said.

"Never been? Get one or another of these grown-ups to take you."

"We'll do that," I said, and the twins lit up.

"Can we really, Dad?" they asked.

"We need to discuss it with your mom first," he said. I saw I might have crossed some boundary.

"But she'll say no," Jane said.

"Don't let that boy who got his hand crushed worry you," the woman said. "They added bars to the sides of the carts. I've got a girlfriend who works out there. It's safer than it used to be."

"Who got his hand crushed?" Jane asked, clearly excited.

"They say to keep your hands inside at all times," the woman said. "But do people listen?"

"We should go eat," said Mid. "Thanks for the tickets."

"Tell Vera up there to give these girls two sausages each," the woman said. "They're too skinny. They need to eat."

We went through the line, and Vera gave the twins extra sausage without anybody having to ask her about it. They were polite, said please and thank you, loaded up their plates with two or three flavors of syrup. We sat down, and it seemed clear Alice had caught Carolyn up on my most recent swing-and-miss. Carolyn wasn't exactly cool toward me—more pitying than anything. Like I'd received some kind of medium-grim diagnosis. I said, "The girls say they've never been to the go-carts. I didn't even know there were go-carts around here."

"There are," Carolyn said. "But they're death traps."

"No they're not," Sophie said. "They're cool. They're from like the eighties or something."

"Maybe we could take them one night," I said. "Alice and I could."

"I don't know about that," Carolyn said.

"Mom," they were both saying now, "Please? Can we? Come on."

"I said I don't know," Carolyn said, her voice harder-edged.

"Maybe we could talk about it another time," Alice said, kicking me a little under the table. "Maybe if we planned it. But surely we don't have to plan it right now, Walter, right?"

The twins kept after Carolyn, trying out various lines of bargaining—they were older now; we would make sure nothing happened to them. Wasn't that right, they asked me. Sure it was, I said, regretting the whole thing, feeling the too-lateness of it grow. I'd buy Carolyn a card to apologize. Surely they had a section for this particular indiscretion at the store—next to Baby's First Halloween, maybe. The raffle woman stood up at the end of the room, sucked on her inhaler, held up a small box. She said, "Let's do some prizes. What we've got first up is a mug that says, WHEN I AM WITH MY FRIENDS, I AM IN HOG HEAVEN. It's got these adorable pigs on it drinking tea." She reached into a basket, came out with a yellow ticket, read off the number. A woman at a table near the door stood up, clapped for herself, went to claim her prize. The raffle woman said, "Now how about we do one for the kids?"

I checked the room: There was Maggie, there were the twins, there was an infant in a car seat two tables over. No question about what was coming. The woman dug into another basket, read out a number from a pink ticket. No winner. Another. Still no winner. She spilled the basket out on the table, squinted at the room, sorted through the pile until she had the one she wanted, and read it out. Jane's ticket. Jane walked to the front, the room clapping, watching her, so grown up, so pretty, and she got the prize we knew was coming—$25.00 at First Coast Speedways—then made her way back to our table. Carolyn did not look at her, did not look at me. Sophie wanted to see it, and at first Jane wouldn't let her, exacting revenge for the flip-flop affair, but Mid got Sophie to ask nicely, and then she was showing everybody. It was a home job, just something Xeroxed onto colored paper, but still: She'd won. It was over. There was no way we weren't going death-trap racing now.

And I could feel all of everything boiling up at the table: Whatever it was that crackled between Carolyn and Mid was there, plus the fault lines running below the rest of Mid's known empire. Also the BOJ, the monitor, the ever-improving version of what Alice and I circled every day. And now this new thing, something concrete, which was nice, which helped—we had the certain coming demise of one or both of the twins at the hands of the internal combustion engine, which would be my fault and mine alone—and you could see that every piece of that was getting ready to come into full and mighty bloom right there at the XMAS IN J.U.L.Y. Pancake Supper and Benefit Raffle, but Delton saved us all. She martyred herself. She came in the door trailing the famous boyfriend, and he was wearing swim shorts and a plain white T-shirt, and she was wearing a little sundress, orange and strapless, something that made her look twenty-nine and her own age all at once. It looked like she'd put her makeup on with a push broom, but that wasn't what mattered so much. What mattered was the inside of her left forearm, where she was sporting a white gauze bandage about the size of Jane's Speedways envelope. Carolyn and Mid were both out of their chairs before she could sit down, asking if she was hurt, if she was alright. No, she was saying, she wasn't hurt. She was fine. Fine. Maggie made sculptures out of the mortar her pancakes had become. Jane and Sophie looked at Delton. All of us looked at Delton. "It's a tattoo," she said.

Carolyn said, "Is it that big?"

"No," Nic said. "They just like to put on extra-big bandages over at Little Charlie's. They're really careful."

"How big is it?" Mid asked, sitting back down.

"You know, like the size of a playing card," Nic said. He pulled the neck of his shirt over, showed us a palm tree on his collarbone. "About like that," he said.

"Oh," Mid said. "OK. Terrific."

"What's it of?" I said, and Alice sunk her nails into my arm. I couldn't help it.

"It's a letter," Delton said. "A character. It's the Japanese symbol for tiger."

"Cool," Sophie said.

"Yeah," Jane said.

Mid said, "I don't get it."

"There isn't anything to get, Dad. That's the whole thing. It's more about being in tune with life."

Carolyn said, "What did you just say?"

"Did you teach her to talk like that?" Mid asked Nic.

"No, sir."

Mid looked him over. "What do you do with your time, anyway?" he asked.

"I'm in school, sir. At Flagler."

"You're in college?" Alice said.

"Yes, ma'am."

"Wow," she said.

"What?"

"Nothing," said Alice. "It's good. It's good to be in college."

Delton said, "I don't get what the big deal is with that. Everybody always thinks it's such a big deal."

"Who's everybody?" Nic asked.

"All my friends."

"What's your major?" I asked Nic.

"Education," he said. "I'm getting my Deaf Ed certification. I'm going to be a teacher."

It was an impossible answer. This was not the answer of a reprobate child who'd just gotten your daughter tattooed. I watched Mid. He took a bite of his food. He took another bite. He said, "Whose idea was this?"

"My major?" Nic said.

"The tattoo," Carolyn said, "is I think what he means."

"Mine," said Delton.

"Why didn't you ask us first?" she said.

"Because you would have said no."

Carolyn turned to Mid. "And this is what happens when you buy a child a Camaro," she said.

"I'll be finished with my degree next year," said Nic. "I'm graduating early. I'll be able to get a pretty sweet job."

Mid set his fork down, lined it up with his napkin. "Why do you keep talking to me like you two are getting married?" he asked him.

"I don't, sir."

"What makes you think I care in any way about what job you'll have next year?"

"Dad," Delton said.

"And what'll happen in five years when you decide this was a completely dumbass move?" he asked her.

"Hey," Nic said.

"No offense," said Mid.

"I'm on the Dean's list," Nic said.

"Let me talk to my daughter for a minute," Mid said. "Then you can give me your résumé."

"Maybe Walter and I should go outside," Alice said, standing up. Maggie started singing "Itsy Bitsy Spider," complete with hand motions.

"Sure," I said.

"We'll just be outside," she told Carolyn, who wasn't listening. "If you need anything."

"Olivia," Carolyn said. "What is this all about?"

"Delton," said Delton.

Alice took my arm, said, "Let's *go*." The twins looked like they'd never seen anything so excellent. I saw Delton reach for Nic's hand under the table.

"I'm coming," I said, not moving.

"Walter. Right now."

"It's a tiger?" Carolyn asked.

"It's the *symbol* for tiger," Delton said.

"Wait till you see it," Nic said. "Dude did a killer job."

"Don't talk like that," Mid said.

"Yes, sir."

"And stop calling me sir. You're driving me fucking crazy."

"Dad," Sophie said, right away.

“This is a special circumstance, sweetie,” Mid said, and that was the last of it I got to hear. Alice pulled me away, hustled me past the raffle lady and out into the parking lot.

“What were you doing?” she said.

“What?”

“You were just staring. You looked like a mental patient.”

“I was watching,” I said.

“You were staring.” The evening had gone very still. The sky was pinking over. Alice said, “She’s not wearing sleeves.”

“Why does that matter?”

“She didn’t even try to hide it. Carolyn will kill her.”

“You think?”

“Maybe not. It’s not like she got arrested.”

I tried to hold her hand a while, but it was too hot, and she let go. “We won’t let Montezuma get one,” I said. “A tattoo.”

“That’s a boy’s name. He was a man.”

“I think it was a volcano.”

“It was a man, too,” she said.

“It could work both ways. Boy or girl.”

“I don’t think that’s true.”

“We’ll just tell her,” I said. “It can be a rule. We’ll say, ‘Monty, no tattoos.’ ”

“Monty. That’s cute.” She put a hand to her belly. A cat stopped out in the open, started bathing itself. “I think they had that rule, though,” she said. “I think they had the rule and it didn’t make any difference.”

“We could still try,” I said.

“I guess.”

I said, “I’m sorry.”

“For what?”

“For earlier. For everything.”

She traced a circle in the sand with her shoe. "What was that with the go-carts?"

"I made a mistake."

"Now we have to take them."

I said, "Surely it's safe, right?"

"Not safer than not taking them."

Something spooked the cat, and it ran for the treeline. "The police showed up today," I told her. "Out at the cabins."

"What did they want?"

"To talk to Mid. They talked to him, and then they left."

"About what?"

"About the store. They want to do some hidden-camera thing."

Part of her was still back inside, I could tell, watching the traveling circus of Delton being fifteen. And part of her was probably still back at the condo, too, watching the monitor watch Monty's room. She said, "Was that all?"

"That's all he told me."

"I'm pretty sure this is just getting worse and worse," she said. "That's what Carolyn thinks."

"Worse in what way?"

"In no way. In all the ways." She rubbed at the side of her neck. "I don't like this," she said.

"I don't like it, either," I told her. "I want you to know that."

She reached for my hand again, and this time she held on. Maybe, for that brief moment there in the parking lot, we were the team Alice wanted us to be. I hoped we were. I was, for once, trying for it.

■ ■ ■

It did not rain the night we took the twins to First Coast Speedways. A storm came in over the flat, almost got to us, but then backed up and stayed put inland, off behind the Intracoastal and the interstate. You could see the lightning strobing the clouds, but you couldn't hear the thunder. Safe distance, we decided. And they confirmed that at the Speedways gate: A guy with his arm in a sling nodded out over the parking lot, back toward the storm, said, "We're fine now, but if that thing gets any closer—if we hear it, we have to shut down for thirty minutes, no exceptions. We'll blow the siren. You'll know. You gotta leave when that happens. Just make sure somebody stamps your tickets for a rain check."

"Are you the person who got his hand crushed in the go-carts?" Sophie asked.

"Naw. I fell down that step the other night." He motioned with the sling arm. "Came out of the booth funny, missed the step, tried to catch myself, fouled my elbow."

"Oh," Sophie said, clearly disappointed.

"Do keep your hands inside the buggies at all times, though, OK?"

"What's a buggy?" Jane asked.

"Fancy word for go-cart," he said.

The twins were tall enough and old enough to ride the kiddie carts by themselves, so of course that's what they wanted to do. Alice and I stood in line with them, made sure they got in OK, and then picked our way up into the bleachers to watch them take laps around a track shaped like a pear. The lights were almost bright enough. There were shadows out at the far ends. Alice said, "Maybe you should have ridden with them the first time."

"They'll do great," I said. "They don't want me down there."

"If we kill one of them, Carolyn will never forgive me."

"She might. Give her time."

"Don't even joke about that."

It was just a tattoo, was where Mid had finally landed. He'd rather she not have done it, but et cetera. And Alice was nearly on board with that, or the idea of it, but when we'd been down on the benches or out walking our evening half-mile, she'd been saying, too, that it wasn't the tattoo at all, that it was the sum total of the body of work in question. That Carolyn would have been fine if it'd been the tattoo and nothing else. I know, I'd been saying, but still. Not still, she'd said. Imagine you were on the other end of that. I'm on the end of some of it, I said. She said: It's hardly the same.

First Coast Speedways featured two tracks. There was the track the girls were on, a flat concrete track, and also one for the older kids and adults, which had banked wooden turns, more turns, bigger carts. The carts on the wood sounded like air conditioners being rolled across Lincoln Logs. Our carts sounded like bees. On the big track, if you wrecked, you were on your own to get yourself pointed in the right direction again. On ours, a guy would come out, lift the front or back end off the ground, spin you around and send you off again. He wore a helmet and shinguards. Any time anybody wrecked, Alice flinched. I did, too.

"The doctor's office called today," Alice said. She had her hand up over her eyes visor-style, watching the girls come around. "They wanted to know if we were enrolled in any parenting classes."

"Right," I said.

"And we're not."

"I know that."

"We're supposed to be, they said. I think there's a law."

"What'll they do, take the kid away?"

Sophie came around the bottom end of the pear. From where we were sitting, her helmet looked four sizes too big. Jane drove by a few seconds behind her, took the corner more cautiously. We waved. They never saw us.

"They have them at the hospital down here," she said. "We can take the classes here even if we deliver in Jacksonville. So we won't have to drive so much."

"Great. Sign me up."

"I did. We start next week."

"Isn't that a little soon?"

"They said we could do it early if we wanted to. There are two sets of classes. Birthing and Parenting. I signed us up for Birthing first."

"That seems like the right order."

Two boys smashed into each other down in front of us, shouting and laughing. The shinguard guy ran out, straightened the carts, and the boys took off again. Alice said, "We only have to take three of them."

The foil on the windows. Now classes. I said, "How many are there?"

"They meet weekly."

"Weekly?"

"I think that's pretty normal. And it could be good for us."

"We'll go," I said. "It's fine."

There was a light stanchion out in the middle of the track to signal how much time there was left in each race—green to yellow to red. In the last minute the red light blinked, then held steady, which meant you were supposed to bring your cart back to the start/finish line. A girl who looked a few years older than Delton wandered out onto the track once all the cars had stopped and handed a boy driving the #31 a cheap-looking checkered flag. I had no idea how they kept track of who won—after the first couple of laps it all seemed scrambled to me. Maybe they just chose a kid out of thin air. The #31 boy stood up in his cart, waved his flag, and his parents, sitting a few rows down from us, cheered more than was necessary. "Now *that's* the way to want it, Gerald Junior!" his dad yelled.

"Wow," I said, too loudly.

The dad whipped around to face me. "You got some kind of issue?" he said.

"No," I said. "I really don't."

"You seem like you do, though."

"I'm good," I said.

"Gerald," his wife said.

"I'm just talking to this dude," Gerald said. "He's got some kind of issue."

That fast: trouble. I felt for the weight of my arms, trying to gin up a plan for what I'd do if he came over the couple of rows at us, which right then seemed fairly possible. The last person I'd hit had been a saxophone player in my high school marching band. There'd been some disagreement over a girl, and he'd been able to hit me right back, no problem, which left us both standing in the instrument room, bleeding and yelling at each other. Our friends broke up what was left of the fight. Gerald looked like he'd be ready to hold his own. Like he had hair plugs, but like he'd be able to hold his own. Alice stood up. "Oh," Gerald said.

"Oh, what?" she said.

"I didn't realize."

"Realize what?"

"You're pregnant," he said. "Right?"

"You don't know that. Now turn around and cheer for your son and leave us alone."

"Sure," he said. "Whatever."

"Peace be with you," I said.

He said, "What did you say?"

"It's something we said in church growing up."

"We're Jewish," he said.

"Walter," Alice said. "Cut it out."

"Congratulations anyway," I said.

"On what?"

"Your son," I said. "The race."

"Oh," Gerald said. "Yeah. Thanks."

We kept staring each other down, like apes. He turned around, finally, and Alice sat back down, whispered, "What was that?"

"I could ask you the same thing," I said.

"I got caught up in the moment."

"You were a wolverine."

"Don't talk like that."

The line was short enough that Sophie and Jane got to go again right away. Gerald Junior came up into the stands, and his parents treated him like he'd won the world. A new race started. Alice and I watched the twins trace that same path over and over, watched the lights flick down the tower. Then they went again. And again. Finally they ran out of tickets, and we got back in the car, headed for the castle. Sophie and Jane were fast friends for the time being, talking endlessly in the back seat about how awesome the go-carts were, how they were totally going to try to go again next week. Alice and I rode quietly up front. My math: What would have happened if Gerald had come across the bleachers at us? If Alice hadn't stood up? If he and I had had to hit each other until one of us learned something? It was all a tryout, I thought, my head alive with the sound of the little engines. A dry run. Every damn thing all the time.

■ ■ ■

I was up early—a Saturday, no cabins, no secret agent men, no nothing. I left Alice and the BOJ in bed and took a cup of coffee down to the beach, walked south toward where the river cut in from the Intracoastal. People were out fishing, bait in plastic coolers and poles propped in PVC pipes shoved into the sand. Once the condos gave way to houses, there were old women in white hats looking for shells, old men in white hats toting metal detectors. Deeply wealthy Scandinavian couples, too, out first thing in their teak-and-canvas folding chairs, their meatloaves of babies sheltering under strikingly engineered tents and umbrellas, eating sand. Bicyclists. Joggers. A man in goggles and a Speedo, headed out for a swim. The sun was almost metal off the water.

We'd been there six weeks. I'd been out of a job for three months. We were only a little more pregnant than that. Even while I was well aware that I should be panicked about whatever had happened to my career, if a word like that even applied anymore, there just wasn't time. Or there hadn't been. We had a roof above us. Food on the table. Cash in the bank—most of which we could not use, or should not, though knowing it was there helped all the same. On a roller coaster, you're only ever playing at being afraid. That's the trick, the thrill. It's all a game. Look: Everyone comes back, strapped in just the same.

I didn't fully register what I was seeing until the parachutist was already a couple hundred yards past me. He came in from somewhere over the Intracoastal, over the houses in a long curve, and he was too low—the motor silent, the black sail not entirely inflated. Something was wrong. He got the rig partially straightened out, at least, but he was falling, and he kept falling until he managed to set the thing down on the hard sand left by low tide. He rolled to a stop. It was the quietest emergency landing I'd ever seen. It was the only emergency landing I'd ever seen. The parachute settled onto the beach like a napkin. He sat inside the cage, not moving.

I ran over and found him staring straight ahead, still belted in, hands on the control bars. "Are you hurt?" I asked him. "Are you OK?"

He held his hands out in front of him, opened and closed them. He was wearing gloves the same green as his cart. "I'm back," he said. "I must have blacked out for a moment." He pulled off his goggles, which left red rings around his eyes where they'd pressed into the skin. "The doctors tell me not to fly, but how am I supposed to give that up?" He unbuckled and got out, checked a couple of levers on the engine. "Yep," he said. "Everything looks fine here. I think this one was all on me."

"Is there someone I could call for you?" I said.

"No, no," he said. "I don't think that's a good idea. I believe we need to get this chariot back up in the sky before anybody brings a sheriff down here."

A man in a flannel robe came out of one of the houses. "Hey," he called, once he got far enough down his walkway. "Do you two need me to call the police?"

"Already it starts," the parachutist said. He looked up at the guy. "I'd prefer you didn't," he said.

"Are you sure?"

"I am," the parachutist said, and turned back to me. "You think a lot of folks saw that?"

There were people headed in our direction. "Some," I said.

"I really need to go," he said. "They'll be all over me if I don't get back up." The flannel robe guy was down near us now, and a small crowd was half-gathering. The parachutist held his hand out. "Hank," he said to me.

"Walter."

"Pleasure."

The robe guy shook his hand, too. "Neil," he said. Then: "What is this thing?"

"It's like an ultralight," said Hank. "But lighter."

"Where'd you get it?"

"Built it myself. Once you've got the engine, you're mostly good to go." Neil apparently knew about engines, and he had questions about governor springs and ccs. I did not know what ccs were. I stayed quiet while Hank answered, while he laid the parachute out flat behind the buggy, folding it in what looked like a precise way. I had questions, too, but I was not asking them: Have you been pointing at me? Who are you, exactly? Is there something you've been trying to tell me? Once Hank had the chute the way he wanted it, he picked it up and handed it to the two of us. "Here's what I'll need," he said. "Run behind me until I get going fast enough, and when you can't keep up any longer, that's when you know to let go."

"Hold on," Neil said. "I'm just wearing this robe."

"You'll see how it works right away," Hank said. "It doesn't take a lot to get this thing to jump. Gentlemen, my great thanks." He got back in, started the engine. It was powerfully loud. The propeller fan seemed enough alone to inflate the chute. Far off down the beach, I saw an ATV cop coming toward us, blue light flashing at the top of a pole mounted off the back. Hank got a little more hurried about his getaway. He kicked something below the steering bar, some clutch, and the whole thing lurched forward, and Neil and I looked at each other—and then we were running behind Hank and his green cart, a string of tiny American flags clipped to the side, holding onto the POW chute until he was going faster than we were. When we let go, the chute jerked into the air with a pop, like a bedsheet, and it bounced him off the beach twice, three times, and then he was in the air for good, swinging back and forth a little before leveling out, gliding up and circling back once to yell something we did not understand. He flew back out over the houses instead of up the beach. The crowd watched him go, and then, not knowing what else to do, went back to their metal detecting, their jogging, their shells. The cop cut his light off, turned around, rode back north. I said, "That was something."

"I've seen him before, up and down the beach," Neil said.

"Me, too," I said.

Neither of us knew how it was supposed to work, the awkward camaraderie of men. Neil tightened his robe. He said, "Do you live down here, or are you vacationing?"

"It's sort of both," I said. "We've been here since June. We're up at the Sanddollar."

"I know that place. It's nice."

"Is that your house?" I asked him, meaning the one he'd come out of, a shingled three-story with huge windows.

"It is."

"It's fantastic," I said, because it was.

"The kids like it. We summer down here."

"That must be great," I said. I did not ask him where he summered from. We squinted in the sun.

"You have kids?" he said.

"A little girl," I told him. "On the way."

"We've got boys," he said. "Ten and five. Just put the oldest one in braces." Braces. I hadn't considered braces, though I could see the metal shining, remembered my childhood friends with rubber bands all in their mouths, the little plastic bags the rubber bands came in. "I'm surprised they didn't come out," he said. "I'd have thought they'd want to see that."

"Yeah," I said.

"They're playing video games. Extreme something. Tennis. You swing your arm and your guy on the screen does, too. These games these days—it's wild."

"I know," I said, even though I didn't know.

The nice thing about having a parachute, it occurred to me, was that when something did go wrong, you already had your parachute ready. Accounting for calamity was built into the design. Neil was saying we should come down sometime, introduce ourselves. I told him we would and thanked him for the invitation. I knew we'd never do it. He went back to his house, to Extreme Tennis, and I walked back up to the condo. I felt like I'd been dropped onto some other planet, one that looked a lot like the one I'd come from, but where something wasn't exactly right, something I knew but couldn't name. Alice wanted to know everything about the crash landing, everything about the parachutist. What he looked like up close. How his voice sounded. Like himself, I said. Like you'd think. She wanted to know why I hadn't asked him what he was up to. I told her it had all happened so fast I hadn't had a chance, which was nearly true. I told her he'd built the thing himself. She wasn't all that impressed. "Did you find out his name, at least?" she said.

"Hank."

"Hank? Really?"

"Why?"

"I would have thought it would be something bigger," she said. "I think I wanted something regal."

"What, like Leviticus?"

"Wouldn't that have been better?" She went to the sliding doors, opened and shut them.

"It certainly would have been stranger," I said, hearing the hum pick back up again.

"Would it?" She opened the doors again, let another amount of air in. We stood there like that, not knowing, while the whole of the outside pressed in against us.

Delton ran away. She wanted to get a second tattoo on her other arm, and what Mid and Carolyn said was no, absolutely not, not while you're living under our roof, young lady, and Delton took them at their word, waited until they were both out of the house, packed up her things, and moved in with Nic. *I am not running away,* her note said. *That's not what this is. Please remain calm.* Carolyn and Mid showed it to us that evening at the house. We'd gone over to stand nearby during tragedy. The note was on Nancy Drew stationery. I was surprised Delton even knew who that was. "She ran away," Carolyn said, folding the note back up again. She was crying. She was drinking wine.

"She didn't run away," Mid said.

Carolyn put her head down on the kitchen table. "I can't believe she ran away."

The crisis had brought Mid back home, at least temporarily, which I'd tried to say was a good thing. Alice wasn't having any of it. "There's nothing good going on here," she said on the way over, and then she turned up the news. For the rest of the ride, we listened to a report on chamber music affecting or not affecting cognitive ability in skinks.

Alice sat with Carolyn. Mid and I stood in front of his giant television. Golf was on. The TV was so large that the close-ups were much bigger than life-size, which made everything feel off. "I guess you've got to give her this," Mid said. "I didn't see this coming."

I didn't say anything about how she'd already stolen the car and come down to the condo. I didn't say that even I'd sort of seen it coming, now that I looked at it.

Mid said, "She's too young to be moving in with a boy, probably."

"Probably," I said.

"It's at least too soon. It's got to be too soon." He looked over at Alice and Carolyn like he was making sure they were still there. "Don't have kids," he said.

"Good advice," I said. "Timely."

"It's a goddamned merry-go-round. Maybe if we kept them in a pen in the yard, never taught them to read or write—"

"Maybe," I said.

"Shit, this kind of thing probably won't happen to you. You guys'll do a better job. And even if you don't, you've got a few years to get ready."

"That helps," I said.

On TV, a golfer took several practice swings. "We're going to have to go get her," Mid said.

I said, "Anything you want. I'm here to help."

He said, "What I want is for her to wipe that shit off her arm and come back home."

"That seems sound."

He said, "Sometimes it gets a little hard to tell."

The one guy never did hit the ball. The coverage shifted to somebody in pink argyle pants, and then they went to a blimp shot. It was a different time of day where they were. There was a lot of green grass, green trees. Big houses. You wanted to be there instead of where you were, a place with mountains in the background instead of a place with runaway notes on the kitchen table. I did, anyway. I wanted to be in the blimp. That had to be why they put it on TV in the first place.

One of the twins came downstairs, looking grave. "Hey, Sophie," said Alice.

"Olivia called," Sophie said, walking into the kitchen.

"She what?" Carolyn said.

"She called. Olivia called me."

Carolyn said, "Is she still on the phone? Is she talking to Jane?"

"She made me promise not to say where she was."

"She's with Nic. It's in the note."

"Oh," said Sophie.

"Where's Jane?"

"Upstairs," Sophie said, "in her room," and Carolyn was up in a hurry, knocking her chair over on her way out. She took the stairs two at a time. We waited, listened. We heard her talking to Jane. Sophie cracked her knuckles and executed a slow-motion tae kwon do move. "This is called back pose," she said, to nobody in particular. "Our instructor says it's useful for a quick strike."

"It's very good," Alice said.

"Thank you." She did a kick next, held her leg out until she lost her balance, had to grab the refrigerator to keep from falling. The door swung open and two or three sodas rolled out onto the floor.

"Sophie," Mid said.

"Sorry." She picked up the cans. "Can I have one?"

He said, "Why not?"

"What about Jane?"

"Just make sure you actually give it to her."

"Cookies, too?" she said.

"How about a piece of fruit?"

"Gross." But she took four or five bananas from a bunch on the table, disappeared back into the house.

Mid got up, opened one of the cabinets, lined up a few juice glasses. "Wait until *they're* fifteen," he said. "What a couple of vipers. If you think having *one's* bad—" He trailed off. He was talking to the dishes. He moved on to another cabinet. "I didn't know we still had these," he said. He had a stack of oversized pasta bowls with fat purple grapes painted on the sides. "I hate these. They're about the ugliest plates I've ever seen."

"Bowls," Alice said. "Those are bowls. Mom gave them to us. One set to you guys, one set to us."

"Do you still have yours?"

"No. I hated them, too."

"Who could even eat this much pasta?" He held one out like Exhibit A, and then walked over to the pantry, started dropping the bowls one by one into the trash. The first one landed softly enough, but the second one broke on the first, and he kept going. Alice and I just watched him do it. It was hard to know what to say to a man dropping bowls in the trash. It was hard to say whether what he was doing was right or wrong. Carolyn came back down the stairs. Mid stopped, holding a bowl out in front of him.

"What are you doing?" she said.

"I hate these."

She said, "I don't understand."

"I'm getting rid of a few things."

"Now?"

He dropped the bowl in. He was tilting. I couldn't blame him.

"You'll wake Maggie," Carolyn said. "And are you not going to ask if that was Olivia on the phone?"

"I already know it was."

"You don't want to know what she said?"

He handed her the bowls he had left. "Let me take a crack at it," he said. "She said she wasn't coming home. She said she was safe at Nic's. She said she's old enough to make her own decisions. Something along those lines?"

"She said she was scared," Carolyn said.

"Of what?" he said.

"Of the world. She said she was scared of the world."

"I get that," I said, and everybody looked at me. It was not my turn to talk, and I had talked. "I do," I said. "That makes sense to me."

"How do you mean?" Alice said.

"How much answer do you want?" I said. "Poisonous snakes. Lupus. Monthly fees."

"You're not helping," Alice said.

"Is that all she said?" Mid asked Carolyn.

"No," Carolyn said, sitting down at the table. "She said all your stuff, too." She looked flattened out, like a paper doll. "She's not coming home, she's old, she's safe, she decides."

"Does she want us to go get her?"

"You're not even listening to me," she said.

"Well, this is fucking great," said Mid. "When did it happen that we don't make the rules any more?"

"Stop shouting," Carolyn said.

"I don't get to be a little surprised that she's telling us where she's going to live or when she's going to call?"

Carolyn said, "And where do you think she got it in her head that something like that would be OK? How about we just start right there?"

"Guys," Alice said.

Carolyn said, "Leecy, has Walter been in jail?"

"Not yet."

"So there we are." She turned back to Mid. "How about you just tell us the truth this one time. You knew they were selling pot in the shop."

"We've been through this," he said.

"Wrong," she said. "We get near it, but you never really tell anybody anything. So come on. You're among friends. Don't tell us that when the police showed up, you thought it was some kind of goodwill gesture. I mean, even Olivia knew, for chrissakes."

He looked genuinely surprised. "What?"

Carolyn knew. Which meant Alice had to know. "She has friends who bought from there," Carolyn said. "She told me a couple of weeks ago, after you moved out."

He pushed a few breaths into his fist. "I wish you'd told me that," he said.

"Why?"

"Does she buy from there? Is she still buying from there?"

"She said she didn't, but why?"

"They set up cameras last week," he said. "In the back. And microphones. If she buys there, she'll be on the tape."

Carolyn said, "What are you talking about?"

"They already set it up?" I said. I hadn't thought about Delton, either.

"You didn't say it was definitely happening," Alice said to me.

Carolyn looked at her. "What are *you* talking about?"

"I knew," Mid said. "OK? I totally knew. Of course I fucking knew. I just tried to hang on to being able to say I didn't *really* know."

Carolyn was still looking at Alice. "*You* knew?"

"Walter told me about the police," she said. "That's all."

"What the fuck is going on here?" Carolyn said. She grabbed Mid's arm. "What have you done to us?" She pointed at Alice. "What have you done to them?"

"Nothing," he said. "This is all going to blow over. I've got it under control."

"Blow over? Are you shitting me? Now there are these cops—"

"Agents," he said. "Revenue agents."

Alice said, "I didn't know they were agents."

"Some fucking *agents* everybody already knows about are going to set up some—some *sting* operation at Island?"

Mid said, "More or less."

"After you and the rest of the world already got arrested? For doing nothing?"

"Almost nothing," he said.

"And they think the kids are stupid enough to keep dealing back there after they already got caught once?"

"I think they do."

"Forget for a second that you didn't tell me any of this, OK? How could you not tell *her*?"

"What would I have said? 'Do take care this week, dear, when you purchase marijuana from Daddy's store?'"

"Something like that would have been good, yes." I kept trying to get Alice's attention, but she was staring at her hands. Carolyn said, "But what would have been easier, you colossal asshole, is if Daddy wasn't involved with any agents at all. If she didn't need to be warned off from purchasing anything from Daddy's store in the first place. Jesus shit, how did we get *here*?" She picked up the wine bottle. "And my God," she said, walking past Alice. "*You* knew? Both of you knew? And neither of you could tell her, either? Or tell me?" She stopped in front of the sliding doors. "You know what I'll bet? I'll bet this is not your typical Wednesday-night-gather-the-family-round-the-dinner-table topic of conversation. I'll bet the Walkers down the street aren't having this conversation." She opened the door. "But wait!" she said, spinning around. "Good news! There *are* no Walkers down the street! We're the only goddamned people in here! *Any* conversation we have is the typical conversation for this street!" She poured wine into her glass, both hands shaking. "Mid, you're a lucky man. Turns out the cops busting your own daughter because it didn't occur to you to even *have* anything occur to you is just fine around here. It is the fucking norm." She stared him down. "You are a complete sack of shit, you know that?"

"Carolyn," he said, but she was already outside, slamming the door behind her. She stood out on the patio, didn't move. There were lightning bugs. She kept her back to us. Eventually Mid got up, went out there with her. They were so still we couldn't tell if they were talking or not.

Alice got herself a glass of water, leaned on the sink. The little muscles in her forearms stood out like vines. "You knew she was buying?" she said.

"That night on the balcony, she told me her friends were. Or that they did, sometimes."

"You didn't tell me."

"She asked me not to."

"What else haven't you told me?"

"I don't know," I said. "I'm so fucking lost I have no idea. Start at the beginning. Ask me anything."

She said, "That's a copout. Don't hide behind that."

"He never goes into details," I said. "The cops turn up somewhere, he talks to them, they drive off again. It's all very secret."

"But how does that strike you as being alright?"

"I didn't say it did," I said. "I never said that."

"I thought you were watching him."

"I am watching him."

"We're not supposed to keep things from each other."

"I'm aware."

"Carolyn's never going to speak to me again."

"Yes, she will."

"Are they like FBI agents? Is that the deal?"

"It's like state FBI," I said.

"That sounds worse than regular police," she said. She pulled a drawer open, pushed it back closed again. "Maybe you can't work for him anymore."

"I don't know what I'm supposed to do here. We need me to work. We need me to have something—"

"But this?" she said. "We can't live our lives like this."

"We're not," I said. "I never see anything. We're safe."

"That's not safe," she said. "That's not anything close to safe. Safe is what we had before, what you had—"

"And that's gone," I said. "Remember? So, not so safe, after all."

"Is this what it's going to be like, though?"

I said, "I have no idea. Maybe it is. Maybe for now."

"I just wish somebody could tell me," she said.

"You," I said. "Line up the people to explain it to me, OK? Schedule somebody every half an hour. Tell them to bring visual aids."

"Don't start in on me. I can only deal with one gaping pit of quicksand at a time." She walked into the living room, vanished around a corner. "Oh, shit," she said.

"What?"

"In here." She sounded exhausted. "Sophie and Jane."

I followed her in. The twins were at the top of the stairs. "Hey," they said.

"Hey," said Alice.

"We heard everything," Sophie said. "In case you were wondering."

Jane said, "We always do."

"That's fine," Alice said, looking at me. I blinked back at her, deaf and dumb. We needed semaphore flags. Lamps. One if by sea, that kind of thing. She looked up at the girls. "So," she said. She smoothed her hands on her legs. The twins held their position. "Is there anything you want to talk about?"

"Are Mom and Dad still fighting?" Jane asked.

Out on the pool deck, Mid had an arm around Carolyn. Her head was on his shoulder. "It doesn't look like it," Alice said. "Though I don't know why not."

"OK," they said, and got up, took off down the hall to somebody's room. A door shut.

"Is that all you needed?" Alice called, but there was no answer. Music came on, something with a lot of noise in it. I wondered if we should be hanging soundproofing in the baby's room instead of tinfoil. Or if maybe it wouldn't matter—maybe we wouldn't even have music twelve years from now. Maybe the ocean would have long since come up and grabbed the buildings, taken us all, swept the sand back clean. Alice sat down on the bottom step. "We're going to have to do something," she said. "We have to think of something. I hate this."

I said, "You wouldn't go get her?"

"Olivia? I'd absolutely go get her. I'd go get her right now. That's not what I meant at all." She stared up into the stairwell, at a chandelier the size of a small car. "What I meant was, I don't know what the hell we do next."

■ ■ ■

What the hell we did next was stand in the kitchen while Mid made calls until he tracked down the kid who owned the little beach house, Robbie, who knew Nic, knew where he lived. "How could it be easier to get there by water?" Mid said into the phone.

"Get where?" Carolyn said.

Mid said, "I do know somebody who has one."

"Has one what?" said Carolyn.

Mid put his hand over the mouthpiece. "A boat," he said. "Wait a minute." They'd come to some kind of agreement outside, who knew why or how. Mid listened a minute. "I can do that," he said. "That'll be fine." He checked his watch. "Half an hour, maybe a little longer. That good by you?" He waited. Then he said, "Thanks, man, OK? I appreciate it." He hung up, put the phone on the table. He said, "Well, I guess we're going to get her."

I said, "In a boat?"

"He's got a house on a spur creek off the Matanzas," he said. "Nic does. Robbie says the road can be bad. Says it's half again as easy if we go by water."

"You're going to go get our daughter in a boat," Carolyn said. "On the advice of a highschooler."

"Robbie's in college," Mid said. "They all are. I need to call Hurley."

"I hate boats," she said.

Mid said, "I know you do."

"I'll go," I said.

Alice said, "You will?"

"I should be there," Carolyn said.

"You can go if you want to," Mid said.

"We could all go," Alice said.

"Except somebody has to stay here," said Carolyn. "With the kids. Jesus. I should be here, I should be there—" Carolyn had the telephone now, was pressing numbers, calling nobody. This I did not want. Not this part. Alice rubbed her shoulders. "I'm sorry," Carolyn said.

Alice told her she didn't have to apologize for anything. Upstairs there was a massive thump. The dishes rattled in their cupboards.

"We're OK," one of the twins yelled down.

Mid went to the stairs. "No injuries," he said, whisper-yelling. "Don't wake Maggie up."

"OK," they said, though even from that distance, you could tell they didn't mean it.

Mid came back in, took the phone from Carolyn. He said, "Whoever's going, we should get ready."

I looked to Alice. Again the secret messages I could not quite decode. "Go ahead," she said.

I said, "You're sure?"

She nodded. "We hate boats."

I said, "You don't—"

"Go," she said. "Call when you get there so you can tell us everything's OK."

I kissed her. Mid reached for Carolyn, who put her head on the table, and he dropped his hand down on her neck like he was praying for her, almost.

"Are they going to take the house?" she said, into her arm.

"I don't know," he said. "They might."

"Just bring her back. I can't even talk about the rest of it right now."

"I will," he said.

"Maybe you should call the Coast Guard."

He said, "I don't think this is in their jurisdiction."

She picked her head up. "Don't die," she said. "Don't get lost at sea."

"I won't," he said.

"Don't come back with a goddamn tattoo, either."

"This can't be happening," Alice said.

"See?" Carolyn said. "That's how I feel all the time. That's how I've felt for years." Then she told us to go, and Alice told us to be careful. Mid called Hurley, detailed the situation, asked about his boat. It was clear from our end that Hurley, without a lot of pushing, was agreeing to take us wherever we needed to go. Mid hung up. I kissed Alice one more time, wanting it to mean, Don't worry, this kind of thing happens all the time, but I knew that was a lie, and she did, too.

■ ■ ■

For the first time, the Camaro felt right—like a yellow Camaro was what was required for a trip like this. Or a purple one. The car wanted for a name, like Rhiannon or Jolene. We rode along with the windows down and the wet salt air blowing in all around us and we needed a shotgun, needed cans of beer, a temperamental CB, a half-blind dog. Instead, we stopped at a gas station for Gatorade. I sat in the car, head singing, watching Mid wait in line inside. The summer before you were born, I thought, Daddy went on a riverboat adventure to save your cousin from herself. She was not yet allowed to make mistakes, so we went to get her so we could keep on making them for her. Mid came back with six or eight bottles in a plastic sack. "Hope you like green," he said.

He drove us a few miles, neither of us talking. He drank one of the Gatorades all the way down and tossed the empty in the back. He turned the radio off. He said, "Look. I'd like to tell you something."

He was going to say he was the Lindbergh Baby. That he was mounting a Senate run. That he had another family in another state.

He said, "This isn't what I had in mind when we brought you guys down."

"It's no problem," I said.

"Not just tonight. The whole thing. I had something else pictured. Something calmer. Fewer police, fewer wayward children, you know?"

"Isn't this how it goes with children?" I said.

He said, "How do you mean?"

The lights went by on the hotels and condos, their oranges not quite enough to do the job, like whoever'd hung them hadn't wanted things all the way lit up. I said, "Won't it pretty much be like this for the next twenty years?"

"I don't know about twenty," he said. "I know about fifteen."

"Has it been like this for fifteen?"

"More or less," he said. "Minus the cops."

"But the cops don't count, right? That's not her."

"Fuck me, Walter, if she's on that tape—if you think they've got me by the balls now, just wait."

"I try not to think about what they've got you by," I said.

"This is not what you expect," he said. "Let me just set that out there right now. When they pull the kid out, after they get her all polished up and get the little hat on her, you do not expect that fifteen years down the road you'll find yourself caught up in some motherfucking crime spree just to get ready enough to send her off to college." He was driving a little faster. "And I know I brought it on myself. You should hear Carolyn. I get it, alright? Mea culpa and all that."

I could feel a new desperation edging in, or another one. A certainty about disaster. "What are we talking about here?" I said.

"All I'm trying to do is make it so we can have a fucking life. That's all. It's not like I'm selling pistols to rapists. I'm not poaching endangered lemurs. So maybe I forgot to dot some i's. Or maybe I did it on purpose. Maybe I owe Uncle Sam some scratch. I'll pay it, OK? I'll pay the whole goddamned thing. I'll pay everybody's bill."

He pushed us under a yellow light. I found myself looking for police cars. "Should we stop?" I said. "Take a minute or something? Deep breaths?"

"All I'm trying to say is you don't see something like this headed your way."

"I believe you," I said.

He reached out his window to work the mirror around. "Probably you don't need me yelling at you about my shit."

"You're OK," I told him, trying to calm him back down. Because that's what I would have wanted if it was my kid we were questing after. Calm.

He said, "You'll make a champion father, by the way."

"Sure," I said.

"I'm serious. I can smell it all over you."

All I could really see right then was our kid, the one we'd have to bring home, thirty hours old and arranged in one of those glass brownie pans at the hospital, sporting a pink watchcap and planning already to move in with her boyfriend. I pulled on the rumble bar up in the ceiling. Changing table. Car seat. Evenings full of word problems, of Train A leaving the station in time to roar by Train B at a point as yet undetermined. Veronica wears woolen scarves and speaks Portuguese, but can't sit next to Michelle, who eats only fish. The whole of it a flip book, a shoebox diorama. I watched our headlights pick up reflectors embedded in the road.

"I didn't mean to go off the reservation like that," Mid said.

"Are you alright?" I said.

"Mainly." He took both hands off the steering wheel, then took hold of it again. "Thank you for coming with me," he said.

"It was the least I could do," I said.

"How about you? You hanging in there OK?"

"Sure I am," I said, and we kept pushing south, two liars in a ridiculous car.

■ ■ ■

Robbie was high. Very. We stood in his bombed-out kitchen, watching him roll a couple of extra joints for the road. "You guys want any of this?" he said, and I couldn't help but wonder where he'd bought it.

"I think we're cool," Mid said.

"Yeah," said Robbie. "You totally are." He put the joints in a bag. "You guys want any of this?" he said again.

Mid said, "It's OK. Let's just go."

"You ever been to the Grand Canyon?" Robbie asked me.

"No," I said. "Why?"

"I don't know, man. It's just really, really something to think about."

"You're sure you know how to get to this place?" Mid asked.

"Nic's? You can't really miss it, if you know what I'm saying. Once you get there, you're good."

"You're certain," Mid said.

"Undeniably," he said. "Let's do this."

He talked a lot about the Grand Canyon while we rode back toward Devil's Backbone. He'd seen some special about it, about rafting down the Colorado. "I'm planning on doing that pretty soon," he said. "But not alone. I gotta get some other people in there to help me paddle. You guys want to go?"

"Why not?" Mid said, and I thought, of course you do.

"That is so bad*ass*," Robbie said. "I try to tell them that at Me Kayak, what a badass you are."

"Thanks," Mid said.

"That reminds me. We got three boats stolen last night."

"We got what?"

"When I counted up this morning, three of them had walked away."

"You didn't call."

"Well, they were still gonna be stolen, right?"

Mid looked at him in the rearview. "What do I pay you for?"

"I don't really know, you know? You've got too many of us down there, anyway. Place only needs like one or two guys at a time."

"Are you trying to quit?" Mid asked.

"No. I need a job bad. But you should let some of the others go. There's kids down there who don't know one end of the paddle from the other."

"I'll send Walter down to look things over," Mid said.

"Yeah," said Robbie. "Send in the muscle."

"Send in the clowns, is more like it," I said.

"Clowns scare the shit out of me," Robbie said. "I don't get what their deal is."

"When's your next shift?" Mid asked.

Robbie said, "Friday."

"Big Walt, why don't you stop in on Friday and take a meeting with young Robbie? Get him to spin you through the inventory?"

"Aye-aye," I said.

"Don't bring any clowns, man," Robbie said. "I'm serious."

When we got to Devil's Backbone, Hurley was sitting out by the iguana cage drinking a beer. He had a fluorescent on in the bait room, and a thin white light was pooling in the air behind him. A pontoon boat was tied up at the dock. *Cindy Rella*. The letters leaned across the back in red cursive. I felt like I was either drunk or dreaming. "Hatchet Man," Hurley said, when we walked up—his nickname for me. We'd had to pull the foundations entirely down, and I was the one who delivered the news. "Hatchet Man and Money Man. Who's the kid?"

"What?" Robbie said.

"Who are you?"

"I'm Robbie."

Hurley waited for more information. When there was none, he said, "That's fine. You're Robbie." He tossed his beer in the water. "Y'all ready?"

"Thanks for doing this," Mid said.

"I was just sitting. This is as good as anything else. Climb aboard."

There were benches down each long side, plus a couple of chairs bolted into a stainless crosshatch floor. Hurley got himself arranged behind the wheel while the rest of us chose up places. I sat near the back. Mid sat in the front, behind Hurley. Robbie stood, holding onto one of the roof supports, while Hurley backed us out away from the dock. He let the motor idle. He said, "Well? Who's the man with the map?"

"Oh," Robbie said. "Cool. South. Toward the inlet. Down past Marineland a little ways. You know Cortez Creek?"

"You can show it to me." Hurley flicked a switch and a spotlight came on up on the roof. He flicked another, and low yellow lights lit the perimeter of the floor, like in a movie theater. He swung the spot back and forth, got it pinned down pointing straight ahead, then throttled up the engine and eased us down the waterway, toward the river, toward Delton.

Robbie sang to himself, something I couldn't place. Mid rode along and stared off into the dark. He looked confused. Not angry, and not sad—more surprised, like the world had turned out, somehow, to be a slightly different place than he thought it was. And who could argue with that? I wasn't totally sure I had good track of the days of the week any more, the time of day. I wasn't sure any of us did. I listened to the sound of the water against the boat and couldn't help but picture the BOJ riding in Alice's belly, turning around in there, floating. And I worked over what Delton being gone might really mean for Mid, after all: Was this the catastrophe, the spaceship come crashing back to earth? Or was it just another outlier, a small thing unexplained, the car keys turning up where you least expect them? Even confused, up there in the front of the boat, even guilty of misdemeanor and felony and whatever else might be on the docket, he still looked like he believed he could fix this, or fix things in general. Like whatever we were doing right then was give or take what we should be doing. Which was what I did not have. Sure, there were things that were recordable enough, and countable: height, weight, number of weeks, kinds and colors of birds, the parachutist flying by. But there was not much left that felt at all solvable anymore. I was as lost, I knew, in that condo, in my whole life, as I would be in the Intracoastal if I fell out of the boat and had to swim back home.

We passed the inlet bridge, passed Marineland all shut down for the night. I had a crazy idea about breaking in, setting all the dolphins loose. We passed a creek off to the right-hand side and Robbie let out a series of low whistles. Hurley did not slow down. "That was it," Robbie said. "Right there." He pointed out the creek as we passed.

"Why didn't you say so?" Hurley said.

"Didn't you hear me give the signal?"

"Hear you give the what?"

Robbie whistled again.

Hurley squinted at him. He said, "What the hell do you think this is?"

"I thought you'd want a signal."

"A signal?"

"Yeah."

"OK, Spenser for Hire."

Robbie said, "Who's that?"

"Forget about it." Hurley swung the boat around, doubled back, and made the turn. Once we were in the creek the water got still, and seemed to get thicker, like oil. It was less a creek than a tidal finger. Every few hundred yards wooden docks pushed out from the land, fishing huts on the ends. Sometimes they were lit, sometimes not. Sometimes you could see a house deep back in the trees.

Robbie said, "It's not too much farther, I don't think."

Mid said, "You don't *think*?"

"I haven't been this way in a while."

"I thought you said it was easier by boat," Mid said.

"It is."

"But you don't go by boat?"

"I don't have a boat."

I said, "How could the road be that bad?"

"It's just low," said Robbie. "If you go at high tide it's real soggy. You can sink a car down in it, so you have to pay attention."

"Kid's right," said Hurley. "I got a buddy lives back in one of these. Go at the right time, you're fine. Get it wrong, you're swimming."

"What tide is it now?" I said.

"Coming in, looks like," Hurley said. Robbie fished in his bag, lit up one of the joints. "You sharing the wealth there, A-Team?" Hurley asked him.

Robbie passed it to him. "I know what *The A-Team* is, by the way."

"Good for you," said Hurley. He pulled on the joint, held it out to look at it. "This is very solid," he said.

"Thank you," Robbie said, and took it back. We passed a refrigerator up on the bank, white with the numbers 209 spray-painted on in silver. "See?" Robbie said. "It's just up here."

"Was that an address?" I asked.

"That was a refrigerator," Robbie said.

I didn't ask any more questions. Neither did Mid. Robbie and Hurley passed the joint back and forth, talked TV—*Cagney and Lacey, WKRP.* Hurley quizzed him a little. Robbie somehow knew *Hill Street Blues.* I sat in the sweetness of the smoke and wondered if I was getting a contact high or if, instead, it was possible I was riding a pleasure boat named *Cindy Rella* down a saltwater creek with a fully stoned twenty-year-old guide and the black-market saffron king of north Florida at the helm.

Robbie said, "So do you want to sneak up on them? Because it's right up here. It's that dock."

Hurley slowed us down to let Mid think. "Yeah," Mid said. "That'd probably be the best thing."

Hurley shut the engine off and sent a trolling motor over the front bow, let that pull us along. He cut off the spotlight. We slid past the dock and there was the house, a huge wooden thing up on stilts, low, somehow, even though it was up in the air. There were lights on inside, the yellows filling out the windows against the blue of the night. The cicadas were so loud they couldn't have heard us coming. Hurley cut the running lights, too, and we sat in the dark watching nothing, watching empty windows. And then there were two people in one window, and then it was clear those two people were Delton and Nic, and they were doing something we couldn't quite see, though the motions were familiar, and then I had it—we all had it, though Mid was the first to say it: "They're in there cooking dinner?"

They were standing in what was now clear was the kitchen, and they were washing vegetables, chopping, telling each other jokes. Nic disappeared, came back holding something green. Lettuce. He held a leaf out and she took a bite, shook her head no, then yes. She leaned down, got a tray out of somewhere, put it on the counter. I wanted a camera, wanted to snap a few quick pictures so I could show Alice later on. "They were cooking dinner," I'd say. "We just watched them do it."

Delton looked up suddenly, looked right at us. I think we all thought it had to be too dark for her to pick us out, or if it wasn't, that she'd think we were any other boat going by. We felt like we had some kind of dazzle camouflage going. She picked up a towel and dried her hands. She kept looking at us. She didn't really have any expression on her face. Then she left the window. Lights came on along the edges of the dock. She opened a door onto a back landing, walked out toward us. When she got to the end of the dock she folded her arms, stared out at us. Hurley turned the trolling motor off. Delton was still holding the dishtowel, orange with white dots. She said, "Dad?"

He said, "Hey, Livvy." I wanted to vanish. I wanted us all to vanish.

"What are you doing here?" she said.

"We came to get you."

"But I didn't want that. I told Mom."

"I know."

"We're making chicken," she said.

He said, "I didn't know you knew how to do that."

"Nic has cookbooks. They're really old, but we think the recipes still work." She seemed to notice the rest of the boat right then, seemed to take in the fact he had people with him. "Uncle Walter?" she said. "You came?"

"I think so," I said.

"Are you mad at me, too?"

"I'm just here to help," I said.

"Who's everybody else?"

"It's me," Robbie said. "Robbie."

"Nic's friend," she said.

"Yep. Sorry."

"And that's Hurley," Mid said. "It's his boat."

"It's a nice boat," Delton said.

Hurley spit in the water. "Thanks," he said.

Mid said, "Why don't you want to come home?"

She shook her head, stared down at her feet.

"You told your mother you were scared."

She said, "You guys don't get it at all."

"Get what?"

"Any of it it." She was rocking from one foot to the other. "Ground me tomorrow, OK? Please. You can do whatever. Just let me do this."

"Olivia—"

"Delton."

"What I don't get, *Delton,* is what 'this' is."

She said, "I don't know how to explain it."

Mid looked at me. I had nothing. I had less than that. I was terrified of this. He turned back to Delton. "Sweetie," he said, "I can't just leave you here. Surely you know that."

"You can, though," she said, and instantly, impossibly, that felt like what was true. How that was, I didn't know, but there it was anyway.

"You mother would kill me," he said.

"She always wants to do that."

"But you've got to see where I'm coming from."

Nic opened the door, stood in the frame. She turned around. "Wait," she told him, and he went back inside.

"Who runs away to cook chicken?" Mid said, to nobody specific. None of us answered. "Shit," he said. "Motherfucker."

"Daddy," Delton said.

Mid looked at the house, then at Delton again. He tapped his shoe on the floor of the boat. He nodded. He closed his eyes. "Fine," he said.

"What?" said Delton.

"Tomorrow morning," he said. "I'm coming back to get you tomorrow morning. Eight o'clock. This doesn't go any further than where it is."

"Really?"

"Don't ask me questions. Don't say anything. Don't give me a chance to think about it."

"I'll come home," she said. "You don't have to come get me."

"Eight o'clock," he said again. "Just try to be— Just don't do stupid things in there, alright?"

"Daddy," she said, wrapping the towel around her hand like a mitten.

"Don't kill each other," he said. "Make sure the chicken's cooked through."

"Nic said you were supposed to use a thermometer."

"Good. That's right. Read those cookbooks."

"He's really smart," she said. "You'll like him when you get to know him."

"*If* I get to know him."

"He's going to be a teacher," she said.

"Everybody keeps mentioning that. Deaf kids, right?"

"That's what he wants."

"He'll be in all the magazines. He'll be Man of the Year."

"Tell Mom I'm sorry."

"No. You tell her yourself."

"I will."

"Tell me, how about."

"I'm sorry," she said.

"Say it like you mean it."

"I did."

"I know," he said. Then, "I love you, sweetheart."

She wound and unwound the dishtowel. "I love you, too," she said, and she turned around, walked back up the dock, opened the door, went in the house, and that was all.

Out on the river, heading back, the hum so present I could feel it buzzing my jaw, Hurley said, "How old's your daughter again?"

"Almost sixteen," Mid said.

"And how old's the kid inside?"

Mid said, "Older."

Hurley said, "Damn, dude, I'm not sure I could have done that."

Mid said, "I'm not sure I could have, either," and the sound of the water off the back of the boat filled in whatever other space there was. I kept looking away to make sure nobody saw me trying to keep from crying.

■ ■ ■

Alice wanted to know what Mid said, what Delton said, what the boat looked like, what the house looked like, how in hell we'd managed to get all the way out there and then come back without her. She said it didn't make enough sense. I said I knew that—but that also there was something about watching it happen, something I wanted to explain but couldn't. If you'd been there, I kept saying, you'd have done it, too. If you'd seen her. If I'd seen her what? she said. No what, I said. Just if you'd seen her.

When Mid and I came back to the house that night, it was Carolyn who'd opened the door, who stood there, taking the two of us in, back home with no Delton. "No," Carolyn said. "No, no, no, no, no."

"Yes," Mid said, and something burned up between them right then, some supply line. But he went and got Delton the next day, like he said—he still had to draw the line somewhere.

■ ■ ■

That week, Alice started spending more time with Carolyn. At dinner, back home, she'd talk about how tired Carolyn was, how worried Carolyn was, how nobody could quite get a read on what the fuck was going on. She'd ask about Mid, how he was acting. He'd been going quiet, I told her—he'd check out for a few minutes while we rode between Me Kayak and Island Pizza, while we drove out to the Twice-the-Ices. "Quiet how?" she asked.

"Quiet," I said. "He goes away."

"That's what Carolyn says, too."

"I think he doesn't have any idea what to say to her."

"I'm not surprised," Alice said. "I don't think he possibly could."

I started sleeping as much as possible. I took naps. I slept late into the mornings, through Alice calling me from the balcony, telling me the parachutist was coming by, that he had a new flag, a fireman's helmet, a tape deck belting out show tunes. I went to bed before the late-night talk shows came on. The way I had it tallied was this: I needed all my rest now, because once we had little Bosporus or Dardanelles in the house, I'd need to spend every night lying awake, being ready at a moment's notice to fail to rescue her by boat.

Hurley poured new foundations. The Twice-the-Ice people sent a man to tinker with the brain inside Number Two, and he got it to make ice as advertised. I went to see Robbie at Me Kayak about the stolen kayaks. They were still stolen. And Robbie was right: There were too many employees by half. Mid told me we shouldn't fire anybody. He said one or two of them would quit soon enough, or, less officially, just disappear, their final paychecks sitting in the office, ready but never picked up. He said kids disappeared all the time. I flipped through the stack one afternoon—a dozen checks for a hundred, two hundred dollars. "You just leave them here?" I asked Mid.

"Writeoff," he said.

I went to the grocery. I bought off-brand Triscuits. Weav-Its. Alice had a thing for the store brand, ate them by the boxful. She started drinking cranberry juice. All the combo flavors. Grape-cranberry, blueberry-cranberry. She'd never liked cranberry juice before. At the classes—we started going to the birthing classes, where everybody was much more pregnant than we were—they said cravings were perfectly normal. The books said that, too, and the pamphlets, and everything all over the Internet.

I hated the classes, not because they scared the shit out of me, which they did, but because of how much shined-up glimmering joy they forced into the room. Everyone smiled at every moment, and when they didn't smile, they cried, and then everybody smiled about the crying. We were in Condensed Baby and Delivery. There was regular Baby and Delivery, but it was full. There was a cheery desperation that hung on the instructors, a husband-and-wife team who seemed sorry for us. "Now, if this was *regular* Baby and Delivery," they'd say, again and again, and then drop some joyful piece of information about birth plans or cervix dilation, and Alice would smile, and everybody would smile, and I would stare off at the wall of brochures. *Mom, You're Beautiful. Post-Partum Questions. Choices and Changes.* The perfect families on the fronts of the brochures were in assorted states of smile.

The extra sleeping left me plenty of time to wake up in the middle of the night, lie in the half-dark, look at all the paintings of birds, and know this: Mid was in a full-fledged racket. Alice was past halfway.

■ ■ ■

"Something I'd like to run by you," Mid said. We were sitting in the Camaro at Twice-the-Ice Number Two, watching people buy ice. We were betting out of piles of quarters on the dash on whether people would go bag or bulk. His heart wasn't fully in it, but he was killing me. He had the knack for it.

“Go ahead,” I said.

“It would be totally fine if you said no.”

“Got it.”

“How would it be if Olivia came to live with you guys for a little while?”

“What?”

“Just a couple of weeks,” he said. A guy drove up in a hybrid. Mid picked up a quarter, spun it through his fingers. “Bag,” he said.

“He’s a bulker,” I said.

“There’s no cooler in there. You watch.”

The man walked around the back of his car, popped the trunk. No cooler. I said, “Live with us how?”

“Like a little summer camp, I guess, is Carolyn’s idea. She and Delton cooked this up.” The man went over to the Twice-the-Ice, put his money in, and the machine delivered a bag. I put another quarter on Mid’s side. “Be the bag,” he said. “That’s your problem.”

“I don’t think that’s my problem.”

Mid said, “You’ll bounce back.”

“Are you serious about this?” I said. “With Delton?”

“As a heart attack.”

“Would she even want to live with us? She barely knows us.”

“Carolyn says she’s got some bond with Alice. And she likes you. She says you’re normal.”

“Normal.”

“She means it as a compliment.”

“I have to talk to Alice,” I said. “I mean, I’d want to do that first.”

“Carolyn talked to her.”

"She did?"

"She thought it'd be best to clear it through her first, and then ask you."

I said, "Could you maybe start over and go a little slower?"

He leaned back in his seat. We had the windows down, had found a little shade to park in. "So we grounded Olivia," he said. "For six or eight years. Or until she hits menopause." The compressor up on top of the Twice-the-Ice was humming. "But it's not going so well. We're not doing a very good job of it, I guess. There's a kind of general distrust around the dinner table. Plus she keeps lodging all these complaints."

"Complaints?" I said.

"We suck, we don't understand her, we don't listen, Nic's going to be a teacher."

"That's not a complaint. The teacher thing."

"You explain it to her. And she's on the tapes, by the way. She's not buying, thank God, so they can't really hit her with anything, but she's there. Her dumbass friends are still buying. Agents Friendly and Helpful called me up yesterday to let me know. I'm supposed to meet them at some Waffle House in Ocala to see the thing."

"Tell me again how this is just the cops trying to bust your kitchen guys, and not something bigger."

"Relax," he said. "You and Carolyn. I think they got some grant to use their tiny cameras, and they're bored."

"That's what you think? Honestly? Doesn't all this seem elaborate to you?"

"I'll give you that much." He took off his sunglasses, put them on the dash with the quarters. "I've got you totally walled off, OK? You're all set. Don't let any of this wad your panties."

"That doesn't make me feel a ton better," I said.

"I can't help that. Anyway. Listen. She's grounded, right? But kids keep showing up in the driveway, and she keeps riding away with them, standing around on videotape while they purchase recreational pharmaceuticals, that kind of thing."

"That doesn't sound very grounded."

"I told you we were doing it wrong."

"How would living with us do anything?"

"No clue," he said. "But we sat her down, told her things weren't working for us, and asked her what she thought we should do."

"And she chose this?"

"She had a lot to say about needing her space. I don't think she knows what that means, but she said it."

"And Carolyn talked to Alice?"

"Yes."

"And Alice said yes."

"She did."

"Are we supposed to keep her grounded, too?"

"We'll all sit down," he said. "We can figure out some rules together, if this is OK with you."

"But you said she doesn't follow the rules now."

"These will be new rules. They'll work much better."

"What's going on with her, anyway?" I said.

He shook his head. "I think she is fifteen in America. I think that's what's going on." A pickup truck, spray-painted green, pulled into the lot. Mid said, "One more time? Double or nothing?"

"Double or nothing won't do anything for me," I said. "I'm too far behind."

"Come on. You choose. I'll take whatever you don't pick."

I looked at the truck. "Bulk," I said.

"You're not even trying."

"Sure I am."

"Bag," he said. "Has to be." An older guy got out, shuffled up to the chute, pressed BAG. "See?" Mid said.

"How can you tell?"

"You have to have a feeling."

"I had a feeling."

"You have to have a different feeling. Let's get you home."

I slid another quarter his way, and he swept his winnings off the dash.

■ ■ ■

Alice was in the bathroom, sitting on the toilet, pants down around her feet. The door was open. "I'm bleeding," she said. She'd been crying. She wasn't anymore.

"How much?" I said.

"Not very much."

The inside of my head went church-still. "It's probably the same thing as before."

"It's not the same. It's new. Something's wrong."

"We don't know that."

"We have to call the doctor," she said.

"Is Delton coming to live with us?" I was floating, confused. "Did that happen?"

"Walter. Go call. Please."

I went to the kitchen, dialed the number off the fridge magnet, waited while music played on the other end of the line. I could only see directly in front of me. Everything on the edges blurred and dimmed. A nurse picked up and I told her Alice's first and last name, her date of birth. I told her about the blood. She wanted to know how much. "Not very much," I said.

"Well, we're probably not supposed to be bleeding at all, are we?" she said. Everything was always very *we* at North Florida Fertility.

I said, "Probably not."

"So let's just go on and get you in here this afternoon, then. How's two-thirty?"

I checked the digital on the stove. One o'clock. "Sure," I said.

"Super. Now the most important thing we can do between now and then is to relax. Can we do that?"

I figured it was best to give her the answer she wanted. "We can do that."

"Great," she said. "So we'll see you soon, alright?"

"OK," I said, and hung up the phone.

One thing I knew without question—of the many places where my life didn't add up anymore, here was a good one: I still and still did not want a child, did not want to be up at three in the morning singing Steely Dan into a screaming baby's ear, did not want to have to decide between cloth diapers and whatever disposable chemical weaponry was on sale at the big box. And I did not want, later on, to have to explain the vagaries of half-cooked semi-sexual attraction in our busted species to a crying twelve-year-old home too early, heartbroken, from her seventh grade Winter Ball—if they even had such a thing in a place like Florida.

But in equal and opposite measure—and this was true, gravitationally so—I did not want anything to be more difficult for Alice than it already was, than I'd already made it. I did not want the bogeyman arriving at our doorstep in the form of undercover cops, of Mid kicked out of his house, of Delton running from Mid, or from Nic, or from herself. And I knew this, too: I surely did not want calamity to present in the form of two teaspoons of bright red blood in the toilet. As much as I was wholly unprepared for a child to arrive, bidden or unbidden, in our lives, I did not in any way want Alice to bleed her into the middle of Aunt Sandy's ducks-and-geese wallpapered bathroom on the fourth floor of a beachfront condominium we had no business living in. That we had no real business living anywhere else anymore didn't play much into the equation. Nothing did. There was no equation. There was only Alice, and there was only me. And even those numbers weren't exactly right.

We got her dressed and out the door and down to the parking garage, got her belted in, got us out on A1A and then the interstate. Alice was far away, off somewhere else—back in Charlotte, maybe, before any of this. Back to when we could grow flowers out by the little brick stoop of our little brick house, when we could sit in the lawn and do nothing other than watch the weeds grow. I held my hands at ten and two, checked my mirrors. I wanted to throw up. Palm trees and pine and swamp ran by us on both sides of the road, interrupted only by the occasional crane supply company or low-rise call center. We went over the river and I looked down at the naval base, at the outline of the few downtown skyscrapers there were. Jacksonville. It could have been any city. I found our exit. Everything was still in the same place it had been last time. I drove Alice right up to the door, stopped there in the drop-off lane.

"I'm OK," she said.

I said, "I'll walk you in."

"I'll be fine. Just park the car."

"Are you sure?"

She stared out the windshield, ran one finger along the smooth hollow of her neck. She didn't get out.

"I love you," I said.

"I love you, too."

"We'll be fine," I said, hearing it, knowing I sounded like Mid. "This will be fine."

"You can't know anything about that," she said.

"Sure I can."

She said, "I thought you were the one who was panicking."

"I am," I said. "That's me."

"Then what's this?"

"I'm on morale," I said. "For right now. I'll go back to panic soon."

"The BOJ is not happy," she said.

"I know that."

She sent the lock up and down in the door. "I told Carolyn that Olivia could come and live with us," she said.

"Mid was saying."

"I think she needs something. I think maybe we could give her whatever that is. Is that alright?"

I said, "I think it's the same as anything else."

"What does that mean?"

"It means we'll learn to live through it," I said.

A couple crossed in front of our car. "Do you think I'm ruining our lives?" she said.

"Do I think you're what?"

"Ruining our lives. Yours, at least."

"No," I said. "That's me. I'm the one doing that." I was supposed to have found some way to stand between Alice and the world, between Kitchenette and the world. That was my job. It was all of our jobs, what we were supposed to do for each other. "I know I'm supposed to be better," I said. "I know I'm supposed to be some kind of father."

Alice took my hand and held it, rested it on the gearshift. A bus rattled by out on the road. "Park the car," she said. "Park the car and meet me in there."

"I'll take you," I said.

"I want to do it."

"Alice," I said.

"I want to do it. Really." She sounded recorded, her voice drained out of a jar. She got out, shut the door softly, then turned and walked inside the building. The mirrored double doors opened and shut for her automatically, swallowing her, and then all I could see was the wavy reflection of our hatchback, of some dumbass guy—me—sitting behind the wheel. I checked her seat for blood. There wasn't any. I found a space and parked the car.

The waiting room was completely empty. No Alice. She was gone. All the frosted windows up at the desk were closed. I heard a child crying somewhere behind one of the walls. I stood there as long as it took the Muzak to cycle through a song, or maybe two or three. I couldn't tell. It would be so much easier, I'd thought the whole time, if there was no baby. Now I knew that was not true. That there was no easy thing, no simple place to land. And if we lost it—would she think I was secretly happy? That this was what I'd wanted all along? My ears were ringing. Another song came on. A nurse in turquoise scrubs opened a door, leaned out into the waiting room like she didn't actually want to set foot in it. She said, "Mr. Ingram?"

"Yes," I said.

"Why don't we come back this way."

"Where's Alice?" I said. "My wife?" I walked toward her.

She checked her clipboard. She said, "Let's get set up with the doctor, and he'll answer all your questions." She moved to one side to let me through the door, and when it closed behind me, there was quiet. No music. Nothing. "We're just right down here," she said, easing past me, and I followed her down the hallway, past scales and benches and bathrooms. When she got to the last door, the door that had to be Alice's, she stopped. "Sir?" she said. I was too far behind her to see into the room. I stopped walking, stood still. I could feel my heart pushing blood through my body. "Sir," she said again, only this time it wasn't a question at all.

“Hey, there he is,” said Dr. Varden, who was standing at the counter, pulling on gloves. There was another nurse in the corner of the room. “Now we’re ready.”

“Where were you?” Alice said.

“In the waiting room,” I said.

“Doing what?”

“Waiting.”

“You took a long time.”

“I didn’t mean to.”

She was already in the paper gown. Varden rolled a stool over, had Alice put her feet in the stirrups. He said, “All we’re doing here, Dad, is eliminating a few of our questions from the get-go. I think we’re going to find that all’s well, but let’s take a peek to be on the safe side.” I’d expected him to talk to us first. There was nowhere good for me to sit. Three different corkboards covered in pictures of babies hung on the walls. He said, “So here’s one possibility. That cervix is pretty inflamed. He could certainly be our culprit.” He looked up at Alice. “Bright red blood?”

"Yes."

"And only today, right? Not regularly?"

"Right."

"Pain? Any cramping?"

"Not really," she said.

"Mom, when you say 'not really,' what is it that you mean?"

"You didn't tell me that," I said.

She said, "Just let me think."

"Take your time," Varden said, gently. He'd slid across the dial—he was more priest now than motivational speaker. It was impressive. He opened a drawer in the exam table, dropped the speculum inside. There was blood on it, I could see, before he knocked the drawer back closed with his knee.

"Not cramping," she said. "Not pain. Just this morning I felt—weird."

"Weird how?" Varden asked her.

"Weird like something was going on, I guess."

I said, "Why didn't you call me?"

"You were at work. It didn't seem like a big deal."

"Isn't it a big deal now?"

"And here you are," she said.

"We're alright," Varden said. "Really we are. I don't think we need to get too fired up about this yet." He stood up and opened a cabinet, got out a fetal Doppler. "Let's dial the little one in for a minute," he said.

"Ours still hasn't come," Alice said, meaning the machine.

He ran a couple of sliders back and forth. "I don't know why these people can't be in a better hurry. We'll send you home with this one, alright? Give you some peace of mind. If yours ever turns up, just ship it back."

"Thank you," said Alice.

"It's what we do," he said, waving us off. He slid another switch and traced the wand over Alice's belly. Varden was tanner than the last time we'd seen him. He was like something browning in the oven. He held the wand near her left hip, closed one eye, tuned the thing in, and then there wasn't any mistaking the heartbeat, the staticked *wow-wow-wow-wow*. He smiled. We all did. "A mile a minute," he said. He looked at the display. "High 150s. Perfect. Would you like to hold it, Dad?"

"Sure," I said. I was wanting to get his questions right this time.

"Well," he said, "come on over."

I took it from him, held the thing in place while he marked Alice's chart. He pulled a cardboard wheel from a drawer, spun it around, said something about due dates. Then he set the clipboard on the counter, slapped his hands on his thighs, and said, "Folks, we could do a quick ultrasound if you like, but I think that guy in there's telling us just about everything we need him to. That right there is a textbook beautiful heartbeat. Listen to him go."

"Him?" I said.

"Figure of speech. He, she, it, whatever you like. Animal, vegetable, mineral. It's not on the chart, so I don't know. Anyway, let's run through a few possibilities here."

Alice sat up and pulled down her gown.

Varden said, "One thing that can happen with our older mothers—which doesn't mean one thing, except you waited until you were ready—is that sometimes we get a few adventures. Not complications, necessarily. Just a few more balls in the air. So, for instance, that cervix in there—" He pointed at

Alice's belly. "That guy's a little bigger around than we'd like him to be. There's a condition we sometimes see where the cervix wants to go ahead and open up too soon, which is not what we want. Think of it like a door on a submarine. We want that sucker good and closed until the end."

We nodded. We didn't know what else to do.

"So here's a ridiculous term, OK? Incompetent cervix. I hate that phrase, and I still don't think it's us yet—"

I said, "What kind of cervix?"

"It only means it might not be doing its full job. In a very, very few cases, we need to go in with a stitch to hold things shut."

"A stitch," said Alice.

"But listen." Varden held his hands out. I felt like we were at the mechanic, and he'd taken us into the shop, stood us under the lift, pointed up at things we didn't know the words for, and started telling us how bad things weren't. How much worse they could be. "We're not there yet," he said. "And probably won't be at all. This is more than likely just a hiccup. I want you to know that. You'll come back in ten days, and everything will probably be all settled and lined up exactly like it should be." He was talking more quietly, taking us into his confidence. "That's what I'm expecting, anyway."

"We come back in ten days?" I said.

"That's best for now, until we get everything calmed back down in there." He pushed his stool closer to the wall. "The most important thing for you both to know is that you're fine right now. And we'll send you home with the Doppler so you can tune in any time you're feeling hinky. Crank that bugger up and listen in. Does wonders to calm the nerves." He smiled. "And one last thing. I'd like to have us on pelvic rest, see how that goes."

"Is that bed rest?" Alice said.

"No, no. You can be up and around. You *should* be up and around. Pelvic rest means no sex." He winked at me. "Sorry, Dad."

"It's OK," I said.

"Sex can inflame the cervix. So let's lay off until you come back in. And maybe no heavy lifting," he told Alice. "Nothing you wouldn't normally pick up. Just relax a little more. Notch it back a speed."

"I can do that," she said.

"Of course you can. Look. Both of you. This happens. I don't mind a little blood. I don't even mind a little cramping. What I do mind is if we get those things at the same time. That happens, I need you to call me."

Alice said, "Is that going to happen?"

He said, "I can't tell you yes or no, but I think all we've got here is the body saying, 'Hey, now, let's take it just a smidge easier.' And the body knows. The body always knows." He looked at us each again, made sure to make eye contact. I wondered if he might have a list of rules in his desk drawer. Affirmations and reminders. Smile. Eye contact. Be positive. "What I always tell my pelvic rest patients is that they should use this time for other kinds of intimacy. Massage is good. Or just listening. Charting your fears." He walked over to the door. He had other ports of call. "Any questions, you two?" he said. "Anything at all?"

He'd bulldozed us. I felt like we were at the go-carts, maybe, like I should be on the lookout for sucker-punching fathers.

"You're doing a beautiful job," he said. "Just beautiful."

"Thank you," Alice said.

"We'll see you in ten days," he said.

"Ten days," Alice said, and then Varden was gone, and the nurse went with him, and we were alone in the room. There was a yellow biohazard container on the wall. Underneath the BIOHAZARD lettering, it said BIOPELIGRA. That'd be a name. Alice nudged one of the stirrups back and forth. I got her jeans. "Pelvic rest," she said. "And what kind of cervix?"

"He said he didn't think you had that."

She said, "He might be a little intense."

"He knows things," I said.

"He's supposed to know things. He's a doctor." She was dangling her legs off the side of the table. She looked like a kid in a swing. "Do you want to know what I want?" she said.

"Are we charting our fears?"

She balled up the paper gown, held it there in her lap. She looked strikingly beautiful to me in that moment. She said, "You think I've got it all figured out."

"I really don't," I said.

"I just want to be pregnant. I want to get to be pregnant and not have to fight about it and not have to keep coming in here."

"I want that, too," I said.

"Do you?"

"Of course I do."

She got down, got dressed. "We need to go home," she said. "I'm tired. Let's go home."

"Alright," I said.

"We'll go home and not have sex and not drink wine."

"Sounds relaxing."

"I have to call Carolyn. She'll be freaking. Like she needs one more thing." She'd forgotten to put on her shoes, was holding them in one hand. "We need to find out what they want to do about Olivia. I don't know what the hell they think they're doing."

"You don't want to do it? I thought you guys had a thing."

"It's you two," she said. "You're the one who talks to her. And it hardly matters what anybody wants. They're family." She stared at a poster that was all about making sure your baby slept on her back. She said, "I'm sorry I made us come in."

"We needed to come in," I said. "You heard him."

"I just want it to be easy," she said. "Is that so much to ask?"

I said, "I never once thought it would be easy."

She kissed me then—a quick, dry kiss. A competent kiss. She said, "And boy were you right."

I pointed at her shoes, and she put them on. Somebody paged a nurse over the intercom. We followed the maze of hallways back out, scheduled our next appointment, left through the sliding doors. Like that, we were in the world again. Still pregnant. Still chugging along. I wondered if they measured that way, if back inside the office some bell was ringing. We'd get to keep our names up on the tote board one more day.

I hated above all else the crushing uncertainty—if you had to be pregnant, I thought, you should at least get to know that everything in there was dividing and conquering according to plan. You should get to have regular, normal terror. We drove back south with all the sun everywhere making the interstate look even flatter, and what I started wanting—what I thought might really help—was some kind of converter for the Doppler, some way we could plug it into the cigarette lighter and ride along with the heartbeat keeping its own kind of time. Or better: Pipe it into bullhorn speakers we could mount on the roof of the car, play it for the whole world. Then everyone would know how we were holding up. Everyone would know exactly where we were. I felt certain that would make things better. I wanted to tell Alice, but I wasn't sure if she'd trust it. I didn't know if I did. But there it was anyway, a new idea taking up residence, something else for which there was no room.

■ ■ ■

Three days of no bleeding, no cramping. Three days of breaking the Doppler out as needed, Houston to Tranquillity, to check in and make sure. The BOJ slept and spun, made ear tubes, made retinas. I held just outside of Alice's orbit, tried to get her things she needed. I tried to keep us each calm. Monday night we went over to the castle to talk through the prisoner exchange. Alice said I wasn't allowed to call it that. The twins were at a friend's house for a sleepover. Carolyn and Mid took turns reading Maggie down—stories about pigs, stories about foxes driving delivery trucks. That went on for an hour. I looked for corners to hide in while it lasted. I couldn't find any. I ended up on the sofa, with Delton, while she flicked through channels on the TV.

"You're leaking," she said, without looking at me. On the screen: an ad for a station wagon that looked like a spaceship; a show with ten kids living in a house; ice skating.

I said, "I'm what?"

"You're leaking. You're like, not totally put together. That's what we say now."

"We?"

"We," she said. "The youth. You're leaking."

"The youth," I said.

"I'll behave. In case you're worried about that. I won't light anything on fire or smoke or sneak out the window."

"I'm not leaking," I said.

"You completely are. But it's OK."

"How can you tell?" I said.

"It's what we do."

"The youth," I said.

"Right," she said. "Something like that." She turned and looked at me, and for half a second I thought she was about to tell me that this too might pass, or maybe even tousle my hair—but instead she just seemed to be on input, or at least that's what I decided. She was taking it all in, making note of the gory details so that she could repeat it, chapter and verse, the next time she had somebody good to tell it to. That's what I would have done at her age. Check this out, you guys. Wait till you hear this.

"Restriction, is how we see it," Mid said. We'd made it to the kitchen table, and we were working through a lasagna Carolyn had found in the freezer. Delton was hunched into a chair, folded hard in on herself. She'd been alright before, when it was just the two of us, but now, in the spotlight, she looked like she'd rather be hiking across the face of the moon. Carolyn looked like she might have wished Delton was doing that, too, and that she'd taken Mid with her.

I said, "Does restriction still exist? People still call it that?"

"I don't know, but that's what we're calling it."

The deal they'd arrived at was this: Two weeks. That was all. She wanted out, and she was getting it, at least in part. The rules: She could come and go from the condo, but only to specific, preordained places. She could hang out with Nic, but only in restaurants and coffee shops, and not after dark. She could see her other friends, but not after ten p.m. Nothing after ten p.m. By then she was supposed to be home, doing whatever it was she did. Texting. Interneting. Reinventing electricity. Mid had climbed up into the attic, found a little television she could set up in our nursery, which was where she was staying. There was still a single bed in there. Delton was saying she wanted to help paint the room whatever color we wanted, that she could help us get ready for the baby. "I know how to paint," she said. "I'm really careful."

Carolyn said, "Sweetie, I'm not sure they need your help, OK?"

"Mom, I'm just offering. God."

"We'd love that." said Alice. "That would be a big help."

"See?" Delton said.

"And if she doesn't follow those rules," Mid said, pushing ahead with his terms, "then she comes back here. Simple as that." He turned to her. "Does that sound like what we talked about?"

"Yes," she said.

"Those are rules you can abide by?"

"That's such a Dad move, saying that. *Abide by.*"

"That's the move I'm trying to make," he said.

"We're having a little trouble with authority," said Carolyn.

"I am," Delton said. "*We're* not."

"I rest my case," said Carolyn.

"May I be excused?" said Delton. "I need to pack."

Mid said, "You're already packed."

"I need to pack more."

"Go ahead," Carolyn said, and she let her get all the way to the stairs before she said, "Your plate won't clear itself, you know." Delton came back, every movement just barely exaggerated—enough to show injustice had been visited upon her yet one more time, but not quite enough to elicit any sanction. It was a perfect tightroped teenage line. She banged her plate into the sink, left again. "Leecy," Carolyn said, quietly, "You guys are really up for this?"

"Of course," Alice said, but she didn't sound totally sure. She'd been on edge since Varden, waiting for the next thing.

"She's not like this normally," Mid said. "She's having a bad summer."

"Except she isn't." Carolyn rubbed at one eye. "She's having a terrific summer. The Summer of Nic. We're the ones having the hard time." She looked at Mid. "Well, you are, anyway."

"I'm fine," he said.

"You're anything but." Things were definitely broken between them. Delton might have been the only thing keeping that from being on fire. Maybe we shouldn't take her, I thought. Maybe we should leave her behind to give them something to do.

"We'll figure it out," Alice said. "It'll be good for her."

"You're both sure?" Carolyn said. "You promise?"

"You don't know what you're getting into," Mid said.

"Don't say things like that," said Carolyn.

"It'll be like a tryout," I said, which was the safest version of where Alice and I had landed. We didn't know her. She didn't know us. But what the hell. If she thought she liked us, we could be those people.

Mid said, "It'll be like something." He opened the fridge and stared in. "Fifteen. Jesus Christ. Maybe I don't understand anymore. Maybe that's my problem."

Carolyn said, "That's not your problem."

"What is with you?" he said.

"Really?" She held her hands out at an imaginary pile of things on the table. "Pick. Pick anything."

Alice said, “Fifteen was hard.” She was trying to bring them back from the cliff. “It was awful, really.”

“I liked it OK,” said Carolyn.

“You got to go first. You were older.”

“Shouldn’t that make me like it less?”

Alice said, “It wasn’t easy. That’s all.”

“Is it ever easy?” Carolyn asked.

“When you’re eight,” I said.

Mid said, “When’s eight? Is that second grade?”

“You play kickball,” I said. “A ton of kickball. And you turn in reports on birds of prey.”

“Maybe second grade’s easy for boys,” said Carolyn, “but it’s a nightmare for girls.”

“Why’s that?” Mid said.

“Every grade is a nightmare for girls,” Alice said. “First it’s clothes, and then it’s boys and clothes.”

I said, “That seems a little broad.”

Alice shook her head. “It’s easy for maybe five seconds when you’re with one other friend. But then you get a third girl in the mix, and two of you have to gang up on the other one. Or they gang up on you. It’s some kind of rule.”

“But even in second grade?” Mid asked.

“Especially in second grade,” said Carolyn. “How do you not remember the twins? Second-grade girls are awful.”

“Let’s have a girl,” I said. “Let’s have two.”

“Probably better than a boy,” Mid said. “With boys, it’s just shouting and breaking shit until they’re old enough to be jerking off into a sock.”

“Nice,” said Carolyn. “Lovely.”

I said, “Maybe we should forget the whole thing and get a puppy.”

"They chew your table legs," said Mid.

"So do boys," said Carolyn.

"So do girls," he said, and brought a few beers over to the table. He poured one for himself, one for me. I let mine sit there and tried to remember the second grade, but I could only come up with one or two names. Our teacher broke her ankle at the skating rink. I knew that. The ambulance came. It was a hell of a thing to see your second-grade teacher loaded onto an ambulance. The BOJ would be in second grade. She would have a lunchbox. She would have friends. She would be working very hard on becoming her own disaster.

"Mom?" Delton called down the stairs. "Have you seen my yellow shirt?"

"No," said Carolyn.

"Did it get washed?"

"Did you wash it?"

"God," Delton said, and went back toward her room.

Carolyn got up, walked through the kitchen to the laundry, came back with a yellow shirt folded into a tight square. "Here," she said, and handed it to me. "Use it as a peace offering."

I said, "Do we need one?"

"You will," she said.

"You guys are scaring him," said Alice. "We all are."

"He needs it," Mid said.

"I don't," I said. "I'm plenty scared. I work on it."

"That's actually true," Alice said, taking the shirt from me. "He does."

■ ■ ■

Delton wanted to keep the tinfoil on the windows. She walked in the room, turned off the light, shut the door, and we stood like that—us in the hall, and Delton inside, in the dark—for what had to be way too long. Already we were doing it wrong. Finally she said, "I've never seen anything this nothinged-out in my entire life. This is the best thing ever." She opened the door and blinked into the light of the hallway. "Can I leave it? Is that OK?" We told her it was. We had no idea what else to tell her.

Lying in bed, Delton closed into her room and us into ours, Alice said, "Are they cute at that age?"

"They're supposed to be," I said. I was feeling a calmness about her being with us, and had no good idea why. Maybe it was that she came off like a creature it might be possible to understand: She had, as it turned out, a pretty basic set of needs, and they were give or take the same as anyone else's.

"I don't always, always want it," Alice said. "You know that, right?"

"The baby?" I said.

"Catherine of Aragon. Whatever you're calling her. I'm not always a hundred percent behind it."

"I get it," I said.

"No, you don't. You think I'm some cheerleader who wants four hundred kids."

I said, "Did I do something?"

"I know it's supposed to be me. I know I'm supposed to be in charge. It's just hard. It turns out having her actually here is hard."

"Why do you have to be in charge?"

"Well, it's not going to be you, is it?"

"That's not fair," I said.

"I still want it. I completely still want it. But then sometimes I kind of don't. Some days."

"Sure you do."

"Not if she's going to be fifteen."

"I think she's going to be fifteen," I said, sitting up. "I think that's the whole deal. If we're lucky, she turns out to be a normal, impossible fifteen-year-old girl. That's what I was trying to tell you all along. This was the losing argument."

"Then forget it," she said. "I change my mind."

"I think it'd be great if she turned out like Delton."

"I don't understand how you wouldn't be afraid of that," she said.

"I'm completely afraid of that. I'm just more afraid of other things."

"Like what?" she said.

"Like everything that comes first. I'm afraid of never choosing what to watch on TV again. Or the kid getting brain damage. Or CP. Or syphilis."

"She could get syphilis riding around on that motorcycle with that boy."

"Were we not just sitting around Mid and Carolyn's table with you telling *them* not to scare me?"

"Keep your voice down," she said.

"Plus aren't you the one who's supposed to be all cool under fire? Isn't it you who takes the kid to the liquor store to buy condoms and cigarettes before the prom?"

"I'm tired of being cool under fire," she said. "It's wearing me out. I can't do it all the time. And I thought *you* were the one who hated all things child."

"I don't hate all things child."

She rubbed her feet together under the covers, then held herself still. She was wearing an old long-sleeved T-shirt of mine, some wintertime fun run from ten years before. "I just don't have any idea how to have a fifteen-year-old," she said, whispering. "That's all."

"You don't have to know," I said.

She pointed at the door. "In fact, I do. We have one now. She's on loan, but we have one." She was blinking a lot. "I can't believe we did this," she said. "She doesn't know us. I can't believe anybody thought this was a good idea."

"You were for this," I said.

"You said yes, too," she said, right away. "You sat there and you said yes."

"What else would I have said?"

"That's never stopped you before."

"We just have to not kill her," I said. "That's all."

"It's *not* all. We have to be role models. We have to feed her breakfast."

"We'll feed her breakfast," I said.

"We have to send her back fixed."

"She's not broken," I said.

"Then what's she doing here?"

"The same thing we're doing here," I said.

"We have to fix her."

I said, "Why can't we just make sure not to send her back any worse?"

She didn't answer. I didn't say anything else, didn't ask her any more questions. I let her be. She was another creature. A new one. I reached across her to turn out the light, a huge thing with a huge shade, nothing I'd have ever bought, and nothing she would have, either. I rubbed her arm on my way back by, trying to make peace. Also I just wanted to touch her, wanted to make sure she was still real.

■ ■ ■

Mid called. "You don't sound so good," I told him.

"We're a little back and forth over here. We fight, I lose. We fight some more, I lose some more. I think the central problem could be that my argument sucks. How's the teenage wasteland?"

We'd made it through the night without fire or flood. I was making eggs. Alice and Delton were out on the balcony, waiting for the parachutist. In the light of day, Alice seemed more herself. She had her shirt up. Delton reached out to touch her. "Fine," I told him. "I think."

"You think?"

"Everybody's still in one piece."

"How about I pick you up in twenty?" he said. "I want to go see a guy about a flatbed."

"A flatbed?" I asked him.

"I'll explain on the way."

I hung up the phone, stood there in the kitchen. I needed Alice to want the baby. That before all else. Because if she didn't want it, then we were both alone, on separate islands, and the BOJ was off on her own island, too, and we were all going to die. That's how I saw it, anyway. I was tired. I was leaking. We were gone from anything I knew, and we were getting farther away with every passing week. What I wanted was a break. A plainness. I wanted to make goddamn scrambled eggs without feeling like there was some manner of import built into it. I wanted to stand outside and watch Hank fly through the sky without suspecting he had some vital piece of information to pass along.

"Pretty still around the house this morning," Mid said, once we were out on the highway. "Quiet. Nobody going on about how life is so unfair. I'm not quite sure how to proceed, you know? Maybe I have Stockholm Syndrome or something."

"I thought you said you and Carolyn were at it," I said.

"That was last night. This morning we achieved a nice gentle post-apocalypse."

"Got it."

"She yelling at you yet?" he said.

"Alice?"

"Olivia."

I said, "She's only been there twelve hours."

"She'll yell at you."

"What does she yell about?"

"You name it, she's outraged by it. Except that boy—but even that still counts, because in that particular case she gets to be outraged that we're outraged."

"She doesn't seem outraged," I said.

"That's how she gets you. She's reeling you in. You wait."

She didn't come off as the kind of kid who reeled you in, but hell, maybe she was. Maybe she was home right then hollering at Alice. I cracked the window to let some air in. I said, "Where are we going again?"

"St. Augustine, to see a tow truck."

"I thought you said flatbed."

"It's both. It's supposed to be one of those tilt-bed things."

"Mind if I ask you a question?" I said.

"Fire away."

"Do we need a tow truck for any reason?"

He sucked on his lip. "*Need*'s a funny word, I guess. This is more of a grease-the-wheels kind of operation."

"How's that?" I said.

"This guy with the truck?" He changed lanes to let a couple of motorcycles hurtle by. "He's the nephew of one of my county commission guys. I'm to understand that if we purchase this truck for a fairly solid pile of cash, the commissioner's general feeling about my high school might come around a little bit."

I heard him say it, and I tried to let it wash past. Whatever else there was about him, he'd made it so we had a place to live, given me a chance to carve out a new corner of the universe for my family, whether I wanted a thing like that or not. Maybe that's why I hadn't quit. Maybe that's why I made a bad spy. Maybe that's why I was in the car with him one more time.

"Mid," I said. "No."

"I really thought I had the votes," he said, only half at me. "I thought I'd lined up enough fucking votes."

I said, "Are you saying you bought people off?"

He had both hands on the wheel. "I am saying I thought I had the votes."

"Is that why the agents are hanging around? The real reason?"

"All the reasons are real reasons."

"Do they know you're doing this?"

He said, "They do not."

The elevator had cut loose from its cables, was falling from the upper floors. We were goners. "You can't do this," I said. "This is way too fucked up. This is extortion."

"It's bribery, I think," he said. "And it's just a little out of hand."

"But why would you tell me this? Why would you even have me along?"

"You're not an accessory," he said. "Don't worry. I haven't told you anything. All I said was that we were going to look at a tow truck."

"You *just* told me—"

"I said I thought I had the votes. I expressed surprise about that."

"Please don't do this, Mid. This puts people in prison. Real prison."

"I've still got a few ideas."

"Like what?"

He looked over at me—so long it made me nervous, made we want to tell him to keep his eyes on the road, to please not kill us. He said, "Walter, I'm trying very, very hard to put it all back together. And I'm going to make it right. Nobody believes that, but I am."

Finally, there wasn't any question: Something was genuinely and actually wrong. I wanted Alice in the car. I wanted her to see it for herself. I wanted her to understand why Mid's trapeze act could feel for so long like it was off on the periphery somewhere, instead of front and center. And already I wanted it over, the whole of it—I wanted somewhere quiet to sit down with her, do the post-game, compare notes, make absolutely sure we'd witnessed the same thing.

Mid said, like nothing was happening, "How's Alice, by the way? She doing OK?"

I should have made him stop the car. I should have made him take me back home. "She's fine," is what I said instead. "Still no heavy lifting."

"That's it?"

"And no sex." The hum. Always the hum.

"How long?"

"Ten days. But we weren't really having sex anyway."

"Why not?"

We hadn't talked about it, but we'd stopped. It had been two or three weeks. I said, "I'm not sure." I was trying to remember if I knew the difference between bribery and collusion. I could see the local news anchors staring out from the TV and saying *graft*.

He said, “You should be having sex.”

“I’ll pass that along.”

“Once you get the all-clear, she’ll be on you like a zoo animal. Let it happen, my friend.”

“Thanks for the advice.”

“Because when the kid gets here, you’ll never have sex again. Now’s the time.”

“You had sex again.”

“And look what happened,” he said. “Big Walter, all I’m trying to do here is help you out. You don’t like what I have to say, maybe we can swing back through the old Pray N’ Wash, see if we can procure some higher-level intervention.”

“We might need some higher-level intervention,” I said.

“Relax. Let’s just go see this truck. We’re taking a look. Nothing more.”

I said, “No part of this a good idea. Do you get that?”

“To be honest,” he said, “I think you might be right. But it may be the best of what I’ve got left.” He eased us across the lanes toward an exit. Something flew by out the window, some bird. Big. A hawk, maybe. I didn’t know what it was. I needed a book. I should have made him take me home. No doubt I should have made him take me home. It’s what Alice would have done.

■ ■ ■

The same desperate strangeness hung on St. Augustine every time. We came in from the south, toward the Bridge of Lions, which was under repair and only half-open. They were building a new bridge next to it. Everywhere down here had the new bridge next to the old one, like there was some rule against pulling the first one down. We slid past mini golfs and bars and restaurants, long low roadside hotels with views of nothing but the mini golfs and bars. Once you were over the bridge, you were into St. Augustine proper, they way the brochures had it pictured: Flagler College dead center, palm trees on a crayoned quad, and then on both sides of that, the French Quarter thing that went on downtown. Wrought-iron balconies, outdoor dining, horse-drawn carriages, fudge shops. A plague of tourists. The tourists rode trollies, walked the streets. They walked up what passed for a hill at the old Spanish fort. The kids carried plastic swords and plastic shields. There was a historical marker about the Fountain of Youth. The nearest fountain was not that fountain.

On through that, pushing back away from the water: Ripley's Believe It or Not! The Florida School for the Deaf and Blind. The Alligator Farm, with shows on the half-hour. A rehabbed carousel. Scooters for rent. Signs for bus and boat tours. All manner of America's First City paraphernalia at sidewalk stands—pop guns, airbrushed T-shirts, salt water taffy. I kept closing my eyes, opening them again, and finding myself still in the car. Mid pushed us along and got us into something half-residential, turned off the main road past two astrologers in two houses next to each other—KNOW YOUR FORTUNE! KNOW YOUR FUTURE!—and checked a scribbled piece of paper he pulled from his shirt pocket. "We go three blocks this way," he said. "I think."

There were little lots carved out of the mangrove, crushed-shell driveways running up to houses in various stages of rot and sink. Roads with no names. Cars pushing into the ground. We rode slowly, Mid looking out the window, squinting back at his notes. We passed two dogs tied to the same chain. We passed a knot of kids who looked like they'd be perfectly willing to do us harm. Then Mid said, "Here we go," and pulled us into what was either a drive or just a yard gone to bare ground. He stopped in front of a big black flatbed tow truck, and everything was already wrong: The truck had the bottom half of a mannequin mounted, ass down and feet in the air, to the back bed. The legs were in fishnet stockings. She had green and red elf shoes on her feet, with brass bells on the toes. There were Christmas lights strung all over the truck. The lights were on. Mid said, "This isn't quite what I'd hoped for."

"Where are we?" I said.

"Oz?"

"You're making jokes?"

"That truck doesn't look like it'd be for sale," he said.

I said, "Where do you think he plugs the lights in?"

He shut the engine off. "That's your first question?"

"You weren't answering my first questions," I said. "That was just one more."

A man walked out the front door of the house, which was sided in sheets of plywood that had once been orange. He looked at us from the porch. Then he came across the yard in no tremendous hurry, stopped at the hood of the car. He was wearing corduroy pants and a white T-shirt and looked like he'd maybe just finished shaving when we pulled up. Mid rolled down his window. The guy said, "Are you the guys?"

Mid said, "Is this the truck?"

He said, "Yes, sir, it is," and Mid got out, and I did, too, and then we were all shaking hands. The air was still, the heat like a jacket. "Pete Brett," the guy said. "Two first names. They didn't have any left for my brother."

"Mid," Mid said.

"Mid what?" said Pete Brett.

"Middleton."

"No."

"It's a nickname," Mid said.

Pete Brett looked at him closer. "Do I maybe know you from somewhere?" he said. "Different name?"

"I don't think so," said Mid.

He turned to me. "What about you?"

"Walter Ingram."

"Pleasure to meet you. Want y'all both to know I can sell the truck with or without adornment."

Mid said, "Meaning—"

"The legs. We can adjust the price accordingly." Pete Brett got down on one knee to look across some sight line or another on the Camaro. "This is a fairly sporting vehicle," he said.

"It's on loan," said Mid. "I'm trying it out."

"What's to try?"

"My wife doesn't approve."

"Of the car?"

"Of me, more like it."

Pete Brett said, "Excuse me, sir?"

"What?"

"She doesn't approve of you?"

"Not always," Mid said. "Not recently."

"Not sure I can sell a truck to a man whose wife doesn't approve of him," he said. Pete Brett looked familiar to me, too, but I couldn't place him. The lights on the truck blinked. Pete Brett pulled a sleeve of peanuts from his pocket, opened it carefully, ate peanuts one at a time. There was something wrong with his teeth. "Ah, what the hell," he said. "I guess y'all drove all the way up here." He grinned. "Peanut?" he said. I wanted to leave.

"No," Mid said. "Thank you."

He said, "Listen. A lot of people think I'm a pervert when I show them this, but come take a look."

Run, I thought. Run right now. From both of them. I stood in the low shade and I thought about what the chances were nobody knew where we were. "Out," Alice would tell the police. "With Mid." Mid made a half-hidden gesture that I took to mean *surely we'll be fine*, but he didn't seem so sure himself. Pete Brett opened the driver's-side door of the truck, tilted the seat forward, and came back out with a single mannequin leg. It was in fishnets like the two on the truck, but it was mounted foot-down to a small plywood platform. It wore a blue high heel. The leg stopped mid-thigh. In a hole cut into the top, there was a beer cozy. Pete Brett set it down on the ground, pantomimed putting a beer in it. "For when you're sitting around," he said, obviously proud of it. "With your buddies. I make these. I sell 'em. What do you think?"

"It's nice," Mid said.

"What about you?" he said to me.

"I think so, too," I said.

"So how about it? You want one?"

"No, thanks," I said.

"Why the hell not?"

"I have tables," I said.

"I don't get your meaning," he said. "You have tables."

"I'm not meaning anything," I said.

Pete Brett whispered something to himself I couldn't hear, and he looked from me to Mid and then back again. "Well, at least take a look at this, would you?" He put the beer leg back in the truck, reached in behind the seat again, brought out a different leg, naked this time. He pointed it at me foot-first. "Feel that heel," he said.

"Why me?"

"Come on, man, feel it!"

"I don't want to," I said.

He swung it to Mid. "How about you? You want to feel it?" Mid didn't move. He stared at Pete Brett, who held the leg out in the air. We had fallen into something. You're not involved, Mid kept telling me. Except here I was in this driveway. Pete Brett flipped the leg around and rubbed the heel himself. "Y'all are missing out," he said. "Feels just like a real heel. Just like the real damn thing." He turned it back thigh-out to show us a hole drilled into it and threaded for a bolt. "Now why don't one of you gentlemen tell me what that is?" he said. "Take a guess. You'll love it."

Neither of us said anything.

"Guess," Pete Brett said again.

I said, "I don't know."

"It's for truck drivers, man! For gearshifts! I'm gonna sell these in truck stops. They'll take off their gearshifts, screw this baby back on. Then they can drive down the highway, take hold of that heel, shift her through her paces, move on down the line."

A dog barked a few houses away. I imagined every truck on the highway with a naked leg gearshift, and a warehouse of legless mannequins, all the bodies left over from the production of these things. Mid said, "You'll make a million dollars."

"I know it! *Now* you wanna feel it?"

Mid said, "I'll still take a pass."

"I don't get why y'all won't just feel it."

"How are you for funding?" Mid asked. He was getting his feet back under him.

"How am I for what, sir?" He kept saying sir.

"Start-up. Are you selling them yet?"

"I got a plan, if that's what you're asking."

"What is it?"

Pete Brett's eyes seemed to pull back into his head. "I wouldn't go sniffing around what ain't yours, if I was you."

"That's not what I meant," said Mid. "I was only—"

"You know what, dude? I think I see what you two are about. You came in here to steal my shit. Well, guess what? I got a lawyer. We got a patent pending. I got—" He blew his nose out on the ground, wiped his face with his wrist. "I got a fucking business model, is what I got."

"All I meant was maybe we could help you out. Investment-wise. I'm not here to take anything from you."

"I don't need your help, OK, sir? And I don't think I'm going to need to sell you my truck, either." He got up close to Mid. "Plus I still say I know you assholes. I recognize you." We never should have gotten out of the car. I should have made him take me home. Pete Brett said, "How about you two pissants get back in your little candy corn Batmobile and get the fuck off my property?"

"It's alright," Mid said, trying to calm him down. "We're OK here."

Pete Brett shook the leg at him. "You think we're OK? You're gonna be the person who says so? Get this: I will *find* your ass. Do you understand what I'm saying? I will come and find you. And how about you not talk to me like I'm your pet?"

"I apologize," Mid said. "You don't need to get upset."

He got very calm. "Don't say that," he said. "I am not upset."

"This is a simple misunderstanding," Mid said.

He turned to me. "And I do know you. I remember you."

"I'm somebody else," I said. "You've got the wrong guy."

"I don't get upset," Pete Brett said.

"We believe you," Mid said.

In one smooth motion, Pete Brett yanked the leg up into the air, and then brought it down, heel first, into the Camaro's windshield. A shatter-star the size of a dinner plate formed in the glass. "*That's* the kind of thing that could happen if I did get upset, though," he said. "That was a little demonstration. Did you catch that? You want me to play that back?"

"No," Mid said, quietly. He bit on the insides of his lips.

A woman came out onto the front porch. She said, "Pete, time to come inside."

Pete Brett stared at Mid. "How about you give me a thousand dollars, you little fuck."

"Give you what?"

"A thousand dollars. You'd like me to go in the house, right?"

"I wouldn't like anything."

"I want a thousand dollars."

"Forget it," Mid said.

Pete Brett hoisted the leg again, and then whipped a kind of uneven baseball swing through the driver's-side mirror, knocking it loose. The mirror bounced off the window and hung from the side of the car by its wires. Mid didn't flinch. I wasn't sure he believed what was happening. I wasn't sure I did. The summer before you were born, I thought. Pete Brett looked at us, at the leg. He wasn't breathing heavily at all. You would have otherwise thought he was fine. "Who's next?" he said. He lifted the leg again, seemed to be lining Mid up. I would have planned some move if I could have made my brain work, could have thought of anything that might stop or slow what was going on. The woman on the porch said, "Pete."

Mid produced a wad of cash from his pocket, counted off several fifties, held it out. “Here,” he said.

“That’s not a grand,” Pete Brett said.

“It’s what I’m willing to give you.” Even now he was making a deal.

Pete Brett tugged on one ear. “I don’t know,” he said.

“Take it,” Mid said. “Take the fucking money and leave us alone.”

“*Peter,*” the woman said, one last time. He turned and looked back at her. Then he nodded, put the leg back in the truck, snatched the cash out of Mid’s hand, and walked across the yard and up onto his front porch. The woman opened the door for him. They went inside without looking back. I thought I heard a deadbolt. We stood right where we were. Finally, Mid said, “I think we should go.”

We got in the car. I put my seatbelt on. He put his on. He backed us up, got us turned around the right way in the narrow street. He had to lean to see around the broken part of windshield. We found the main road. We stopped at a light. A Ripley’s tour trolley crossed through the intersection, people taking pictures out the open sides. They took pictures of us. When the light went green again, Mid drove us a little ways, then pulled into an empty parking lot behind a closed-down chicken place. He parked and put the keys up on the dashboard. There was something new that was blown-through about him. He kept pinching his nose. He said, “What the fuck would we have done?”

“If what?” I’d been keeping it reasonably under control, but now, with the car stopped, I felt sick, almost like I had a fever. “I think what you did was right,” I said. “I think that was the only thing.”

"Are you alright?" he said.

"Are you?"

"No," he said, and put his head on the steering wheel. "No, I'm not."

"Did you really recognize him?" I said.

"He's that pirate from the grocery store."

"Are you sure?"

"I'm pretty sure."

"How could that be?" I said.

"Same as anything else," he said. "Things happen. All kinds of things." His head was still down on the wheel. "I don't want anybody to know about this," he said.

"Which part?"

"I don't want to tell Carolyn."

"Except you have to tell her," I said. "Don't you?"

"You'd tell Alice?" he said.

"I think I would."

"She'll just say this is one more thing."

"Mid," I said. "Isn't it? Isn't that what's up here?"

He said, "Things are starting to go bad on me." And he began to cry, which was horrible. It made it so I didn't get to wish I could find a leg of my own, bash him over the head once or twice. You destroyed my life, I wanted to say, except it wasn't true. It was only almost true. A tornado skips and jumps and people say God's plan. Nobody ever says luck of the draw. I put my hand on his back. "I'm sorry," he said, and started saying it over and over, sobbing it, almost. I did not stop him to tell him we were OK, or that we were going to come through it one way or another. I didn't tell him we weren't, either. I left my hand on him. I didn't tell him anything. I did not want to lie.

■ ■ ■

Setting the dinner table, Delton was telling Alice, in vivid Technicolor, about a TV show she liked to watch, a dance contest show for groups of dancers. Alice was asking questions: There are judges? People call in and vote? This was not a show we watched, but she was trying. Here was the nuclear world: Home from battle, dinner as a family. Alice had placemats out. Candles, even. She'd gotten candles. We looked every bit the part.

"What do these people do when they're not on the show?" Alice said.

Delton said, "What do you mean?"

"Are they professionals? Do they dance for a living?"

"No. They do other things."

"Like what?"

"This one girl who was on last year was a pharmacist. She just really liked to dance."

"Did she win?" Alice asked.

"No. Her group was pretty bad. They went out early."

They had something going, Alice and Delton. They talked to each other easily. Not that Delton was cozied up to either of us and confessing secrets—she had her actual friends for that. But this was working. It was fragile, but working.

Delton went to the sink, filled her glass with water. "So," she said. "What did you and Dad do today?"

"Me?" I said.

"Yeah. How was your day? What did you do?"

I thought about how to tell them. It was pretty much all I'd thought about. I said, "I'm fairly sure we got mugged." They both stopped what they were doing. "We went out to see some guy about buying his tow truck," I said. "He ended up shaking Mid down for a few hundred dollars."

"What are you talking about?" Alice said. "Are you guys alright?"

I looked at them—my wife and my imaginary daughter. "It's hard to say."

We'd spent the afternoon ignoring it. He didn't want to talk. He wanted to drive by Me Kayak, drive by the sunglasses hut, make sure everything that was supposed to have four walls and a roof still did. For a little while he worked on a plan to call in a favor from the state agents, get them to go out and rattle Pete Brett an appropriate amount. You could see him trying to hold it together, go through the motions—but he definitely wasn't the same. He dropped me back at the condo, and when I came through the door, Alice and Delton were already making dinner, laughing about something, privately, it seemed like, and so all I'd done was say hello and seek shelter in the back bedroom. Our bedroom. I stood in the window and watched some people out on the water having real trouble making a catamaran go any other direction than the way it wanted to go. Then Alice and Delton called me in to eat, and there we were. "The guy was strung out or something," I told them. "We were standing in his driveway, talking to him about his truck, and he snapped. He told Mid to give him some money. Mid gave it to him."

"That doesn't sound like Dad," Delton said.

I said, "He was threatening us."

"With what?" Alice said.

"A leg."

"A what?" they said, almost at the same time.

"He had this thing he wanted to sell, a gearshift made out of a mannequin leg. He smashed the windshield with it."

Delton said, "Did he hit you guys or anything?"

"Mid got us out of there before things turned too hairy."

"I don't understand," said Alice. "He just asked you for money?"

The whole thing was like waking from a dream you were already forgetting. "Pretty much," I said. "He smashed the windshield, and then he asked for a thousand dollars."

"You had a thousand dollars?"

"Mid did," I said. "More than that." Suddenly I felt like I'd sold him out by telling them that. Surely this was not the kind of information you were supposed to hand over to somebody's daughter.

Alice put both her hands on her placemat, spread her fingers out wide. "Olivia," she said. "What does your dad really do?"

"Alice," I said.

Delton said, "Follow me around. Tell me not to get tattoos after I've already got them." She cracked an ice cube in her teeth. "He's OK?" she asked me. "For real? You're telling the whole thing?"

"He was when he dropped me off," I said.

Alice got up, walked to the sliding doors, opened the blinds. The louvers clacked together at the bottoms. "What life is this, Walter?"

I said, "Maybe now's not the time?"

"Go ahead," Delton said. "Don't mind me. This one sounds familiar."

"What kind of job do you have where you can get assaulted by a guy with a mannequin leg?"

"I don't think he was expecting that," I said. "I don't think that's what kind of job it is."

"Was anybody hurt?"

"No," I said.

"*Could* anybody have gotten hurt?"

"I don't know," I said. "Probably. Yes. But it didn't happen that—"

"He's got children," she said, pointing at Delton. "And you—you can't be—"

I said, "You're not even giving me a chance to talk."

"Can I call him?" Delton asked. She already had the phone. "I'm calling him, OK?"

"Could you wait?" I said.

"Why?"

"I don't think he's ready to talk about it yet."

"Why not?"

"He was still working out how to tell your mom."

"Carolyn will climb the walls," Alice said.

"That's what he was worried about," I said.

Delton said, "I could use a beer. You guys want a beer?"

"You can't have a beer," I told her.

"Worth a shot. I really can't call him?"

I said, "Can you maybe let me think about it a second?"

"What's to think about?" Alice said.

"They're going to get a divorce, right?" Delton said, and that really started the room spinning for me.

Alice said, "What makes you think that?"

Delton said, "Doesn't everybody think that?"

"Sometimes things seem worse than they are," Alice said, but we all knew she was just reciting lines.

Delton's phone rang. She put ours back on the charger and answered hers. "Hey," she said. "Just eating dinner. Hold on." She covered the mouthpiece with her thumb. "It's Nic," she said. "Can we go get coffee?"

"You're not supposed to go out after dinner," I said.

"After dark," she said.

Alice said, "It'll be dark in an hour."

"I'll be back in an hour," she said. "Please?"

"An hour," Alice said.

"I swear."

"Take the phone," said Alice. "Call us if anything happens."

"He's here," she said. "In the parking lot. Can I go now?"

Alice looked at me. We were parenting. "Sure," I said. "Go ahead." And she was into the bathroom in three steps, and then back out again, wearing a tiny black skirt and a tank top. She had high-heeled sandals. I didn't understand how she'd changed clothes so fast. She told us goodbye and walked out the door. We listened to the drum of her footsteps down the concrete walk to the elevator. When it was quiet again, Alice said, "He smashed the windshield?"

"Yes."

"With a mannequin leg."

Both of us were still looking at the front door, like Delton might instantaneously appear back inside it: Puff of smoke, half-tall girl. "He had this idea," I said, trying to find a new place to start. "Mid did. The guy with the leg is connected to the county commission. The school vote. Mid was going to buy this truck, and that was supposed to help—"

"No," Alice said. She closed her eyes. "No. Let me just stand here."

The air in the room had gone thin. I said, "Do you want to sit on the balcony?"

"No."

"I'm not happy either," I said. "Believe me."

"That doesn't help."

"Do you want to go down to the beach?"

She walked over to a painting of seagulls, stared at it like she was waiting for them to tell her something. "You can't work for him anymore," she said. "You just can't. You have to quit."

"I know."

She ran her finger along the top edge of the frame and checked for dust. Then she turned back around. "I guess we might as well go down to the beach," she said. "We live here."

■ ■ ■

The turtle pickup was back. The woman had her headlights on even though it wasn't dark enough to need them. She was half a mile down the beach, and coming our way. Alice said, "We can't give her back. Not now."

"What?"

"Olivia. Delton. She can't go back to that house. Carolyn's got to get out of there. She's got to get the kids out."

"Slow down," I said.

"Don't tell me that," she said. "Now he's out there bribing thugs?"

"I don't think he was a thug. I think he was off his meds or something."

"And on top of that, the school—" She stopped walking. "This is it. It has to be. This is too much."

"He didn't bribe the guy."

"You said he did."

"I said he was going to try to."

"Oh, great, then. Never mind."

A few condos down, somebody set off a few bottlerockets. I said, "I don't think he knows for sure what he's doing anymore."

"Is there anything that makes you think he's ever known?" she said.

"Today was different," I said.

"In what way?"

"He didn't—" I was almost at a loss. "He didn't take that very well."

"How could anybody take that well?"

"You didn't see it," I said. "You didn't see him."

The shrimp boats out on the water were starting to pick up the pink of the sun. It was a hell of a thing to be standing there. I felt sure we were on the edge of the world. Beyond here there be dragons, is what it felt like. Alice said, "I think something's happened to our lives."

"We're having a kid," I said.

She folded her arms across her chest and faced into the breeze. "A girl," she said. "I think it's a girl, too."

"You didn't say so."

"I'm saying now. When I talk to her, it feels like a girl."

"Do you want to find out next time we go in?"

"You do," she said.

"I'm fine either way."

She said, "I still want to be surprised."

"We could name her Olivia," I said. "It's a good name. And she's not using it."

"I think that's bad luck."

"We could name her Middleton."

"Do you ever imagine her?" she said. "Can you see her?"

"I've been able to imagine her all along."

"But is it—is it getting any better?"

"Sure," I said.

"You're lying."

"I'm walking," I said. "I'm walking on the beach with you."

"I need to know where you are," she said. "I need to know if you're alright."

I was not. I knew I was not, and that there was little chance I would be, and that I could tell her neither of those things. I knew that until the kid was born, or until Alice got the next all-clear from Varden, and then however many more all-clears we'd need after that, that I'd be damaged. And I was coming to rest pretty surely on the idea that, give or take, that was the ride I'd be on for the rest of my life—that the only real calm I'd ever see again would be the demilitarized zone between one crisis and the next. As soon as somebody stopped by to let me know something was alright, that the threat had passed, the next new thing would ride over the horizon at us, whip out a naked leg, and shake us down for lunch money. Maybe Mid was right. Maybe I did need the Pray N' Wash. What can we pray for today? the kid would ask. All of it, I'd tell him. Every single piece of it. Here, I'd say. I brought a list.

"I do like it down here," I told her, which was no kind of answer. The turtle woman was closer now. You could make her out behind the windshield. "I like Delton. She seems like a person."

"She is a person."

"And I like Mid," I said. "I—"

"I like him, too, Walter, but Jesus Christ."

"I think he's not right," I said.

"No kidding."

"What I mean is, I don't think he understood how all that was supposed to work today. And that's not him. Or it doesn't seem like him."

She said, "Is this supposed to be making me feel better?"

"It's not supposed to be doing anything. I'm just trying to talk to you. I think it scared the shit out of him. It scared the shit out of me."

"Say it," she said.

"Say what?"

"Say something terrible could have happened."

"We don't know that," I said. "We don't know anything like that."

"You could have been killed."

"I don't think that's totally true," I said.

She said, "You have to take care of him."

"Take care of him how?"

"You can't let something happen to him. Carolyn couldn't take it."

"I thought you said she had to get out of there. Take the kids. That was just now, right?"

"She does, Walter, but that doesn't mean he can— And you. You guys can't be out there—"

"We won't be out there. I'm quitting. Like you said. There's no 'you guys.'"

"You have to take care of him. You have to watch him for a little while longer."

"You're not making any sense," I said.

"Just promise me, OK? At least while we still have Olivia. Until whatever this is with the police works out. Stay with him until then. Promise me you'll make sure—"

"You want me to quit," I said, "and you want me to save him."

"You're the only one he might listen to."

"He doesn't listen to me," I said. "There's no listening."

"But maybe you can keep him from— Maybe you can stop

things like today from happening. That can't happen anymore. Whatever that was can't happen. Not while she's in our house. We have to keep them safe."

It was lunatic, what she was asking me. It was plainly impossible. And I told her I'd do it. Because it was right. Because it was one thing, finally, I could say yes to and know I meant it. She moved toward me, fit her body up against mine. I took hold of her hands. There was water in the air, spray off the ocean, but if you looked north, you could still make out the St. Augustine lighthouse. You could figure out, in one small way, where you were. We stayed down there until it was nearly dark, until it was time for Delton to come back home—time for us to be back upstairs, waiting, hoping hard for the sound of her key in the door.

For the first few days, we survived: I kept going to work, kept coming back home. We fed Delton. We fed her friends when they came by to check out the arrangement. We fed Nic a sandwich one afternoon while we all stood around waiting for Delton to get out of the shower. They were going to the go-carts. "Drive carefully," I told him, feeling for all the world like I was the one on some security camera, like someone somewhere was watching me. "Check your blind spots. Use your turn signals."

"I will," he said.

"The car is not a toy," said Alice.

Delton arrived in the hallway, towel wrapped around her, armpits to knees. She said, "But the go-carts *are* toys, right?"

"It's complicated," I told her.

"Is it?" She laughed at her own joke and disappeared into her room.

She'd covered all four walls in tinfoil. Her first official act under our roof. She said it made her feel like she was in the future. It took almost twenty rolls of foil, and Alice drove her back to the grocery two or three times to get enough. They were bonding, she said. I looked in there while they were out getting the last of it. It looked horrible. Most of it was crooked. I'd have loved it if I was fifteen.

I found myself keeping an eye out for the Pete Bretts of the world. Something like that happens once, and it begins to seem possible around every corner. Everything's a potential threat. I was waiting for signs and signals. Every day, I told Alice, it felt like we were getting closer. That's because we were, she said. No, I said. That's not quite what I mean. One morning, Alice and Delton gone somewhere—off buying more foil, or scouting for some new project—Hank flew by in his parachute, and I stood on our balcony, pulled my own shirt up over my own belly, and waved. He snapped a fast salute, like what I was doing was as ordinary as anything else, and sailed on by.

■ ■ ■

Sunday morning, early. I'd been up since before dawn, sneaking around my own house and trying not to wake anybody. I was on my second pot of coffee, shaky but more or less awake, and flipping through one of Sandy's bird books: descriptions of plumage, nesting tendencies, variant foot coloring in juveniles. I found a category called "Casual or Accidental Seabirds." I looked for my own picture. Mid didn't even ring the doorbell—he just came through the door and stood in the front hall, looking like a lit match. "You should probably knock," I said.

"Somebody fucking stole one of the Twice-the-Ices," he said.

"It's seven in the morning," I said.

"And somebody stole one of our machines."

Delton opened her door. "Daddy?" she said.

"Hi, sweetheart."

"What are you doing here?"

"Having an emergency." He looked in behind her. "What did you do to the walls in there?"

"It's tinfoil," I told him.

"Why?" he said. "Never mind. Walter, who fucking steals an ice machine?"

"Curse jar," Delton said.

"Diplomatic immunity," said Mid.

"Stole it how?" I asked.

"I mean it is no longer there. There is no Twice-the-Ice. There is an empty concrete pad and no machine. It is absent. Gone. Goodbye."

I said, "Are you sure?"

"How could I not be sure? I already called Friendly and Helpful. They're meeting us out there."

"What does it have to do with them?"

"Nothing, probably, but I asked them to meet me, and they said yes."

"Did you tell them why?"

"I said it was an important business matter."

Alice came out of our bedroom wearing a tank top and red fleece pants. Her belly was clear under the shirt, obvious in a way I was coming to like. "What's going on?" she said.

"Somebody stole one of the Twice-the-Ices," Mid said. "Some fucker."

"Who would steal an ice machine?" she said.

"My point precisely. It has to be an act of war."

"War?" Alice said, looking at me.

He said, "Walter, we have to go get it back."

"Let's get some breakfast first," I said, wanting to slow him down. "We can talk about it on the way."

He turned to Delton. She looked eleven now instead of fifteen, looked sleepy the way a little kid does. He said, "I guess that could be the right idea."

"What?" she said. "Is it something you can't talk about in front of me?"

"We can talk about anything you like," he said. "This is just something I need to get squared away, alright?"

"I guess," she said.

Alice said, "I'm not sure if—"

"We'll be careful," Mid said. "No need to worry about us."

"Why do you have to be careful?" Delton asked.

"We don't," I said. "It's only breakfast."

"And a small amount of avenging," Mid said. He was hyped up—he was having trouble holding his hands still, kept putting them in his pockets and then taking them back out.

Delton said, "You guys are weird."

"Not as weird as you, Livvy," he said.

"Nobody's weird as me."

"Keep it up."

"I'm trying."

"I know you are," he said, and they stared at each other, some parcel of information trading hands, until she stretched up on her tiptoes to kiss him on the cheek. Then she went back in her room and shut the door.

Alice said, just above a whisper, "Maybe you should let the authorities handle this?"

"I can still hear you," Delton said from behind the door.

"We are," Mid said. "That's what we're doing. We're meeting them out there." I knew Alice was wanting me to think of something—come up with a way, any way, to send Mid off on some other mission. "We're the victims," Mid said, but she didn't hear him, or didn't act like she did. She put one hand on her belly. She waited for me. When she saw I had nothing, she turned around, headed for the bedroom. She was mad. It wasn't me, I wanted to say. Or, I'll do what I can. I'll try. I'll be back soon. "You ready?" Mid said, and even though the answer was a sure no, I put my shoes on, checked our closed bedroom door, gave up all over again, and followed him down to the car.

■ ■ ■

"They don't look open," I said. He'd driven us to Pomar's, the little roadside place.

"Pomar'll be here, though. He's always here."

"This early?"

"Usually."

I stood behind him while he knocked on the closed door. Soon enough a guy wearing a white button-up and swim trunks opened it. None of his clothes really fit right. Pomar. "What?" he said.

"Somebody stole one of my Twice-the-Ices."

"Wasn't me," said Pomar.

"Shrimp on toast?" Mid asked.

"If you help me cut some lemons. I'm behind on prep."

"Deal," Mid said, and we went in.

Closed, the restaurant felt like an exhibit. All the TVs were off but one, which was playing a cable financial show on mute. Stock prices scrolled along the bottom of the screen, red for losers and green for winners. It was hard to remember a life where those had actually meant something. Nothing had been the same since they switched from fractions to decimals, one of my buddies at the bank used to say. Fred Fairhead. A tall guy who'd take you to lunch and draw graphs on napkins. I wondered what work he was doing these days, what town he might've landed in, who he was supposed to keep watch over. Pomar set us up at the bar with cutting boards and a five-gallon bucket of lemons. "I can't believe somebody stole the fucking thing," Mid said. "Just the logistics, you know?"

Pomar poured coffee into rocks glasses. He said, "I can see not believing it."

"You'd need a truck, for starters," Mid said. "Who has a truck like that?"

"Circuses," said Pomar.

"Circuses?"

"Ever passed a circus out on the road? They got trucks. They carry things."

"You think the Ringling Brothers took my machine?"

"You asked who had trucks," Pomar said. "I gave you a good answer."

"You made the payments, right?" I asked him. "It is actually stolen?"

"Nobody came and repossessed the machine. I made the payments."

Pomar said, "It's a fair question."

"Fuck off," Mid said. He halved a lemon, then held his knife up in the air. "But I'll tell you who's got a big enough truck."

"Who's that?" I said.

"That goddamn pirate. It's him. I bet you anything."

"And the circus was a bad answer?" Pomar said.

"We met this guy," said Mid. "He had a truck that would about do it."

"How would he know it was yours?" I said.

"He would. He would have some way."

"Like an actual pirate?" Pomar said. "With parrots?"

Mid said, "In a grocery store, more like. But he had this tow truck."

Pomar looked at him like he had more questions, but maybe knew better. He was pulling on some history I didn't have. He took a handful of lemon wedges out of Mid's pile, put them in a little bowl. "Sixths, OK?" he said. "Not eighths. You keep these skinny ones for your toast." He turned around and went through the swinging doors into the back.

Out the big front windows, the sun was burning us into true morning, still and cloudless again. Quiet. Mid cut lemons. I cut lemons. Pomar dropped a lid in the kitchen, cursed at it. "Don't worry about the foil in Delton's room, by the way," I said, aiming for something good to tell Mid. "We let her do it. Alice helped her hang it up."

"I'm not worried," he said.

"It couldn't be the pirate guy," I said. "He can't have put that together."

"I'm on file with the county to operate there. I pulled permits. Or he could have worked it backwards through his uncle."

"It took a crane to put them down," I said.

"He didn't strike you as the kind of guy who might be able to figure his way around a crane?"

I said, "He struck me as the kind of guy who had bodies in the yard."

"Here," Mid said. "Feel this. Feels just like a real heel."

"Right."

"So that's my point," he said.

"What is?"

He picked up a lemon, turned it in his hand. "We need to go out there. Go pay him a visit."

"No way."

"Somebody has to go out there."

"Get your buddies to do it," I said. "Your cops. Get them to park in the driveway and flash the lights and do what they do."

"Maybe," he said.

"What would we do, anyway?"

"If what?"

"If we went out there and he had it?"

"Fuck, man, I don't know," he said. "I haven't gotten that far. Ask him for it nicely?"

"What, like it was a ball we hit in his yard?" I said. "And then what?"

"Why do you have to make it so complicated?" he asked me.

"I'm not trying to," I said.

He said, "Alice has you keeping tabs on me now, right?"

Up on the TV, more numbers went by, mostly losing bets. "Yes," I said. "She does."

"Because of—" he said.

"Because of everything," I said.

He nodded. "Can't fault her." The TV host had his sleeves rolled up like he was actually doing work. The show went to commercial. "Get this," Mid said. "Carolyn wants us to go to couples therapy. She's got all these conditions now, shit we have to do. We're supposed to go sit down and pass the talking ball back and forth." He looked at the blade of his knife. "And also Maggie needs tubes in her ears. The doctor told us yesterday."

"I had tubes," I said.

"Sophie started her period."

I could see where we were headed, could see this ended in fire. "Congratulations?" I said. "Is that what you say?"

"Last month. She asked Carolyn not to tell me. But then

Carolyn told me. Jane hasn't started hers yet, and Carolyn says she's freaking out." He halved a lemon, then halved it again. "Shit," he said. "Sixths." He picked up another. "You know what I could go for? Six or ten days of real quiet. A vacation. Branson, Missouri. Or one of those Alaska cruises. Somewhere with no ice machines. No kids. No threats of bodily harm."

"I could do that," I said.

"You're already on vacation," he said.

"I'm not. I'm working a Saturday, even."

"How many weeks is she?"

"Twenty-two. No: Twenty-three."

"Subtract that from forty. That's how many weeks of vacation you're on." He looked up at the money show, which was back on again. "This fucking guy," he said, pointing up at him. "What does this guy even do? He just reads the shit out as it comes across. He's like one of those books for the blind."

"He tells us things," I said.

"What things?"

"We should buy stock in sugary cereals. We should not buy stock in napalm."

"You ever miss your job?" Mid said.

Paychecks. Bonuses. A set of bright lines to play between. I said, "Depends on when you ask."

"Is it me?" he said.

"No," I said, and that was the truth. "Not all the time. Mostly I like this pretty well."

"But you're gonna quit. I'm trouble. I'm the bad guy."

"I don't want to," I said.

"Why not? You could do other things. You'll land on your feet."

"I can't even think of anything," I said. "I'm just out here floating."

"You didn't think of this, and it came along."

"Yeah," I said, "but—"

"What do you miss? When you think about it?"

I spun a lemon around on the bar. "Everything," I said. "I miss everything. Our whole life back there. I felt like I knew what that was."

"Even though you didn't."

"I thought I did. I really thought I did. But maybe it was the same as anything else, and I couldn't tell."

He nodded. "See?" he said. "*That* is what I'm talking about. That shit. That is the very center of it right there."

Pomar came through the doors with six or eight pieces of toast on a plate, a bowl of boiled shrimp, an institutional jar of mayonnaise. He'd stood a bunch of parsely up in a glass like it was flowers. "Here we go," he said. "The works."

"Tell me how to do this," I said.

"Listen to the master," said Mid.

Pomar handed me a rubber spatula, unscrewed the huge mayo lid. "Thin layer of mayonnaise on a piece of toast," he said. "See-through thin. Open-face. The shrimp over that. Two or three. Then lemon, then parsley. And here." He banged a salt shaker down on the bar. "A little salt."

"That's it?" I said.

Mid smiled. "Just try it," he said. He was happy and unhappy in the same moment. He scraped his lemons off to the side of his cutting board. He built his sandwich. We each did. The three of us ate. Whether it was a last supper or just communion, I didn't know. But it was good.

■ ■ ■

In the car, Mid got going again about wanting to buy in with Pomar. How if that ever happened, he'd get him to open up for breakfast. "We'd be famous," he said. "We'd be in food magazines. That could be the only thing on the whole menu. Shrimp and toast. Nothing else. Come if you like it, go the hell someplace else for some crap biscuit if you don't." He was sketching out how it would work when we pulled into the strip center. The Crown Vic was there, his agents, but there were also two local squad cars, white with green lettering on the doors: ST. AUGUSTINE BEACH SHERIFF. "Oh," Mid said.

"What?"

He was staring at the sheriff's cars. "This seems bad."

The Twice-the-Ice was definitely stolen. The electric service coming off the pole had been disconnected, and the water pipe was cut all the way back to the shopping center. No water, though. At least whoever'd done it had shut the valve off. A little decency among thieves. The two sheriff's cars swung around behind us and switched their lights on. "Yeah," Mid said. "This doesn't smell right. Something's up."

Two men got out of the Crown Vic and walked toward us. It was the first time I'd ever seen Friendly and Helpful. They looked related—same shoulders, same walk. One of them tapped on the glass. Mid rolled down the window. "I hate to do this," the one on the right said. Friendly, I decided.

Mid said, "Then don't."

"What happened to your windshield?" he said. "And your mirror?"

"That's what I wanted to talk to you about."

"I'm sorry they stole your ice machine," said Helpful.

"Who's this 'they'?" Mid said.

"Whoever it was," he said.

"Do you have any leads?"

"No," Friendly said, leaning down. "But we need to go ahead right here and advise you to stop talking. If you want to. You have the right to not be talking, is what I mean to say."

"The right to remain silent," said Helpful.

"You gotta be kidding me," Mid said. "You guys are awful at this."

Friendly said, "Please step out of the car, please."

Mid said, "Two pleases?"

"I really apologize," said Friendly. "Not our decision. Came from higher up."

"Where higher up?"

"I'm sure you'll be able to work it out," he said. "The DA up here's a good guy. If it even gets that far. This is mainly a formality." He opened Mid's door. "You want my opinion, they're just trying to squeeze you, but it's not ours anymore."

Mid said, "You couldn't just give me a call, ask me to turn myself in?"

"Flight risk," Helpful said.

"Flight risk?"

"That's what we were told."

"Where would I fly to?"

Helpful pulled a piece of paper out of his pocket. I felt a kind of hush seep in around everything else. "Francis Middleton, the State of Florida hereby charges you with fraud by telephone, obstruction of justice, intent to conceal—"

"What the fuck is fraud by telephone?" Mid said.

"That's what it says here."

"You had to write it down? You couldn't remember it?"

"Mid," I said, trying to bring him back a little, trying to do my job.

"Why aren't you guys out somewhere looking for my ice machine?" he asked them. "Go do police work, would you?"

"We did find some receipts," Friendly said. "Might be from our perpetrator. Might have fallen out of his car."

"You two geniuses think somebody stole this with a car?"

"Truck," Helpful said. "Come on. Just get out of the car. We'll take you in, get you charged, get you out on bond, get you home so you can start straightening things out."

"Bond? I thought you said I was a flight risk."

"Can't work toward resolution if we never begin the work," Helpful said.

"Did you make that up?" Mid said. "That's terrific. I need that needlepointed into my forehead."

"Mid," I said again.

"Oh, I really do not think so," he said, and pulled his door back shut.

"Mid," said Friendly. He put his hand on the door, in the space of the open window.

"I know who did it," Mid told him. "It's this pirate guy who works the deli at that new Publix. I know where he lives."

"We can discuss that once we bring you in."

"This wasn't the deal," Mid said. "This wasn't the deal at all."

"What deal?" I said.

Mid looked up at Friendly. "What happened?"

"I'm sorry," Friendly said. "Truly."

"But what the fuck?"

"Listen. We went on and lost that tape. The one with your daughter. We misplaced it." Delton. If Mid hadn't burned through his fuses, he would now.

He said, "You did?"

"This morning," Helpful said. "After we got the call about the change in strategy."

"Did you guys steal my Twice-the-Ice?"

"We did not."

Mid looked at me, at the empty concrete pad. "Like forever lost? For real?"

Friendly said, "For real."

"Thanks for that, at least."

"So let's just get out of the car," said Friendly. "Alright?"

Mid picked at the smashed windshield. It would definitely leak in the rain. "Your kids getting tattoos?" he asked. He'd slipped into an eerie, careful calm, which made me nervous.

Friendly said, "Not yet, thank God."

"You know Maggie had colic for a year?" Mid said to me. "An entire year. One full year with no sleep. Hard to believe you can survive a thing like that."

"We should get out," I said, hoping there was still something I could do to keep the lid on. An officer showed up at my window, one of the sheriff's deputies. His uniform was green. He didn't knock. He just stood at the ready.

"I'm not getting out," Mid said.

"You have to get out," said Friendly.

"No. I'm going home."

"You can't go home," Friendly said. "Not right now."

"Maybe I am a flight risk," he said. "I might like the sound of that. It sounds fierce, you know? Dangerous?" Then he said, "Except I'm pretty tired. Are you guys tired?"

Friendly said, "Sometimes I am."

"Fucking pirate stole my ice machine and you're here talking to me."

"We're on that, OK?" Helpful said. "That's definitely a felony."

Mid said, "I'm feeling better already."

"We have those receipts. We'll start there."

"Maybe you could make plaster casts of the tire marks," Mid said.

Helpful said, "There aren't any tire marks. It's a parking lot."

"Maybe it was done by helicopter," Mid said.

"I have to ask you to get out of the vehicle," Friendly said. "Please. Right now."

Mid said, "I hate to disappoint you, but I just don't feel like that's what's going to happen." He took a long breath. He put both his hands on the steering wheel. He looked dead ahead.

I could see Alice, could see Delton. Out in front of us somewhere, I could see the BOJ, age three, age seven, age seventeen. I said, "Don't do it." I didn't even know what he was going to do. Helpful took a step toward the car. The deputy on my side knocked on the window. I got a metal taste in my mouth. I saw the Twice-the-Ice on the end of some long webbed straps, soaring away underneath one of those two-rotored Coast Guard helicopters that came up and down the beach while they were training for whatever the Coast Guard trained for. Mapping. Rescues. I saw Pete Brett at the throttle of that thing, flying it with a naked leg. And then Mid floored it. He drove us right across the empty parking lot, through the flowerbed next to the sign, over the curb and out onto the street. The bottom of the car scraped as we went over. When the wheels caught the road, they squealed. I turned around. One of the deputies had his hand on his hip, but nobody drew a gun. No shots were fired. Friendly and Helpful got smaller the farther away we got. Mid kept gaining speed, and there was no sound except the engine pulling harder and harder. Nobody chased us. They just watched us go. Mid ran a light at the end of the block, but nobody was coming. Nobody hit us. We were not killed. I couldn't believe it. We were gone.

■ ■ ■

At first, Alice hadn't wanted a kid, either. In fact, while we were dating, I was the one who talked about having kids, who would sketch out what it could look like: evenings at a ball game, vacations in the national parks. She'd listen but say she'd never really imagined having kids. I used to tell her I could see maybe a thirteen-year-old girl and a ten-year-old boy, the two of them often enough friends, his sister explaining the world to him when he asked nicely. Someone he could eventually go to for bra-strap advice. But I was playing with dolls. It was for some other time. It was an easy fantasy to have.

And then the morning after our wedding, driving east and headed for the beaches, for a quick honeymoon we couldn't afford, Alice started talking. We were riding through the sandhills and the military bases, fighter jets coasting across the sky like impossible models. She'd had a dream the night before, she said, about one of our friends who'd been at the wedding, a woman so pregnant you thought she might give birth right there while we cut the cake. I dreamed she lost it, Alice said. The baby. I remember what the light looked like while she told me, all that new summer green, the silhouette of another jet taking off, another one coming right behind it. It made me want a child, she said. It made me start thinking about the rest of our lives.

At that moment I wanted badly to think only about being

married to Alice, about sitting by the hotel pool with a gin and tonic in an insulated mug. I wanted to think about driving home four days later, married, walking through the front door of our same house and back into our same lives, just glued together a little more firmly now. I wanted to think about putting a roof on in a couple of years. I wanted to think about sometime we might go to Italy. And I said so, a few days after we got back. I just want to be married to you for a little while, I said. I want to do that first. She said that was fine. She apologized, even. But we'd set some kind of clock, I knew: We were headed for Collar or Cholera, Orange or Orangina. No matter what game we made of it, I was pretty sure I knew where we'd end up.

■ ■ ■

I said, "Mid, you have to go back." He'd turned off A1A, and we were aimed inland. I was starting with reason. I felt nothing close to reasonable.

"Forget it," he said.

"We can't go on the run in this thing," I said. "They can probably see it from space."

"I know that."

"We can't go on the run at all," I said.

"I know."

"So we have to go back."

There was nobody behind us. There was almost nobody on the road at all. He said, "Let me ask you a question."

"OK," I said.

"Do you own a gun?"

"What?"

"Easy one, Big Walter. Do you own a gun?"

"No," I said.

"Perfect. Neither do I. So we can't really be on the run here. Nobody goes on the run without at least a pistol."

I said, "But you can't really think—"

"This is a planning session. All we're doing right now is planning our next move."

"Mid," I said. "This is pretty straightforward. They'll find us, they'll set up a roadblock—they have guns, alright? That's who has guns."

"No real need to plan, then, under your plan."

"That wasn't a plan."

He said, "Let me tell you something about daughters."

"No," I said. "No. I need you to tell me you're in there, instead. Tell me you understand what you're doing."

He was driving with his knees. He said, "How about *you* tell *me* something about what's happening right now. How about I ask the questions?"

"You're driving away from state agents who tried to arrest you. Plus the St. Augustine Beach Sheriff's Department. You're resisting arrest."

"I'm fleeing the scene," he said.

"Whatever you want to call it," I said.

"Good. That's what I thought was going on, too."

"This isn't the kind of thing you get away with," I said, watching gas stations go by out the window, pay phones bolted into the ground next to the air and vacuum pumps. I could dive out of the car, roll to a stop, call Alice. "Unless you plan on sailing to Cuba and living the rest of your life there. Which you're not. Right?"

"I'm not. But I like where your head is. Do me a favor and check in the glove compartment there, will you?"

"What for?"

"Open it up. I have something for you."

"What was all that back there about a deal?"

"Just open up the glove, alright?"

I looked inside. I found the owners' manual for the car, a tire gauge, and a flashlight. "There's a flashlight," I said.

"That's handy. We might need that."

I held it out for him to see. "It's not that big," I said.

He said, "Keep digging."

I found a box, like a check box from the bank, but taller. It was about the size of a brick. "This?"

"That," he said. "Yes. Open it."

I felt the engine in my spine. He checked both sides of an intersection as we came up to it, ran another light. The scrub outside the window smeared by. We were the only people on earth. I opened the box. Inside were hundred-dollar bills, all stacked up. They were squeezed perfectly into the space.

"Happy birthday," he said.

"You can't possibly—"

"What that is," he said, "is a little something nobody can ever find. A little something to tide you through."

"You definitely can't do this."

"I definitely already did. Too late."

I flipped a few corners like playing cards. "How much is in here?" I said.

"Sixty-thousand-some-odd. I wanted it to be seventy-five, but it wouldn't fit."

I said, "Can we please stop the car?"

"Not yet."

"You don't think whoever ends up in your books is going to see sixty thousand missing?"

"Twice that. There's a box for Carolyn, too. And no, I do not."

"And why is that?"

He said, "Work it all the way through."

"Because it's not on the books," I said.

"Hey, there we are. On to the bonus round."

"So you're in all of it," I said. "Right? Island? The cops? The undercover shit? Have you been in it all along?"

"It's not like that," he said.

"What is it like?"

"I'm not going to tell you. Which is better, by the way, because that way you won't know."

I said, "I think I'm owed some kind of—"

"Listen to me," he said. "They still don't have anything. Everything they've got is circumstantial. Secondhand."

I couldn't get all the way to being angry with him, which pissed me off. The problem was that it left me too alone, too stranded. And there was that same blank want, back again, filling up in me like water. I said, "Are you not getting that you just left the scene of the crime?"

"That was not my crime. We both know that. That was the scene of someone else's crime."

"*Do* we both know that?"

"Are you accusing me of stealing my own machine?"

"I don't know what to accuse you of," I said. "I don't know what the fuck is happening. You have to tell me. I'm here. I'm in the goddamn car, too."

"You're fine. I took you against your will."

I wondered if that would be enough. I said, "But are we talking about—what are we talking about here?"

"It's only ever money," he said. "Nobody ever gets hurt. That's why I hated what went on at Island. You don't want actual police showing up around actual kids. Those jackasses, selling dope out of the back of the kitchen. What idiots. They can't have been clearing more than a couple grand a week."

"Is it drugs?" I said. "Is that what all this is?"

"Look. Between you and me and anybody else who can count to four, Hurley's got to have a field or two out in the swamp somewhere. The crocus shit can't be the only thing paying him. But it doesn't matter. It's all just money. Just numbers. Move little packets from one thing to the next. Do it enough times and finally not everybody knows where all the little packets are anymore, and you can put a few away. That's all. It's pretty simple laundry. You know how this works."

"I don't know how it works," I said.

"You did it for a living!"

"I sold loans."

"Call it what you want. That's the same thing."

"It's hardly the same thing."

"I thought you had expertise in this field," he said. "I thought you guys knew all about this."

"Is that why I'm down here?" I said. "Is that why you brought me on? So I could mop up after whatever the fuck this all is?"

"I brought you down here because you needed a job and place to live, and we had those things. There is nothing else. Like I said before, this is an unfortunate sideshow. I did not mean for this to happen. I am truly sorry. I humbly repent."

"How much of it is bullshit?" I said.

"What?"

"Me Kayak. The Twice-the-Ice. How much is bullshit?"

He eased off the gas some. "None of it is. All that is real."

"A sea kayak rental doesn't make a hundred thousand off the books," I said.

"They do fine over there." He slowed at a yellow sign with a silhouette of an alligator on it, turned onto a gravel road. After a hundred yards he stopped the car at a wire cable strung between two sawed-off phone poles. He got out, unhooked it, got back in. It was clear he knew exactly where we were. "I'm not walking you through it," he said. "I'm just not. We want for you not to understand. That way, later on, you can explain, in full, your complete lack of understanding to the authorities." He got us going again, fought the wheel against the ruts in the road. "All you need to know is what you know right now. That Me Kayak, for instance, rents and occasionally sells some generally beat-up sea kayaks for a fair price." He looked over at me. "And I need you to keep those kids on the payroll. Make sure they don't fuck off too much on the job. Make sure they're getting everybody to sign the insurance waiver before they go out."

I said, "Are you committing suicide?"

"Jesus," he said. "No. Not this time. No guardian angels needed, OK? I'm fine."

"You don't seem fine."

"And yet I am," he said, turning again, off the road and onto something that wasn't much bigger than a deer trail.

"What's going to happen to you?" I said.

"I'm optimistic I can still make a trade," he said. "Just need to row up a few more ducks."

"What kind of trade?"

"Couple of guys on the commission might be persons of interest in another investigation. A larger investigation. And I might have some useful information for somebody who wanted it."

I held the money in my lap. I was back in the kitchen, our old kitchen, and Alice was coming around the corner with the test kit, asking if I was sure. There was nothing I could do to stop what was happening. The inside of my head was completely lit up, every circuit flashing full. "Pete Brett?" I said.

"That was actually separate. That was when I thought I could take care of everything on my own."

"You were going behind Friendly and Helpful—"

"And now I'm not."

"Except they're who we're running away from."

"This isn't running away," he said. "This is buying time."

I said, "Persons of interest in what way?"

"You really don't want to know."

"Try me."

"Short version is they siphon off airline-grade diesel from a few regional airports and then resell it at some gas stations they've got between here and the Georgia line. They don't see most of the taxes that way. Pretty sweet deal, really. Friendly and Helpful think they're hooked into some Baltic crime syndicate, but I'm almost positive they're just assholes stealing gas."

I wanted to say: Let's go find Carolyn. We can figure something else out. What I said instead was: "Are you hooked into all that, too?"

"Hell no, man. What do you take me for, a thief?"

We broke out of the woods and into a clearing. There was a metal barn, and behind it a long flat field of mown grass, a windsock out at the far end. The door on the barn slid back and then there was Hank, the parachutist, standing in the open door. The back wall was open, too, and light flooded through around him. "No," I said. "You don't know him. You can't."

"Of course I do. Why not?"

"He flies up the beach—"

"Everybody knows him. We had a gig lined up to sell his ultralight things, but it didn't work out."

"What's he doing here?"

"I asked him to be here today in case things became complex."

"So you knew all this was coming?"

"I got the money out after they took me in the first time, if that's what you're asking. I wanted to be ready."

"For this?"

"Among other possibilities."

I said, "Where are you going?"

He got out, tilted his seat forward, rummaged around in the back until he came out with that same pink duffel. Delton's. "Nowhere," he said. "I'm going nowhere. Tell the cops I'm all theirs as soon as I'm done."

"When will I talk to the police?"

"You said it yourself. You can see this thing from space. You'll probably get pulled over on the way back home."

"Fuck you," I said.

"You don't mean that," he said. The car was still running. "Tell Carolyn this was not my original plan. Tell Alice I'm sorry. Tell her I knew what she wanted, and I ran you over anyway. And tell the kids at Island the state has a goddamn camera back there. No sense in me holding up my end anymore." He leaned in, took hold of my shoulder. "I'll see you in a couple days. This won't even make the papers. I'll be back to help you get everything straightened out. No worries, alright? You know how to get back home?" The question seemed made from some other language. He pointed behind the car. "Turn right at the end of the driveway. Turn right at the end of the road. Go straight until you hit the ocean. Turn right again." I held where I was. I pushed my feet against the floorboard to make sure it was still there. "I'm sorry, Walter," he said. "I really am. But sometimes this is how it goes." He opened the duffel, moved things around in there, and then zipped it back closed. He said, "That kid'll break Olivia's heart, by the way. You know that's what's coming."

"What?"

"He's the nicest boy in the world, but she can't even drive. How long do you think that'll last?"

"No idea," I said. Like every other thing in the world.

"She's a smart kid," he said. "If you talked to her, she'd listen."

"Why me?"

"She likes you," he said.

"She likes *you*," I said. "You let her stay with him."

"It's not the same."

"What would I tell her that would make any difference?"

Hank slid the door open a little further, and the metal groaned. There were planes in there with their wings folded up. "You're right," Mid said. "Never mind. I'll call you later, OK? I'll call Carolyn. Tell her I'll call." Then he turned around and walked away, toward the barn, or the hangar, or whatever it was. He shook Hank's hand. The two of them walked through the building and out to the grass runway, where I saw there were already two parachutes set up, two buggies. Mid got himself strapped into one of the carts, and Hank climbed onto the other, his usual ride, and soon enough Mid was rolling out across the grass at what seemed like far too slow a speed until he bumped up into the air anyway, a white wing over his head, blue letters and numbers along one edge like a sailboat sail. He went up like he was tied to a string somebody was pulling. Hank followed, the POW-MIA chute unfurling behind him, and then he was off the ground, too, and they flew out toward the treeline, engines whining away, and then I couldn't see them anymore, and then I couldn't hear them, either. They had vanished. Where had they gone? the cops would want to know. Away, I'd tell them. Did you see which direction? West, maybe, I'd say. Inland.

It was our flyer, I'd tell Alice.

It was not, she'd say.

It was.

Of course it was, she'd say.

I sat in the car, cool air blowing on my face and out Mid's open door. I checked the gas gauge: Full enough. I could sit there a while longer. I was somewhere in Florida in a vandalized Camaro with a box of hundred-dollar bills in my lap. I didn't have any idea at all about what to do next. I looked through the barn to the field, hoping hard that something would come to me. What were you doing? Alice would want to know. Waiting, I'd say.

■ ■ ■

At the end of the gravel road I turned toward the interstate instead of the beach. It was like somebody'd spun me around a couple of times, hollered out go. I took inventory: Mid was gone. I needed to call Alice. She had the cell. She had the car. I had the Camaro and the cash and who the hell knew what in the trunk. Illegal furs. Automatic rifles. Bodies. I stopped at a fruit stand, got out to look. Jumper cables. The little doughnut spare. Nothing else. They were selling twenty-five pound bags of oranges at the fruit stand. I bought one, put it in the trunk. A mile down the road I knew it was a mistake, knew that when the cops asked, the dude would remember. The Camaro. The huge sack of oranges. All those oranges, he'd say. Just for himself.

What plan I had was to turn around, though, before anybody was hot on my trail, before anybody was asking around about a person who looked like me. I needed a little pried-open space first, was all. I was headed back as soon as I knew what I might say to somebody—Carolyn, Alice, Friendly and Helpful—when they asked. Some version of: I have done this wrong. All of it. I apologize. My wife is pregnant. Here is the car. He left me there, flew away. He did not say where he was going. No, I'm not helping him. No, I don't think he'd hurt anybody. No, I don't think he'd hurt himself. Because I asked him. Because I thought I should. The cash was just like this, in this box. Give it to orphans. To amputees. To orphaned amputees. I don't know anything. I have never known anything. This is what I'm trying to tell you.

I drove. I watched the sky for Mid.

At the interstate there was an old Howard Johnson, light blue with an orange roof. I pulled in. She'd kill me, I knew. I pulled in anyway. I parked the Camaro behind a Dumpster. I had the urge to cover it with branches, but there weren't any. I found the front desk. I paid cash. That part was simple enough. My room was on the top floor, the third floor. I passed the cleaning people with their cart. It was still morning, or something like it. Inside, my ceiling featured the long fifties slant of the roof, triangled windows above some sliding doors that led out onto four feet of concrete balcony. Brown carpet. Two queen beds. I lay down on one. There was a water stain in the ceiling, which felt unfortunate, like a bad letter. I switched to the other bed. I could hear the trucks out on the highway. Did fathers do this? Was this fatherly behavior? I called the front desk and ordered a patty melt and a 7UP from the restaurant. I turned on the TV, set it to the channel that ran previews of the movies you could order. We owned no furniture. Alice was bleeding, Mid had flown away. Once the channel had cycled the preview through so many times I knew the exact sequence, I called Alice.

"How are you?" she said.

I started peeling an orange. "Terrible," I said.

"How's Mid?"

"Better than I am," I said. "For the most part, anyway."

"Did you meet with the police?"

"Yes."

"And?"

Half the movie trailers had stars in them I'd never seen, too-skinny twentysomethings with perfect skin and excellent teeth. I was losing track of who was supposed to be famous. I was already out of touch with the BOJ's generation, and her generation wasn't even here. "I'm in a Howard Johnson," I said.

"You're what?"

"In a HoJo." I felt myself measuring out the words. I put the orange down on the nightstand. "I'm out by the interstate. I checked in. I got a room."

"If this is a joke, I don't get it."

"It's not a joke. I'm in a hotel. I have the car. Mid's gone." It felt better, saying it out loud like that. It also felt true, which arrived with its own set of problems.

She said, "I don't know what any of that means."

"I don't know what it means, either," I said. "He drove me out into the woods and got out of the car, and Hank was waiting for him in some hanger, and they both flew away. I'm pretty sure he had it planned."

"What woods?"

"When we got to the Twice-the-Ice, the police tried to arrest him. He drove off. I tried to talk him out of it. Then he gave me sixty thousand dollars and flew away."

She said, "Flew away in what?"

"A parachute. Like the other one, like Hank's. He had one waiting for him. Another one." I looked around the room, which seemed to be getting dimmer. I wondered if they'd built all the Howard Johnsons the same in any given year—if they'd just traveled the same set of blueprints around the country, and if somewhere in Wichita right now there was someone sitting in room 303, talking to his wife, and trying to keep his head from separating from his body. "I don't think I feel right," I said.

"What do you mean? How?"

"Like I could be losing my mind, too," I said.

"Are you? Did those things really happen?"

"Yes," I said. "Also, I bought some oranges."

"Stop screwing around. Are you screwing around?"

"I really did buy oranges," I said. I pulled a section off and put it in my mouth. "They're pretty good."

"Give me the number where you are. I'm coming to get you."

"Don't," I said.

"What do you mean, don't? I'm coming to get you right now."

"I wanted to be still. Just for a minute."

"Which one are you in?" she said.

"Which one what?"

"Which Howard Johnson." I could tell she was trying to keep her voice even, that she was upset. I'd upset her. It made sense.

"I don't know," I said. I thought it was possible I might be remembering what was happening instead of it actually happening. "This one."

"Walter, stick with me, OK? Are you still in the state?"

"Yeah," I said. "I don't think we drove more than a few exits one way or the other." I checked the desk for a pad of paper or a phone book, but there wasn't anything. "Listen," I said. "Don't tell Delton."

"Of course we have to tell her," she said. "We have to tell everybody."

I said, "He could still come back. He said he would."

"Have you called the police?"

"No."

"You need to call the police."

"We need to call Carolyn," I said.

"I'll do that."

"He said she'd understand. He said this wasn't the way he had it set up originally."

"He said she'd *understand*?"

"Maybe not exactly that way," I said. "Let's wait until you get here."

"For what?"

"For everything. To tell her. To tell anybody. Can we just wait until you're here?"

She said, "Did he say where he was going?"

"No."

"Did you ask?"

"I tried."

"What *happened*?"

"That's what I'm trying to figure out."

"You don't sound like yourself," she said. "I'm worried about you."

"He told me he needed a few empty days," I said. "I think I need that, too."

"Read me the number off the phone you're holding, OK? Read it to me right now."

I did that. She wrote it down. She made me read it again to make sure it was right. She told me not to go anywhere, and I asked her where she thought I might go, and she told me again: Stay there. Stay right where you are. She made me promise. I promised. She hung up the phone.

Most of the movies on the preview channel seemed to want to be about two people having a very fine time until some manner of adversity or confusion arrives, and then one of them has to run through the rain or the night or both in order to set things right. There was also porn, but after a few times through, those plots seemed to be about the same as the regular movies. I sat on the floor between the two beds so I could see the light flashing from the TV, but not the picture itself. That helped. Alice telling me not to go anywhere—all along I'd wanted to go somewhere. Everything was upside down now. I pulled a comforter off one of the beds and lay down. Sure I'd wanted there to have been a third buggy for me, a third parachute. Sure I'd wanted to be off the ground, too. But then also this: All I wanted right then, in the entire open landscape of my life, was for there to be a knock on the door of my room and for Alice to be there, pregnant, on the other side.

■ ■ ■

Things that had come out of Delton's mouth in the week she'd been living with us: Kids were sending naked pictures of each other back and forth on their cell phones, but she wasn't. Not because she thought it was wrong, but because she thought it'd be too easy for somebody to hit the wrong button. Kids were off birth control and using the rhythm method because birth control made them fat. She was sticking with the pill. Anything else was too risky. Some kids had sworn off having actual sex. Not for religious reasons—it was just easier. They were doing everything else, everything but. She was trying to shock us. She wanted us to have to ask what "everything but" was. Maybe she thought we'd never been to high school, had never parked a car at the St. Jude's Catholic Church playground, never frantically, desperately tried to decide whether asking Janet Rosenthal for a little help getting her pants down would break the mood.

"Some kids are getting their genitals pierced," she'd said. "But I don't think I will." She pushed her sleeve up past her tattoo like that'd be plenty, thanks. We sat at the dinner table and acted like we pierced our genitals all the time. We told her we liked her tattoo. She said Mid and Carolyn had threatened to make her sand it off.

Alice brought Delton with her to the hotel. They knocked, and I stayed on the floor, trying to remember if I'd thrown the deadbolt. "Walter," Alice said. "Let us in."

"I'm coming," I said, but I stayed still.

She knocked some more. "Come on," she said.

"Yeah," Delton said. "Open up."

There was an escape plan on the inside of my door. In case of fire. Somebody'd hand-drawn a long red arrow telling me where to go, but the outline of the building was backwards from the way I'd pictured it, and I couldn't figure out whether the map was actually wanting me to run in the direction of the arrow as shown or if in fact I was supposed to go the opposite way. That, and the map had me in 304. I thought I was in 303. When I opened the door, I checked: 303. I had the wrong map.

"You've been sleeping," Alice said.

"I was going in and out."

"Cool hotel," said Delton. She was wearing gray cutoffs and a tuxedo shirt. It was a huge relief to see her. I didn't know why. "Does it have a pool?"

"You can see it from the room," I said.

"Does it have a diving board?"

"Come look for yourself." I stood back from the door. "I have oranges, if you want any."

"I hate oranges," she said.

"You do?"

"If you'd grown up here, you'd hate them, too. Is there a soda machine anywhere?"

I said, "By the stairs, I think."

"Can I borrow a dollar?" I gave her a few ones. "Either of you want anything?" she said.

I said, "How about a bucket of ice?"

She said, "How about a bucket?" I got the bucket from the bathroom, brought it back and handed it to her. "Coming right up," she said, and walked off toward the stairs. I swung the latch around so the door would close but not shut. Alice came in and sat down, and there we were.

"That was graceful," I said. "Her leaving us alone."

"That's how she is."

"She's taking it well?"

"She's not taking it at all," Alice said. "She's ignoring it. Plus, she's convinced he'll be back in an hour. She thinks it's not a big deal."

"You're mad at me," I said.

"You know, I was trying not to be, but that's not working out so well."

"This is not my fault," I said.

"This part is. The me-rescuing-you-from-a-hotel-room is."

"I don't need rescuing."

"If all you have is a hundred oranges, you need rescuing." She folded one leg up under her. She was looking everywhere in the room but at me. "Tell me you're not covering for him right now."

"I'm not."

"Are you stalling for him?"

I thought about that. I was, after all, in the Howard Johnson instead of at the police station, turning the car over so they could dust it for fingerprints. "He said he had things to take care of," I said.

"What things?"

"He was talking about telling the cops about these guys on the commission who're selling illegal gas. He thinks he can trade that for some get-out-of-jail-free deal."

She said, "You have to be kidding me."

"I want to be," I said.

"What else is there?"

"I don't know."

"Bullshit. How could you not know?"

I wanted to crawl into the bed and sleep. I wanted to stand in the shower and use every one of the little prewrapped soaps, one after the other. "He already had the thing waiting on the runway," I said. "The parachute. I don't know a hell of a lot more than you do."

"But why are you *here*? Why didn't you come home?"

I wanted to make an apology out of something, knit it together somehow. I wanted to tell her about sickness and health. "I ended up here," I said. "This is what happened."

"Is this about the baby?"

"No," I said.

She got up from her chair, walked over to the glass doors. "You know what we were doing when you called?"

"What?"

"Watching giraffes give birth. Online. It was some website Delton found." She slid the door open, stepped outside, leaned over the railing. It felt dangerous. "They're so relaxed," she said. "They just stand in the grass, and then they start breathing a little more deeply, and then, bang! Baby giraffe. Like it doesn't hurt at all." She leaned out farther. "Did you park the car behind the Dumpster?"

"Yes."

"You *hid* it?"

"I guess so."

"I don't believe this," she said. She was back inside now. "How could you be doing this?"

"Do you want to see the money?" I said.

"What money?"

"The box of money. The sixty thousand."

"You were serious? That exists?"

I opened the little drawer in the desk. I'd been keeping the box in there with the Bible, which somehow seemed the right choice when I first walked in the room.

She said, "We have to go see Carolyn. We have to go over there right now."

"It's not about the baby," I said. "It's bigger than that."

"There is no bigger than that," she said.

I held the box out. "This?" I said. "This isn't?"

She sat down on a bed, leaned forward until her head was

between her knees. Her hair nearly touched the floor. “It’s all part of the same thing,” she said. “I don’t know how you don’t see that.”

“I tried to stop him.”

“Like hell you did.”

“That’s not fair.”

She sat back up. “This doesn’t have anything to do with fair. If this were fair, I wouldn’t be here right now. We wouldn’t be doing this.”

“I don’t not want her,” I said.

Something played through her face I didn’t recognize. “That’s the best you can do?” she said. “That’s what you spent your morning at Howard Johnson coming up with?”

Delton knocked on the door. She had the bucket of ice and two cans of a brand of ginger ale I’d never seen before. She went in the bathroom, came back out with three plastic cups in plastic sleeves. She poured one for each of us. I wondered how long she’d been out there—if she might have been listening behind the door. She said, “Don’t worry, you guys. He pulls stuff like this all the time.”

She was wrong. She’d lived with him for fifteen years, and I’d worked for him for six weeks, and still I knew she was wrong. “Are you OK?” I asked her.

She took a long sip of ginger ale. She flashed me a too-big smile. “Are you?” she said.

“No,” I said. “Not at all.”

“Don’t tell her that,” said Alice.

“Tell her,” Delton said. “Tell her everything.”

“What have you told her?” I asked Alice.

"Nothing," Delton said. "She said you guys got pulled over or something, and then Dad took off."

"That's about what there is," I said. "That's the problem."

■ ■ ■

And if you did pull the young man aside to have a talk with him, to speak as men speak, what would you say? Nic, she's fifteen. You're nineteen. Brainwise, yes, this still leaves her a good bit out in front of you, but that doesn't matter so much as you being *nineteen*. Finally there's no getting around that. You operate in an entirely different era. So come up with a good way to let her down easy, and then go to Dollar Night somewhere on your fake ID and find a nice girl your own age who will take you back to her dorm room and make you listen to her albums, who will take pity on you, who will invite you into her single bed. Do not be dating a fifteen-year-old child who, as soon as she wises up or ages six months, whichever comes first, will hopefully dump you on your ass for someone sophisticated enough for her. Get out before she realizes what the deal is with that whole Vespa–through–the–streets–of–St. Augustine thing.

And that's of course if she's lucky. If she's unlucky, you either do or don't speak with the boy, and he either ignores you or it makes no difference, and he lands at Dollar Night anyway, and without telling her, because that's what he's been doing all along. Not because he's vicious. Because he's nineteen. Or it's even less his fault: He's at a party one night, a party no parent in her right mind would let a fifteen-year-old go to, and for whatever reason she hasn't lied. She's asked for permission. They've said no. So there's Delton at home, or in her foiled-over room at the condo, and she's got three wishes, each one of them that she not be fifteen anymore. She doesn't yet know that it doesn't ever get any better. And while she's uploading adorable photographs of when Nic took her for that picnic at Fort Matanzas—there they are in sunglasses; there they are laughing, laughing—he's standing across the keg from a girl, a kind of quiet girl, and pretty, probably, because the new girl is always pretty. He finds out she's in Deaf Ed, too, that she has a deaf sister. Nic's stepbrother is deaf, of course, and what that's like is so hard to explain to someone who doesn't already know that he usually doesn't even bother. But she knows. So he tells her. And while they talk he's deciding no one has ever really *gotten* him like this before, which is what he explains to Delton over pancakes a couple of mornings later at the IHOP. At least he breaks up with her in person. At least he tells her at all. He's not vicious. But there's our little girl, pouring too much boysenberry syrup over her food, listening to this boy break up with her for someone she surely can't compete with, someone who can drive and vote and go to fucking *college* and even under certain circumstances probably even rent a *car,* and the thing is—the real problem is that her parents will have been right all along, *the whole time,* which more than anything else is what's going to play over her inner airwaves while she fails to fall asleep at night for the next ten weeks. They were right. He was too old. She was too young. They were right all along.

So let her change her name. Let her get a tattoo. Let her pierce what she does or doesn't want to pierce and let her date this boy four years older than she is, so much older that you probably lie about his age at parties so people won't judge you, won't score your parenting. It probably never matters what you tell her, how right you are or were, how clearly you could see this one coming the very minute it walked through the door. She was always going to do it. She is always going to do it all, and it doesn't make any difference: That's still your kid in there, hobbled by the world, completely by herself, and you cannot save her from any of it, and you never could.

■ ■ ■

The three of us stood on the doorstep, looking somber. Delton rang the bell and Carolyn opened the door, and we knew we'd screwed it up right away: She thought he was dead. She started saying no, no, and her legs went out from under her, and she caught herself on the wall, slid down to the floor. Alice went right at her, telling her it was OK, that *he* was OK, which was only true so far as we knew, but that was the only thing anybody could have said. Alice held her until she calmed down, caught her breath, and in that little space Alice was able to explain that he hadn't died, that he was only a fugitive, that everything would somehow be alright. The twins showed up in the hallway wanting to know what was going on. Delton took them away. Carolyn wiped her face with her sleeve. The little rug they had on the floor was all piled up underneath her. She pushed her hair out of her face. It was the same move I'd seen Alice make a thousand times. I was still standing in the door. I hadn't moved. I could smell the newness of the house. "A fugitive from what?" Carolyn wanted to know.

Alice wanted to call the police, wanted to tell them he was incapacitated, wanted to declare him a missing person. It was Carolyn who wouldn't do it. "He's not missing," she said. "He's an asshole."

I assumed we wouldn't have any need to call the police. I stood in the front of the house, in the big bay window, waiting for six or eight squad cars and a SWAT van to pull into Pelican Pines, roll down the empty road to the house. I had an idea about opening the door, putting my hands up. I had a speech that addressed my innocence. I could deliver it to the SWAT team and to Alice at the same time. The basic problem: I was trying to make sense of something that couldn't be made sense of. Mid, flying over the trees. Mid, master of the corner hustle. Mid, leaving Delton at Nic's house, and then leaving her with us, and the growing possibility that both of those moves had been the right ones.

Delton called Nic. The twins went out to the backyard to try kicking things off a stepladder. Maggie decided she wanted to swim. It took twenty minutes to get her suited and floatied and buoyed, by which time she no longer cared about swimming, but Carolyn sent her out there anyway, enlisted us to help watch her. The grass around the pool almost glowed green. The sky was more white than blue. It was hard not to think Mid was about to land in the backyard. Carolyn wanted to know if anybody wanted Bloody Marys. I said sure, what the hell. Alice said it hardly seemed like the time, and Carolyn ignored her. She made a pitcher of V8 and hot sauce and lemon juice, and she set out a bottle of vodka and some tall glasses. Delton came through and wanted one. Carolyn said no problem, but no booze. Delton poured herself a glass, and then she stared Carolyn down, very carefully topped her drink with an ounce or so of vodka.

"Olivia," Alice said.

"Look," Delton said. "Delton has two mommies." It wasn't mean the way she said it, but it still hung in the air wrong. She looked a little sorry, and then she disappeared off into the house.

Carolyn watched her go. "I quit," she said.

"You don't," Alice said.

Carolyn poured a drink for herself. "You don't think I'm doing it right," she said.

Alice said, "I didn't say anything like that."

"An hour ago I thought he was dead, OK? Give me a few minutes, and I'll call the police. Give me half an hour of peace and we can call anybody you want."

"That was Walter's argument," Alice said. "Back at the hotel."

"Let's just sit down," Carolyn said. "Outside. Half an hour. You can set the clock."

We got ourselves huddled in what shade there was from the

table umbrella. Maggie paddled side to side across the shallow end, and the twins worked through an elaborately scored contest having to do with how high up the ladder the thing was that was being kicked, plus how far it went when you kicked it. Beach balls. Plastic flowerpots. There was a lot of subjectivity. Much disagreement. They seemed like kids. I said so.

"They are kids," Alice said. "They don't seem like it. They are."

"Be nice to him," Carolyn said. "He was the last person to see Mid alive."

"How is that funny?" Alice said.

"It isn't," Carolyn said.

"That's not funny, either," said Alice.

Carolyn worked on her drink. She stared off into the yard. She said, "Did he leave you money, too? A ton of cash in a box?"

"Oh, God," Alice said. "Really?"

"Yes," I said.

"I found ours this morning," said Carolyn. "He's never coming back."

I said, "He's coming back."

Carolyn said, "How do you know that?"

I felt heavy in my chair. I said, "I just have a feeling."

"A feeling," Carolyn said. "You'd at least call, right? You'd have probably called every hour on the hour."

"Who knows what he would have done?" said Alice.

"He'd have called."

"Here's what I'd like to know," Alice said.

Carolyn looked at her. "What's that?"

Alice said, "Did you know how fucked up he was before we moved down?"

Carolyn waited a long time before she answered. "I knew he wasn't right," she said. "I didn't know this."

"OK," Alice said, and it was clear she was spinning a little bit. "That's fair. That's good. But could I ask you another question?"

I said, "Alice, hold on."

"It's fine," Carolyn said. "Let her do it."

"*Let* her do it?" Alice said. "I get to decide what to do."

I said, "That's not what she meant."

Alice turned back to Carolyn. "How the fuck could you not know?"

Carolyn set her glass down on the table. "Maybe the same way you ended up pregnant without Walter really wanting to be," she said. "I just went on ahead with my life."

"Take it back," Alice said.

"You take it back. I told you, alright? I told you almost from the moment you got here that he wasn't himself."

"I thought you meant he needed help," Alice said. "I thought you meant he might need a therapist. I had no idea you meant he was some kind of criminal mastermind."

Carolyn said, "I did mean I thought he needed help."

"He needs something."

"He's not a criminal mastermind."

"That's obvious now, isn't it?" said Alice.

"How about you back off a little?" Carolyn said. "Your husband's right here. We know precisely where he is. He's not gone. Mid's *gone*. Do you get that?"

"Wait," I said. "Please."

"Don't you fucking lecture me, Leecy," Carolyn said.

Alice said, "You're the one sitting here doing deck chairs

while—" She stopped. I knew she didn't mean this. I at least knew she didn't mean it this way.

"While what?" said Carolyn.

"Nothing."

"Is it anything I can't figure out? Are you getting ready to point anything out to me that I can't figure out on my own?"

Maggie started splashing water out over the concrete. She looked like she was trying to empty the pool. "I wanted a baby," Alice said, maybe to Carolyn, maybe to me. "OK? I wanted a child. I knew I was supposed to have a child."

"And I thought he had things under control," Carolyn said. "That's why I didn't say anything specific."

"But why did you think that?"

"Because he always had before."

Alice said, "Do you know where he is?"

"No."

"Do you know places where he could be?"

"Who are you, the police?"

"I'm your sister," Alice said. "Why aren't you more worried?"

"I'm worried," said Carolyn. "I'm plenty worried. But you don't know how it goes with him. You're sort of always worried. It's a little hard to tell the difference between this and anything else."

"That just can't be true," Alice said.

"It's been true," Carolyn said. She leaned back in her chair. "Lately, anyway."

One of the twins kicked the ladder instead of the flowerpot, and went down in a pile on the lawn. She was holding her foot. What rattled through my mind was that if he didn't come back—if we never saw him again, or if she never let him back in the house, then this was what our life would be. These kids. Carolyn. Alice and me on the sidelines, only partly able to help. "Mom," the standing twin called, and Carolyn went to tend to her wounded child. She got down on one knee to assess the damage. She convinced Sophie-Jane to stand up, test it out, take a few limping steps. Carolyn told them to stop kicking things off the ladder. They complained. She backtracked, told them at least to be more careful, please, to stop kicking the ladder itself, and they said OK. Delton turned up in the back door. Carolyn saw her. She said, "If you drank that, I'm going to kill you."

"There's a van," Delton said.

"What?"

"In front of the house," she said. "A van. Just sitting there."

Carolyn got the twins to watch Maggie, and the rest of us went to the front window. Sure enough, there was a van, plain navy blue with tinted windows, parked across the street from the house, and down a sewer inlet or two. Why anybody would bother with secrecy in a neighborhood of a single house was beyond me, but there it was: An unmarked van. "Are they watching us?" Delton asked.

"Probably," I said.

Alice said, "This is so far out of control."

"We'll fix it," I said.

"How?" she said.

"We will," I said, but I had no idea. I just knew that was what you were supposed to say. You were supposed to say it would get better. You were supposed to believe that it would.

"We'll go get him," Carolyn said. "We'll go looking for him."

"I know where we can start," said Delton.

"Where?" I said.

"Nic's place," she said. "You can't find it. I got lost twice trying to get there last week— I mean, we got lost trying to find it when we went. When we went before."

"You're grounded," Carolyn said. "And your dad found it."

"He had help. Also, I'm already grounded."

"You were on restriction. Now you're grounded."

"You need me to get you there," she said.

"What makes you think that's where he'd be?"

"It's a great place to hide," she said. "And doesn't it seem like him?"

Carolyn closed the blinds, and we all stood in the fake-dark of the room. "Fine," she said. There was some new note in her voice, something worse. "We'll start there. Let's go."

"I thought I was grounded," said Delton.

"You are. Just not right now."

"Excellent," she said.

"Be quiet," Carolyn said. "Go get your sisters ready."

Delton aimed for the backyard. Carolyn looked at her watch. "I didn't even get my half-hour," she said. Alice reached for her, but she slipped away, went off into the house. Alice picked up Carolyn's drink, wiped the table with her sleeve, and then she turned back around, pushed one slat of the blinds back up. "Still there," she said. I thought about Mid being out there, checking things off some list, while we sat in his yard and yelled at each other and drank Bloody Marys and tried to make sure his kids didn't find new ways of maiming themselves. I took Alice's elbow, held on. I expected her to try to pull away, too, to shrug me off, but she held still, did not move at all.

■ ■ ■

We were in Carolyn's SUV, a monster of a thing, and Alice was riding shotgun. I was in the back with the kids. The whole truck smelled like Cheerios and ketchup and karate robes. Delton had her headphones in, and the twins were playing a video game with Maggie. I watched the back of Alice's head, plotted complicated ways to make things up to her—marching bands breaking into formation, spelling out her name.

The van didn't follow us. Carolyn, very much in charge and channeling what I hoped was not yet the ghost of Mid, had everybody put their heads down when we pulled out. I couldn't see how that would have made any serious difference. Still, I kept checking behind us, and we kept being alone. There'd been some talk of not bringing everybody, a conversation about danger and harm's way, but Carolyn shut all that down by saying that wherever we ended up, she was the only one getting out of the car. Alice and I were only there in case of emergency—and we couldn't be there in case of emergency if we were back at the castle watching the kids, so there we all were, the Swiss Family Robinson, marauding and search-partying in leather seats at fifty-five law-abiding miles per hour. Carolyn stopped at stop signs. She signaled to change lanes. A state trooper passed us on the right-hand side and we all waited for the lights, the siren. Nothing.

Once we were on the island and as far south as the second bridge, Delton leaned up between the seats to give directions. Turn there, she said. And there. We left the highway, rode inland. That one, Delton would say, but then change her mind. I was already lost. But she started claiming she recognized landmarks, took us through a few last turns, and finally eased Carolyn onto a sand-and-shell path. We drove a couple hundred yards before the road turned soft. "Put it in four-wheel drive," I said.

"I don't know how," said Carolyn.

"Walter?" Alice said.

"I don't know, either," I said. "I just thought—"

Alice said, "Isn't there a button?"

"I thought so," Carolyn said, looking at the dash.

Delton reached through, pulled a lever next to the shifter. A red 4 lit up on the stick. "It's that thing," she said.

Maggie'd fallen asleep a couple miles back, and the twins were keeping quiet, looking out the windows on either side. They were zen. Carolyn let the truck inch itself forward, and even though it groaned through a few of the wetter patches, we seemed to be making it alright. That kid Robbie had been right that night—the road was not good, and I couldn't help feeling like we'd all have been better off to have Robbie or Hurley or somebody along with us. I was hard-pressed to name what expertise we might be bringing to this mission. Alice had been developing a heightened sense of smell, she'd been saying. The books said that was normal. So we had that and maybe not much else.

I didn't recognize the house from the back. We came up on it suddenly, climbing out of the swamp and into a clearing featuring a long strip of grass and weeds that looked almost built for landing something, even if it did need mowing. There was nobody there—no car by the house, no buggy on the runway, no swath of fabric. No second cart, either. No Hank. No POW chute. I'd expected him even if I hadn't expected anybody else, I realized. He'd pointed at me. So here I was. Carolyn put it in park, closed her eyes, said a prayer to some god—and then she got out of the truck, left the door open, and walked away. The warning chime played until Alice leaned over to pull the door back closed.

Carolyn stood in the high grass and looked at the house, looked up at the sky, then back at the house again. After a while, she sat down. The grass was so tall that we could really only see her head. Delton said, "What's she doing?"

"She's melting down," Alice said.

"Maybe she's just taking a minute," I said.

"Maybe it's both," said Alice.

"I'm going out there," Delton said. "I want to talk to her."

"Me, too," said Sophie-Jane.

"No one's going out there," Alice said. "That was the deal."

Delton said, "I wish Nic was here. He's good with stuff like this."

"Like this?" I said. "Really?"

She said, "He'd have ideas."

Maggie woke up. "I have to go potty," she said.

"Can you wait, sweetheart?" said Alice.

She said, "I have to go now."

"I have a key," Delton said. "I could take her in."

Alice said, "We're not doing that."

"She can't pee in here," I said.

"I can't pee in here," Maggie said, already edging up on tears.

Alice blew a couple of breaths through her fingers. "Here's what we'll do," she said. "Delton and I will take Maggie in to pee, and Uncle Walter will stay out here and keep track of everything else."

"Cool," the twins said.

"Not cool," Alice said. "Just plain and simple. Everybody else stays in the car."

"OK," they said.

"OK?" she said to me.

"OK," I said.

"Nothing happens," she said.

"He's not even here."

She said, "And isn't that the problem?"

Alice got down out of the truck, holding the small of her back with one hand, something I'd seen her do several times in the past few weeks, but somehow hadn't fully processed—and in that moment, I'd never been more aware of her being pregnant. Of her being so apart from me, but so bound to me at the same time. The fact of it tightened the skin across the backs of my hands. The way she walked had changed, I saw, and the way she moved and stood. Her hair was getting longer. Her jawline looked different. Her eyes. And it wasn't the pregnancy itself, all those cells choosing up sides. It was Alice. It was this new Alice. I had missed it. It had been happening without me. But it was right there. And I wanted, suddenly, to tell her there was more I could do. I wanted to tell her I would not flee the scene. I wanted to get out of the truck and get my feet planted in what ground there might be and wrap both my arms around her and push my face into the back of her neck and just see how long that could hold us—see if that would be enough to start.

But she reached back in for Maggie, and all my halfassed gallantry receded into the busy simple need to get the child out, find her a bathroom. The twins unbuckled her and passed her up, and Delton and Alice lifted her to the ground. Maggie took hold of each of their hands. Alice shut the back door, and that fast I was sealed off from her again, had to watch them through the windshield as they passed Carolyn, who glanced up, but maybe didn't really see them. She was too far inside a world of her own. Maggie looked tiny between Delton and

Alice. They swung her up the front steps, making a game out of it. Delton shuffled through her purse, produced a key, jimmied the bolt on the front door and got it open—and they were inside the house, and when the door swung shut again there was only Carolyn, still sitting on the ground, and only Sophie and Jane and me in the truck. And then there was the Crown Vic pulling up beside us, a shimmering mirage, out of nowhere. Friendly and Helpful. It was not quite fear I was having. It was certainty. "Stay here," I told the twins.

"Who's that?" they said.

"They're helping look for your dad."

"It's the cops," they said.

I said, "In a manner of speaking." With just the three of us in it the truck seemed gigantic, insane. I got out. "Stay here," I told them again.

"She told you to stay here, too," they said.

"I know," I said, and shut the door. I walked to the Crown Vic and waited for them to roll down the window. Which did not happen. Instead, Friendly got out and stood next to me. Neither of us looked at each other. We both looked at Carolyn, who was still watching the sky.

"You're not supposed to be here," Friendly said. He was tan. Everybody was tan. "You know something we don't?"

"I doubt it," I said.

"He's supposed to be here. Not you."

"Which is why you're here?"

"Which is why we're here."

"I haven't understood one piece of this the whole time," I said.

"That's what Mid keeps telling us. Hopefully that'll be true."

"It is true."

Friendly looked around. "This place is big. What the hell is it?"

"Fishing cabin?" I said.

"It'd be a lot of fishing."

"Then I don't know," I said, and I felt the hum set up along my spine.

Helpful got out, too, and pointed back behind us at the trees. "Adding a few to the dance card," he said.

"What?" Friendly said.

Helpful held up a radio, but he didn't need to. Two green-and-white squad cars—maybe the same cars from that morning—came down the road and parked at the edge of the clearing. Green-shirted officers got out. With rifles. Friendly stared them down, said, "Motherfuck." He took his sunglasses off and wiped a line of sweat from his forehead. "Who's in the car with you?" he said.

"Me?" I said.

"You."

"Everybody. Some of them are in the house. Maggie had to pee. The youngest."

"What is this, a field trip?"

"Something like that," I said.

"You gotta get them all out of here," he said. "Everybody."

I said, "What's going on?"

"How did those guys end up here?" Friendly asked his partner. Helpful shook his head. "Who needs the goddamn infantry?" Friendly said.

"You need me to get them out of the house?" I asked him.

Friendly said, "Just get everybody the fuck out of the way.

Please." To Helpful, he said, "Any chance of raising their people on the dial, see if we can slow this down some?"

"Already tried," Helpful said. "Nobody's talking."

"I thought he'd at least be ours to bring in," Friendly said.

Helpful said, "Guess not."

"Call somebody," said Friendly. "Call anybody."

We heard him before we saw him. The breeze slacked off and the birds went quiet, and then there was that telltale buzz and whine, and Mid came right over the top of us, low, just above the treetops. He dipped a little at the field before he saw everybody, and then he pulled back up. He was by himself. No Hank. Carolyn stood up. Friendly and Helpful were both already on their phones. Two of the local cops got back in one car, wheeled it around behind the SUV, bumpered us in to where we couldn't go anywhere. They left the lights turning. I went over to explain to them about how Friendly and Helpful actually wanted me to move, but they weren't paying a lot of attention to me. They were both back out of the car, looking up. They were impossibly young. Mid flew over again, this time yelling something down nobody could hear over the top of the engine. He was gesturing, pointing, waving us off, and every time he did the whole rig swung around with the effort of it. His face was red. Cords stood out in his neck. Whatever he was yelling was long and complicated. Instructions, maybe. Accusations and amendments. Alice and Delton came back outside. Alice had Maggie on one hip, and she was trying to keep Delton pinned to the porch railing with her other arm. They were staring. Everybody was. Carolyn tried flagging him, waving him down, and she was screaming at him, telling him to land, calling him a bastard, telling him she loved him. He disappeared again, but we could still hear him. We knew he was coming back. The engine thinned, then swelled, and he flew over a third time. As he passed across the front edge of the clearing, he started shooting. One shot. Another. The cops on the ground scattered, took cover behind the open doors of the squad cars. My whole head emptied out. Something hit the roof of the Crown Vic. They would kill him. They would kill him in front of all of us.

Except something already didn't balance: His gun was funny, for one. It was like he was shooting firecrackers—though they were bigger than that. One hit the ground and did nothing, a black sphere the size of a golf ball. Another landed in front of the squad car that had us parked in, bounced underneath it, rolled out the other side and burst into pink flame. They were flares. He was shooting safety flares. Alice pushed Delton onto the porch floor, got down there with her, held onto Maggie. I opened the door of the SUV that was furthest from all of it, dragged the twins out, ran them up to Alice. "What are you doing?" she wanted to know. I pushed the twins closer to her. It was the only thing I knew to do. I would have pushed them inside her if I could.

Mid was circling now, holding the gun in his left hand and firing cowboy-style, letting his whole arm bounce with each shot. He wasn't even aiming. It was a show. He was laughing. Or singing. The white sail over his head looked like a rip in the sky. The grass was smoldering where the flares burned. He was going to take down the whole forest, the house, everybody. He'd make the news after all. A hundred acres burned to ash. Story at eleven.

And I did not see what happened next so much as imagine

later what it must have been, paint it out by numbers once things had sufficiently slowed: He'd stopped shooting—I knew that much—and as he flew away from us, toward the far end of the field, one of the sheriff's deputies near us stood back up, put his rifle to his shoulder, aimed, and fired. It was a smooth, simple motion. The noise of it. The sheer noise. Nothing happened. Mid flew on. He did not evaporate in a fireball, did not turn, did not try to land. The deputy shouldered the rifle again, and I took off running from the front porch, started counting steps—ten, eleven, twelve—and I focused on his ear, stared at his ear as I got closer and closer, the folds, the pinches of skin, and I was in the air and through him before it ever occurred to me to worry about what would happen after we landed.

We hit so hard that at first I could not tell the difference between ground and sky. I huddled on my side trying to figure out what it might take to breathe again, trying to make note of what I could still feel and what I couldn't. I had grass in my mouth. Blood. I held my arms up at my ears, waiting for them to start beating me, kicking me. I listened for Alice. I saw the rifle lying well away. The cop I'd tackled was still on his back. We'd hit our heads together. I wasn't sure if he was conscious. I saw the deputy who was still standing drawing his pistol, aiming the gun at my chest, yelling at me to freeze, to put my hands in the air, two competing ideas I didn't think it was right to leave me to choose between. I saw he was shaking. It wasn't Mid they were going to kill. It was me.

Over the deputy's shoulder I watched Mid continue on his line down the field, only lower now—lower, I could see, than the tops of the trees—and he did nothing other than sail directly into them. It was hard to call what happened a crash. He did not swerve or bank. He just flew into the trees. The cart hit first, bounced off and fell a few feet, and then the parachute caught him, snagged up in the branches so that the whole rig hung in the air. The engine ran a full beat, maybe two, before it cut off. The only sound left was Carolyn screaming to him, and him not answering. The deputy kept his gun on me. Nothing moved in the cart. Friendly and Helpful had their guns drawn, too, but they were aiming at the deputy. He didn't even look like he'd need to shave every day. The other cops were coming at us on the run, yelling at everyone to wait, to holster their weapons. Carolyn made it to the end of the field, was standing directly under him, and now she was yelling back to us, screaming, "Somebody help!" Begging us. "Somebody do something! *Somebody somebody somebody!*"

Friendly grabbed the deputy who had his pistol out, spun him around, and punched him in the face. It was an uncomplicated thing. The arc of his fist. The sound of it against the kid's head. The kid went down. Then Friendly got in the Crown Vic and drove to Carolyn, to Mid, or almost to them, because he hit something down there, something metal in the grass, hit it hard enough to spin the car sideways, put it up on two wheels for a moment before it came back down again. He ran the rest of the way and started trying to climb the tree. Helpful called whoever it was he had on the other end of his fancy phone, said he wanted a helicopter. The deputy I'd tackled was sitting up now. He was cut along the bridge of his nose. I felt like I might have knocked one of my shoulders loose from the socket. Nobody put me in handcuffs. Nobody shot me. Up on the porch, Alice had pulled all four kids back through the front door of the cabin, and she had her body between them and everything else. She was staring at me, not blinking, not moving. My head hurt. My shoulder hurt. I got up and went to her, asked her if she was alright, if the kids were. "I'm sorry," I told her, wanting that to stand in for everything. "I love you. I'm sorry. I am."

"What happened to Dad?" Delton asked. She was crying. "Did they just shoot him?"

"I don't know," I must have said, reaching for Alice, for all of them. I almost could not hear, could not see, could not taste.

Delton said, "Is he going to be OK?"

I was cold, I realized, for the first time since we'd moved. "Somebody's coming," I told her. "There's going to be a helicopter."

"How are they going to get him down?"

"They'll get him down," I said. Friendly was halfway up the tree, standing on a limb in his suit. Still no movement in the cart. "There are people who know how to do this," I said, wanting to make it true. I felt Alice's hand on my back, a small circle of heat. I turned around just to make sure.

■ ■ ■

At the hospital, we ate candy bars from the machine. We bought out their supply of anything with peanuts in it. They'd already told us we wouldn't get to go back to see him. Maggie stretched out along a row of seats and tried to go to sleep, kept pretending to wake from a nightmare. She'd sit up, eyes wild, and one of the twins would pretend to calm her back down again, pat her hair. It was not quite a game, but it was enough to keep them busy.

What we knew: He'd been hit. That he'd already had one surgery, and they were talking about a second. That one of his lungs had collapsed, or was collapsing. Carolyn was back there with him. She'd ridden in the helicopter. It was Carolyn who was coming out to give us updates, to tell us they had him sedated, to tell us they'd posted an officer outside his room. Friendly and Helpful had one of their guys out there, too, she said—they had guys—to watch the officer watching Mid. He had broken bones. He had pieces of the cart in his shoulder. The bullet had done something Carolyn couldn't quite explain, had hit one thing and bounced off another. He'd lost a lot of blood. A GSW does a lot of damage, she told us. Alice asked what that was. Gunshot wound, Carolyn said. She'd learned the lingo. She had emergency powers. They were trying to decide when to wake him up, she was telling us, and they didn't want to wake him up until they knew if they wanted to go back in.

We hadn't seen Carolyn in an hour. Alice thought that meant they were back in surgery. I said we did not know what it meant.

When we'd first gotten to the hospital, the sun was going down, and it lit the sky three hundred shades of orange on its way out, turned even the parking lot into something it wasn't, something fabulous, something adorned. But now night had come on, and out the window there was only the same darkness everybody everywhere else got, interrupted by the same sodium lights. Somewhere out there was the ocean. Somewhere out there was the Twice-the-Ice.

They'd flown him to Jacksonville, to the same hospital where we expected the BOJ to make her appearance sometime around Christmas. Maybe we'd get a helicopter ride, too. Or at least a star in the east. Mid would be healed by then, would be showing off his scars. "That's where it went in," he'd say, showing us his shoulderblade. Then he'd turn around, face us, pull his shirt to one side, show us a cigar burn of a scar, and say, "And that's where it came out." Whether he'd show us in the visiting quarters of the state penitentiary or in his own wine pantry, I had no idea.

Delton sat down between Alice and me. She looked other-worldly. Exhausted. We all must have. "Nic wants to come," she said, holding up her phone like he was inside it. "Is that OK?"

"Of course," I said.

"Cool," she said.

"Tell him to bring some burgers or something," Alice said. "The kids need to eat. You need to eat."

"I will," she said. She got up again, walked back over to the wall where she'd been sitting, curled herself into a ball.

"Do you think she's alright?" I asked Alice.

She said, "Would you be?"

"I'm not," I said.

"Well, there you go."

"Do you think she will be?" I said.

"I don't know," she said. "Maybe we'll all get lucky like that."

Earlier, after Carolyn had come out to bring us the first piece of news—that he was alive—Alice had said this to me about tackling the deputy: "What if he'd shot you, too?"

"I wasn't thinking about that," I said.

"What were you thinking about?"

"I don't think I was. I just did it."

"I need you," she said. "We need you. You can't leave."

"I'm not leaving," I said.

"Are you sure?"

"I am," I said. "I'm right here."

She said, "It's different now. You have to know that."

"I do know it," I said.

"We don't know anything," she said. "That's what's so crazy."

"We'll learn it," I said.

"How?" she said.

All this was at the coffee machine, which was next to the candy machine. There was also a soda machine and a water machine. We could see everybody from where we were standing, all four girls, could make sure everyone was where they were supposed to be.

"We need to think of a name," Alice said. "A real name."

"We will."

"I want to start. I don't want anything to happen and us not have a name."

"When we get through this," I said. "We'll get through this, get home, and we'll get her a name."

"Or him," she said.

"It's a girl," I said.

"I know. I know it is."

"Or him," I said.

Mid strafing us from an ultralight. A baby girl up there on the television screen, live from the belly of the whale. There was nothing that was not possible anymore.

■ ■ ■

We slept at the hospital because that seemed right, but by morning what seemed better was to get Alice home, get her in a true bed. They had done the second surgery, and everybody was happy. He was critical but stable. There were other classifications, Carolyn told us. Worse ones. Given the conditions, he was in good shape.

The idea was for Delton and Nic to take a real turn at playing house, take the twins and Maggie back to the castle for showers, breakfast, changes of clothes. Some kind of normal routine. We offered to do it, but Carolyn and Delton seemed to have arrived at a new arrangement, however temporary. What I thought Carolyn might know was this: Her pregnant sister needed rest. Her husband had been shot out of the sky and was now hooked up to tubes and bags, reactors and centrifuges. He needed someone to sit by him in his time of need, watch fluids go into his body and come back out. She could only do so many things.

We drove south. With the sun streaming through the windows and into our laps, Alice soon enough fell asleep, which left me to spin the radio dial back and forth. I wanted something to half-hear underneath all the noise in my head. My shoulder hurt, my back, my whole body. I watched signs for golf courses go by, for amusement parks two hours' drive from where we were, surf shops even farther still. If we were not in paradise, there was at least a billboard every five miles that would tell us how many exits were left before we got there. I saw egrets in the medians, stark white against the persistent green of everything else. The only time the land was not green was when it had been blackened by fire this year or last, and even then, out at the edges of the char and up above the burn lines on those trees left standing, there was new green. The flatness. There was nothing anywhere to make you believe the land did not extend this way forever. I punched in radio stations from our old life, familiar numbers. For whatever reason it seemed to me that they might carry down out of the hills and travel this far. I got nothing, of course. Static. We had left behind nearly anything I'd ever known.

I got us parked in the lower level of the garage, got Alice upstairs and into the bed, brought her water and juice and half a cup of coffee, told her to call me if she needed anything. I said I was going to take a quick ride, look in on Mid's life and make sure everything was still alright. Be careful, she said. Of what? I said. Of everything, she said. I got back downstairs, got in the hatchback, put it out on the highway, and headed for St. Augustine. I'd do what she asked, I was telling myself. I would keep a fair distance. I would exercise caution. But there was something I needed to know.

When did we move here? Our daughter would ask us. Before you were born, we'd say. I thought about my parents' stories, how when they'd talk about the lives they'd led before my brothers and I were born, it felt invented. Flickering. They had not been real people until we were there—we were sure of it, even if we never said so. Before you were born, I would tell her, there was nothing. No heavens and earth, no sky, no sea, no fish, no birds, no air. Thank God you came when you did. Your mother and I had begun to think we had certain things figured out. We wrote them into the lease. We felt sure we knew those things were true.

I drove over the bridge, through downtown, and out the other side. I found the two astrologers' houses. I shut the radio off, the AC off, rolled the windows down. I got lost. I ended up back out on the main road more than once. But I found it—I found the orange house, the empty yard, the flatbed with its mannequin leg, its Christmas lights. The lights were not on. There was no other car. There was a chicken sitting on the ground by a rusting toolshed. It was not moving, but it was alive. There was no Twice-the-Ice, which was what I'd come to see. I'd wanted to know if Mid was right—about that, about any of it. I guess I'd thought it would be there in the yard, the brilliant white fact of it plugged in and hooked up, Pete Brett dressed in full pirate garb and filling cooler after cooler with brand-new ice. But it was not. And without it, all the answers crowded in again, all at once: The company had repossessed it. The crime syndicate had stolen it. Pete Brett had it hidden somewhere else. He'd junked it for parts. He'd dumped it in the sea. It had never been there in the first place, or it had only winked into being when we were there to see it. The front door of the house opened, and I drove away, heart drumming hard. I did not wait to see who was coming out. I did not want whoever it was to see me.

Alice was still asleep when I got home. I called the hospital, and the nurse said Carolyn was sleeping, too. I hung up and walked out onto our back balcony, looked down at the beach. It was crowded—umbrellas, tents, children everywhere. There was a sand bar a hundred yards out into the water, and some older kids were trying to surf the few small waves it was kicking up. Every now and then one of them would get up, ride all the way in to shore.

It terrified me, what had happened to Mid. Not the shooting. What spooked me was what had come before—whatever it was that nudged him past the vision of himself he thought he'd mastered and into whoever it was flying that thing, singing and shooting flares. I held tighter to the railing, looked down at the grass between the building and the dunes, wondered if I'd survive a fall. I wanted to know if Mid had felt it coming. Not if he'd known *what* was going to happen, necessarily, but that *something* was. If he'd known how close it would come to killing him. I looked south, looked for Hank. I wanted to see the POW-MIA chute, the green cart, whatever extra flag was called for on a day like today. But he wasn't there. The sky was empty. I went back inside, crawled into bed next to Alice, listened to the steady rhythm of her breath.

▪ ▪ ▪

"Maybe if you guys move, I can still use this as a place to hang out," Delton said. This was days later. Mid was still in the hospital, though he was out of ICU. Shattered clavicle, shattered shoulder, broken arm, collapsed lung. Screws and pins. Carolyn and the kids were sleeping at home again. Delton was still with us. We were taking the foil back off her walls. Her idea.

"Why would we move?" Alice asked. The strips were coming down in smaller pieces than they'd gone up. We were balling everything together in the center of the floor. Delton was up on a ladder, pulling thumbtacks out and dropping them in a cereal bowl.

"After Dad goes to jail or whatever. Except there's no way he's going to jail."

"Why not?" I said.

"Nic says he did it on purpose."

"Did what on purpose?" Alice said. She sat down on the end of the bed. Delton uncovered a window, and light washed in.

"He says he has to be going for the whole insanity thing." I wasn't in any way certain you could get out of drug possession and tax evasion and whatever else they'd have him on with an insanity plea, but I didn't say so. "Nic says it's brilliant," she said, smiling at everything that came with that.

"Sweetie," Alice said, "you know you can talk to us, right?"

"Sure," Delton said. "Why?"

"We just want you to know that if you ever need somebody to listen, we're right here."

Delton frowned. "Mom's always saying stuff like that, too."

"Well, you've got a lot going on."

"I don't have a baby," she said.

Alice said, "Would you like to—" I was trying to catch her eye, but she was focused on Delton, up on her ladder. "I mean, if there's anything at all—"

Delton said, "I went to health class, OK? We saw the video."

"That's not what I meant," Alice said.

"Still," Delton said. "Let's really not talk about that."

Alice said, "Just tell me you're being safe. Or that you feel safe. Anything like that."

Delton curtseyed on the top step. It was like ballet. "Uncle Walter and Aunt Alice," she said, in her fake deep voice, "I am practicing the safest of sex. Practicing and practicing."

"You don't have to share that kind of thing," I said.

"Anything she wants to tell us is fine," Alice said.

"Too soon?" I said.

"Just in time," Delton said, turning back to the wall. "Hard to say when the world's going to end."

I said, "What does that mean?"

"It's something Nic says."

"All we're trying to say is that we're really sorry all this is happening," said Alice.

"Why are you apologizing?" she said.

"Because you shouldn't have to—"

"Because a normal fifteen-year-old shouldn't have to blah, blah, blah," said Delton. "Fill in the blank. Dad in the hospital. Is that what you mean?"

"It's part of it," Alice said.

"But there are no normal fifteen-year-olds," she said. "There is no normal anybody." She pulled another pushpin out. "This is pretty wild, though. I never knew anybody who got shot before."

Alice said, "Hopefully you never will again."

"He doesn't look like his normal self, hooked up to all those things."

"He will," I said.

"He looks smaller," she said.

We'd only been to see him once—he was pretty drugged up, and they were looking at X-rays of his collarbone, trying to see if the screws were in the right places—but she was right: He did look smaller, like someone had sent him through a machine, and he'd come out the other end reduced. Seeing him was like seeing him from far away. He'd said, "Should have taken evasive action."

"Right," I said.

"Those things don't move so great. Terrible getaway cars."

"Now you know for next time," I said.

"I pissed everybody off," he said.

"They'll get over it."

"Exactly," he said, but the drugs had him not quite fully there, and he leaned back into his pillow. There was a tube in his nose to help him breathe, an IV in his arm to feed him. I wanted to tell him: I can't find your ice machine. I don't know where to look. Instead I held still while Carolyn asked the doctors questions. There was a bruise that ran out from under the bandages and up the side of his neck. I wanted to ask him if it hurt, but I knew the answer. What I really wanted to know was how *much* it hurt.

"We're going to the go-carts tonight," Delton was saying. "We're taking Sophie and Jane."

"You are?" I said.

"Mom said anything on the ground was fine."

"Do you want us to go with you?" I asked.

"We're good." She picked at something up on the ceiling. "But I might not be home by ten," she said, and you could tell she loved the idea. "Because we have to drop them off and everything."

"Will you call us?" Alice said. "Call when you leave the park, and call when you drop them off?"

"No problem," Delton said.

"We just want to know you're OK," I said.

"I get it," Delton said.

"Are you?" I asked her. "OK?"

"You mean other than Dad?" She got down off the ladder, put the bowl of thumbtacks on the nightstand. "Yeah," she said. "Sure I am. I always am."

■ ■ ■

The name: Try to imagine it on a report card, on the back of a jersey, on a driver's license. On the front of envelopes addressed to her, color-coded for major holidays and special occasions. Said over the radio, or blocked up in white letters underneath her on the TV screen while she delivers expert analysis on the news of the day. On an album cover. On a runoff ballot for council selectwoman. On a passbook for her own savings account. See her writing it inside the covers of her books, at the top corners of her papers, signing it to a marriage certificate, a mortgage, a contract. Try to hear it coming out of her cousins' mouths. Her uncle's. Her mother's. Try to hear it coming out of your own.

■ ■ ■

The police were finished with the Camaro, and Hurley knew somebody who did auto glass, so we'd had his guy go get it, replace the windshield, drop it back off at the condo. Alice and I stood on the front balcony after I paid for the work and signed for the car. The only other vehicle in the parking lot was a golf cart.

Alice said, "That car keeps being the dumbest thing I've ever seen."

"He likes it," I said.

"But he can't give it to Delton."

I said, "Maybe not."

No one had asked about the cash yet. Nobody seemed to know about it. We were letting it be. The lawyers were telling Mid not to say anything, so that's what he was doing. He wasn't even talking to Friendly and Helpful anymore. Our idea was to tell the truth to anybody who asked, but not volunteer anything. The whole thing belonged to Mid, was our feeling, and we were trying to keep it that way.

Alice looked out over the water. It was low tide, and the Intracoastal had pulled back from all the grass spits again, left rings of sand around them. “Carolyn told me he almost died,” she said.

“When did she say that?”

“This morning. On the phone. One of the pieces of metal lodged in his rib. She said if it had gone through, it would have cut his heart in half.”

“Did she say anything else?”

“Like what? What would you say after that?”

A rubber motorboat came around the back side of one of the bigger islands. There was a circle on the side, a seal with some lettering. Maybe one of the universities. Or the same agency as the turtle woman. One person was up front, driving, and two more were in the back, with nets. They were all wearing white hats, white shirts. One of the net people dipped in, came back out with nothing.

“What do you think they’re doing?” Alice asked.

“Fishing?”

“It looks like science,” she said.

“I want that job.”

“Me, too,” she said, but she wasn’t really paying attention anymore. She rubbed at her side.

“You alright?” I asked.

“She’s kicking me. Do you want to feel?”

“Sure,” I said, and she put my hand to her body.

“I like knowing she’s in there,” Alice said. “It’s just—” The people on the boat had gotten something out of the water, something dead. “Oh,” Alice said. “Is that a bird?”

“I think it’s a possum,” I said, even though it looked very much like a bird, like maybe a heron.

“What’s it doing in the water?”

"I'm not sure," I said. One of the science people opened a clear trash bag, and they dropped the thing into it, put it down in the boat.

"That's horrible," Alice said.

"Maybe not to them."

"I think it would be horrible for anybody." She left me there, went inside the condo, came back out with her purse. "Let's go for a ride," she said. "The twins were telling me there's a carnival up in Butler Beach. Let's go see it."

"What time is Delton supposed to be back?" I said.

"Later." The scientists were back at it with their nets. "Let's please get out of here. I don't want to see them find anything else."

We went downstairs, got in the car. "It's like a cave in here," she said. "Or a cockpit."

I said, "It's like something."

"Turn it down as cold as it'll go," she said, and I put the AC on MAX. Once we were out on the road, she said, "I want to be able to see my breath."

"There's no way it goes that cold," I said, making sure the lever was pushed all the way to the end of the blue.

"Try," she said.

"I'm trying."

"I want to make it so cold we have to open the sunroof to save ourselves," she said.

"OK," I said. "Bundle up."

The highway north took us through almost all of Mid's known empire: Island Pizza, Devil's Backbone, Me Kayak Sea Kayak. We went past Pomar's. We went past the grocery. We went past where we'd turn for the castle. I got a quick flash of him hanging in the trees, belted into the parachute, bleeding and certain he was dying, knowing that even if they did get to him, even if they did cut him down, it wouldn't make any difference.

"I don't want to go to the doctor tomorrow," Alice said. "I don't ever want to go back."

"I'll call and cancel," I said.

"We have to go."

"We could go next week," I said. "We could make something up."

"I don't want anybody looking at me anymore," she said. "I just want to help her grow hair and fingernails."

"Is that where we are?"

"You have to read the books," she said.

"I'll read the books."

"I want them to tell us we're safe," she said, pulling her knees up under her chin. She looked a lot like Delton. "I can't take it if they say something else."

"They'll say it," I said. "We're safe."

"You always say that."

"We always are."

"Not always," she said. "We haven't been. You weren't."

"I am now."

"No, you're not."

"I'm better," I said.

"You're lying."

"Only sometimes," I said. "The rest of the time, it's almost true."

"Tell me you'll get it figured out," she said.

"I will."

"Tell me that's the truth."

"I want it to be."

"I miss you," she said. "I've been missing you."

I shifted down, then back up again. The engine revved and released. I said, "I missed you, too," only seeing in that moment how much. I eased the car into the empty oncoming lane to avoid a case of beer in the road. "I still like Olivia," I said. "For a name."

She pushed the lock button a few times. She said, "Do you really think he did it on purpose?"

"Which part?" I said.

"Any of it. Do you think he meant all that?"

"I don't know."

"How did he learn to fly one of those things?"

"I don't think it's that hard," I said. "The sail does most of the work. You just hang on underneath, and whatever happens next is what happens."

"My God, what if he did have it all planned?" she said.

I said, "Isn't it worse if he didn't?"

It was easy enough to find the carnival. As we came into Butler Beach, the police had a lane blocked fully off, were directing traffic into a parking lot at one of the public beach access points. As we got closer we could see it: a pirate ship, a Tilt-a-Whirl, a massive slingshot that launched people in a huge arc down along the ground and then thirty, forty, fifty feet up into the air. There were carts and trailers selling cotton candy, elephant ears, popcorn. "So there it is," Alice said.

"Yeah," I said, looking at it.

"Let's go. I want to ride the rides."

I said, "No small children, no pregnant mothers."

"We'll ride the kiddie rides," she said. "We'll eat corn dogs."

"Are you sure?"

"Come on," she said. "I really want to go."

It was five dollars to park, two dollars a ticket. Some rides cost one ticket, others two or three. They rang a bell, like a schoolhouse bell, right before they shot the slingshot each time. The bell would go off, and everybody would turn to look, and the cables would go tenser and tenser, and then they'd ring the bell again, and that was it: The highschool kid—invariably it was someone Delton's age, with her friends cheering her on from the ground—was let go along that tight curve, rushing down and then sailing back up toward the sky. Every time, I'd hold Alice's hand a little tighter, sure this would be the moment the ride would fail and the kid would just keep going, out over the parking lot and the cars and the road and into the Intracoastal. Maybe she'd tuck into a dive when she hit the water, and maybe she'd live. Or maybe—maybe she'd never hit the ground at all. Maybe she'd be the first among us to figure out how it worked, swoop in low over the cheering crowd and then fly off, away, never to be heard from again.

We rode a kiddie Ferris wheel that was barely taller than a house. We had our pictures taken in a replica Model T. We rode a roller coaster made to look like a pig. The whole thing was pink. Alice and I got our own car near the back, watched the kids in front of us, watched their parents watch them from behind the plastic gating. The metal of the cars was nearly too hot to touch. This was a one-hill ride, and that hill took us just high enough to see over the dunes and out onto the beach, the ocean. It lasted five laps, five times around, and then it was done. When we got off the ride, Alice wanted a sno-cone. We bought red and blue. She ate them both.

The sun crushed down on us. Inside the tents it was hotter

than out, so we stayed away from the skeet ball and the guess-your-weight-and-age guys, played the games on the perimeter. Alice won the ring bottles on the first try. The girl running the booth said she could choose a prize, and she picked a stuffed yellow gorilla as big as a dog. It had an expression on its face like it wasn't sure what town it was in, like the carnival stopped in thirty towns in fifty days, and this must be one of them. "We can take him to Mid," I said. "He could probably use somebody to talk to."

"He's mine," she said. "What if I want him for the baby's room?"

"We could loan him to Mid until she gets here," I said.

"Let me think about it," she said.

Alice had to go to the bathroom, so I found a piece of shade behind one of the bigger rides, waited. She left the gorilla with me. There were kids everywhere, knots and huddles of them, kids in bunches. Parents chased them, trying to make deals to keep them happy. One more hour. Two more rides. Either the funnel cake or the ice cream, but not both. We would have to have a second one, a second child. I knew that now. The bell rang, and they hoisted a shirtless boy into the air over at the slingshot. Because you had to give a kid an ally. It wouldn't be fair to leave Kitchenette on her own. Or—or maybe we could get Maggie to be her big sister. Maybe we had that part already wired in, and we'd be alright. Maybe we'd at least be able to wait until we knew if we could do it. That would be the one miracle we might be owed. The second bell went off, and they let the kid go. He flew with his arms out from his sides. The wind pushed his hair off his face. Alice came out of the bathroom, looked around. She didn't see me. I waited, just for a second, watching her stare out into the spinning crowd, before I lifted the gorilla up in the air, waved him back and forth until she saw. She smiled. The kid sailed back by again, turning a flip. He was a pro. Alice came right for me, right through all the people. Tomorrow we would go to the doctor, would go to the hospital to see Mid, then out to the castle to see Carolyn and the girls. After that, I did not know. After that, anything. Right now I still had paper tickets in my pocket. I got them out. I handed them to Alice. She had tears in her eyes. "What is it?" I said.

"Nothing," she said. "I just really like the carnival. I'm glad we came."

Behind her, a girl who couldn't have been more than five years old was getting ready to test her strength, to play the hammer game. HY-STRYKER, it said on the tower. She'd picked up a hammer bigger than she was and was lining things up. She had long reddish hair pulled back in a braid, was wearing a plain brown dress. "Watch out now," the barker was saying. "Folks, we got a natural on our hands. Better stand back." From our angle, I could see the guy doing something with his feet, probably rigging the game—but the girl had already swung the hammer through the air and brought it down square on the metal plate, and the needle took off up the tower, all the way up, rang the bell. Her parents cheered. The little crowd that had gathered to watch her cheered. The girl didn't even smile. She looked directly at Alice—I swear I saw her do this—and she put the hammer back down on the ground like it was nothing, like that was the result she'd expected all along.

ACKNOWLEDGMENTS

Thanks so very much to Kathy Pories, who believed all along, who saw things I didn't, and who just kept being right. Thanks one more time to Peter Steinberg for working such magic. Thank you to everyone at Algonquin for every moment of your hard work in bringing this up off the page and into the world; thank you, all of you, for making me feel so utterly at home.

Thanks to the Sustainable Arts Foundation for its generous support.

Thanks to my parents, Tom and Judy, and to my brothers, Neil and Josh.

To AMR, and to all those beasts beneath our roof: I've never been more delighted to be so, so wrong.